WRAPPED
UP IN
CHRISTMAS

JANICE LYNN

To my real-life Hallmark Happy Ever
After, Michael. I love you.

-Janice

Table of Contents

CHAPTER ONE

AFTER MONTHS OF SWEAT, GRIT, and sheer determination to get to the picturesque Kentucky town he'd only recently heard of, Bodie Lewis had finally arrived in Pine Hill.

He turned off his pickup's engine, ruffled his dog Harry's scruffy black and white fur, and let out a long breath. Put him on a dangerous overseas mission, and he was in his element. Searching out a little elderly lady in the civilian world to express his gratitude? Not so much.

"We made it," he told the dog who had been at his side nonstop for the past few months.

A dog and a quilt.

Not exactly things he'd expected to call his own, nor to have made such an impact on his life.

If he added the just-purchased truck he was sitting in and a rarely touched bank account, he'd be listing all his worldly possessions. Until recently, he hadn't been in one place long enough to justify his own transportation and had always driven government-issued vehicles when the need arose.

He ran his hand over his dark hair. Although an average length by most standards, the strands felt out of place. He'd worn a crew cut most of his adult life—a cut he was no longer required to maintain, thanks to his honorable discharge.

The "honorable" was enough to gut him.

There had been nothing honorable about the demise of the rest of his unit.

Pain shot across Bodie's chest. Pain of grief and emotion so raw he longed to scream. His ever-present anger, threatening to boil over into rage, constantly simmered at the loss of his brothers-in-arms, and at the loss of his career.

All he'd ever wanted was to be a soldier. To serve and protect his country.

So much for dreams.

He glanced around the town square. Mom-and-pop storefronts provided a fresh facelift for old brick buildings. That's what he had to do—give his old dreams a fresh makeover. Surely his upcoming job with iSecure would fill that driving need inside him, wouldn't it? His need to do more? To be more?

He had been more, and now...

His gaze shifted to a flag that whipped in the November wind atop a pole in front of the stately brick courthouse. The material stretched and stood at attention within the wind's invisible fingers, saluting him.

Bodie nodded his head in silent acknowledgement of that flag and all it represented.

Of what he'd been willing to give to defend that flag.

In acknowledgement of what many had given.

Feeling the pain tighten his chest again, he sucked in a deep breath and stopped his mind from going where it went too often. Wasn't that what the therapist the military had required he work with told him? To refocus when his mind wandered into dark places?

Fine. He concentrated on the reason he was here in Pine Hill: to find the elderly woman who'd affected his life with her kindness.

His task shouldn't be too difficult for someone used to tracking down terrorists. Pine Hill, Kentucky, wasn't exactly the mecca of booming civilization.

Even though he'd never stepped foot in the town, he'd pictured it so clearly. Sarah's description was burned in his mind, offering him a safe space to escape when memories overpowered him. So, seeing his safe haven come to life brought him an unexpected sense of belonging. Apple-pie America at its best.

And a far cry from his childhood home in Houston, where he was headed after this slight detour.

Not that there was much of a home in Texas. Just his mom, stepfather, and a couple of much-older stepsisters he'd never been close to.

He wouldn't be there long. The moment he got the go-ahead to start his new job, he'd provide top-notch protection to the rich and famous around the globe. Not the life he craved, but staying in the same place for very long made his feet itch. Always had.

Which was why he'd turned down the Army's offer of a desk job. A desk job? For him? Never.

He glanced toward the quilt in the passenger seat. He'd be starting his next journey as soon as he'd had the chance to thank Sarah Smith for pulling him out of a dark, dark place.

He'd never heard of Quilts of Valor prior to being presented with the special gift. But that red, white, and blue quilt had given him something to hang on to—literally and figuratively—while he was recuperating.

Which was why he was in Pine Hill, to thank the quilt's maker in person.

He owed her more than a simple thank-you could convey, but that's what he'd come to give.

A thank-you, and then he'd be on his way.

Humming along with the Christmas music playing over the church's intercom system, Sarah Smith sewed white yarn through a cut piece of plastic canvas. The snowflakes she made each year with the pieces of canvas and yarn were some of her favorite homemade Christmas decorations.

She glanced around the room at the mix of women, teens, and children busily making ornaments to be sold at Pine Hill's annual On-the-Square Christmas Festival. Many of the twenty or so volunteers were the same smiling faces who had helped with Sarah's past projects—people she adored.

With her employment as Pine Hill Church's administrative assistant and special projects planner, Sarah was always organizing something. Often, she believed their projects helped those participating as much as—and sometimes more than—they helped the recipients of their work. Giving truly was better than receiving, which was why Sarah loved Christmas so much.

She enjoyed everything about Christmas. The decorations, the smells, the food, the kindness, and good cheer that prevailed. The get-togethers with family and friends that made everything sweeter. If it were up to her, she'd arrange for Christmas to come way more often than just once a year.

"I couldn't do this without you all," she told the group of women working at her table. The Butterflies, as they referred to themselves, had an assembly line going to make the plastic canvas snowflake ornaments.

Sarah's projects would be nothing without the Butterflies to see her ideas to fruition. She could always count on them. The four women had been a part of Sarah's life from the beginning, and she loved them dearly.

"Yeah, yeah." Maybelle Kirby's old blue eyes didn't lift from where she was hot-gluing sparkly white sequins to a finished snowflake. "Use it or lose it, I always say. And these old bones ain't got much more to lose, so I gotta keep using."

Maybelle was Sarah's favorite—possibly because she had been Aunt Jean's best friend. The two women had bonded over being young military widows, neither of whom had remarried or had children. Although in her early seventies now, and the oldest of the group of volunteers, Maybelle was a firecracker and knew how to do just about anything Sarah took a fancy to learn. As the church's previous special projects planner, Maybelle had been adopting do-gooders such as Sarah for years and was a fount of knowledge and encouragement. Sometimes Sarah thought Maybelle missed her role as planner. That was why she made sure she kept the woman involved.

"Besides, someone has to keep you in check," Maybelle muttered, earning a few chuckles from the others at her table. "Don't know how you think you're ever going to meet a man if all you do is work, work, work."

Sometimes, Maybelle's involvement *wasn't* a good thing. Like when it came to Sarah's love life—or lack thereof. Though to be honest, it wasn't just Maybelle. All four women thought it their responsibility to marry Sarah off.

"I happen to love my work," Sarah reminded, smiling at Maybelle as she added, "Besides, who says I want to meet a man? The last man—and I use that term loosely—in my life sure wasn't worth taking time away from work or you ladies."

Richard and his big-city dreams were, thankfully, long gone from her beloved Pine Hill. Although memories snuck in from time to time reminding of how her heart had broken when he'd left her, these days, mostly she just bid him good riddance.

Any man who didn't want a calm, normal, white picket fence, church-going, Christmas-loving life in Pine Hill wasn't the right man for her. Plain and simple.

Sarah added, "With trying to get the bed and breakfast open by Christmas, I don't have time for a man." Renovating the old Victorian ate up all her time and then some. "Fulfilling Aunt Jean's dream of turning Hamilton House into a B & B is my number one priority outside of church and work."

Her aunt had belonged with these women—had grown up with them and been a part of everything in Pine Hill. Sarah's mother had died giving birth to her, but her father's older sister had stepped up to give her niece a woman's guidance.

6

"How's that going?" Ruby asked. Sarah was especially glad that Ruby seemed to have accepted the subject shift away from Sarah's love life. Ruby was happily married to the man of her dreams for going on fifty years and would gladly tell anyone who'd listen about her wonderful Charles. It made her a very determined matchmaker, since she wanted everyone to be as happy as she was. Ruby and Charles were a sweet couple, but the Butterflies often teased Ruby about her longtime love affair with her husband.

"Yeah, about that." Sarah's shoulders sank. "I placed another handyman ad, if that tells you anything."

Four concerned faces winced in unison.

"Did you fire another one?" Ruby asked.

Maybelle's eyes narrowed. "Or did this one quit, too?"

Sarah shrugged. What did it matter? This time, the sloppy handyman had splattered paint on the hardwood floor. When she'd gotten upset, he'd only picked at his teeth with his dirty fingernail, saying it would clean. He hadn't been the right handyman for Hamilton House, any more than Richard had been the right man for her.

"Girl, your aunt didn't mean for that house to take over your life," Rosie Matthews reminded her as she attached ribbons and hooks to Maybelle's decorated snowflakes. Rosie was a mover and shaker and sometimes made Sarah's head spin with her crowded social life. Flaunting her energetic, youthful spirit with her bright blue hair, Rosie liked men and they liked her. No doubt the woman had broken more than a few hearts over her sixty-plus years. Although she'd been married three times and had gotten a few proposals since, she'd remained single after her last husband had passed a few years back.

"I listened to Aunt Jean talk about restoring Hamilton House to its former glory those last few weeks before her death," Sarah said. "She knew what I'd do when she left the house to me, that I'd find a way to bring it back to life even if I can only do so a few rooms at a time."

If she wanted to keep the sprawling Victorian home, it had to bring in enough income to pay for its upkeep. Not to mention paying back the hefty loan she'd finagled at the bank to make needed repairs and updates.

With her background from old money and lots of it, Maybelle had offered to fund the restoration, but Sarah had refused. She needed to do this, and thankfully, the loan officer had approved the loan.

Hopefully her determination would pay off and be the perfect legacy to her darling aunt whom she missed so much.

"Jean should have told you to sell the place for every penny you could get and travel the world," said Claudia while dusting a completed snowflake with snowy glitter. Though she'd stayed in Pine Hill all her life, she was known for wishing she'd spent her life dashing from one exotic locale to another, or at least gone on a vacation or two with her husband.

Maybelle rolled her eyes. "As if you could pry our Sarah out of Pine Hill."

Sarah laughed. "Are y'all trying to get rid of me?"

"Pine Hill would be lost without you," Claudia assured her, the others nodding their agreement.

"*We'd* be lost without you," Ruby clarified. "My Charlie is always marveling at how much joy you add to our lives."

Smiling at the love she had for and received from these ladies, Sarah tied off a knot at the end of the plastic canvas piece she was working on. "Good thing you think so, because I'm not leaving. Pine Hill is home."

It had been for four generations of Sarah's family. Even if she and her dad were the only ones left, the small Kentucky town was a part of who she was.

"I can't imagine living anywhere but here."

Clicking the completed piece of canvas into another she'd already done, she surveyed her work. It would be even better once decorated with the sparkly glitter, tiny pearls, and sequins. The snowflakes had been a big hit last year at their church booth at the Christmas festival. In fact, they'd sold out—which was why they planned to double how many they made this year. The proceeds helped fund backpacks filled with school supplies for needy kids each fall, goodie baskets for hospitalized patients' family members, and so many other charitable projects that came up throughout the year.

Sarah loved the warmth within this community and the care people showed for each other. She truly wouldn't want to live anywhere other than where her parents met, fell in love, and had planned to grow old together.

"Me, either," Ruby sighed, a bit nostalgically. "Pine Hill is the perfect backdrop for my love story with Charlie."

A noise that was somewhere between a gag and a snort harrumphed from Rosie's throat.

"Don't listen to her," Claudia warned, cutting plastic canvas pieces to be used to make more snowflakes. "You sell that place and go see the world. London, Paris, Rome...the world is calling for you."

"That's not the world calling for her," Maybelle advised drily, gluing down a row of faux pearls. "That's your hearing aid squeaking and squawking."

More good-natured laughter sounded around the table as their assembly line of snowflakes continued.

"I'll remind you, I don't wear hearing aids. Even though I am the world's greatest grandma, I'm still younger than you old biddies." Chin held high, Claudia gave each of them a pert "so there" look, then tilted her head toward Sarah. "Except that one, and she seems destined to toss her life away fixing up Jean's crumbling old mansion, rather than expanding her horizons."

"Aunt Jean's house isn't crumbling." Not anymore, thanks to her loan and her having spent every spare moment over the past year working on restoring the outside and the downstairs to their former glory. She'd worry about the upstairs once she got the bed and breakfast up and going. "It just needed some TLC."

And a repair guy to stick around to finish up the job. She'd had a few good contractors for the bigger jobs, thank goodness. But none of them were currently available, and the independent handymen weren't working out. Didn't anyone take pride in their work? If so, she'd yet to find that elusive handyman who paid attention to details.

Hopefully God would answer her prayers and

the right person would reply to her help-wanted ad. Otherwise, she'd have to delay her planned Grand Opening of Hamilton House.

The thought of that made her heart hurt a little. She wanted to do this for Aunt Jean.

Please, Lord, let them respond.

The door to the community room opened, and all heads turned to see who'd shown up to join their ornament-making festivities.

Sarah's eyes widened at the unfamiliar six-foot-plus man wearing jeans and a sherpa-lined blue jean jacket. He rubbed his hands, warming his bare fingers from the chill outdoors as he surveyed the Christmas chaos Sarah adored.

Ask and the Lord shall deliver.

Literally.

Okay, so she didn't really believe the stranger was there to answer her prayers, but still, his timing was impeccable. Who was he?

Apparently, she wasn't the only one wondering. It wasn't that one could hear a pin drop—not with the holiday music playing—but there was a collective curiosity pervading the now-muted room that had been loud with chatter prior to his arrival.

"I've been extra-good this year and Santa's delivering early," Rosie whispered under her breath, elbowing Claudia. Her lively eyes sparkled with mischief. "That's exactly what I asked for."

Giving the newcomer a once-over, Maybelle snorted. "You ain't been that good your whole life."

Claudia snickered. "That's the truth."

"That one there makes me wish I had been," Rosie sighed, fanning her face. "He's easy on these old eyes.

A few years back, I'd have invited him over for some of my grandma's cinnamon bread. That never fails to warm a man over to my way of thinking."

"Charles didn't think much of your grandmother's cinnamon bread," Ruby reminded, a cheeky smile on her face as she happily sewed white yarn in and out of the plastic canvas piece she now held.

"Only because that was my first attempt at making it," Rosie defended, obviously annoyed at the reminder. "Be grateful I didn't have the recipe down yet or your Charles would've been my Charles."

Knowing better, Ruby just smiled and kept on sewing.

Still amused at the timing of the man's arrival, Sarah's lips twitched. Rosie's grandmother's cinnamon swirl bread was the stuff legends were made of. Women had been attempting to copy the recipe for years without success. Rosie closely guarded the recipe, as she swore it was guaranteed to put a sparkle in a man's eye. She wasn't about to let the other town women in on her little secret.

Maybelle's penciled-on brow arched and she made a loud tsking sound at Rosie. "If you really thought you had a chance with Mr. Tall, Dark, and Stoic there, you'd have fired up the oven and started stirring the batter."

Rosie's gaze narrowed but with good nature as she intoned, "I'll stir your batter, Maybelle Kirby."

The women laughed as one Christmas song ended and another began.

With almost every eye on him, the man scanned the room, apparently searching for something, or someone. He didn't look impressed—more like he didn't belong in the room or around happy people in general. With his observant, stern expression, he stuck out like a pumpkin on Christmas morning.

Despite the stranger's serious demeanor, Rosie was right that he was easy to look at. Give the man a smile, and he'd make women of all ages swoon.

Who was he and why was he there?

"You should go say hi, Sarah," Claudia suggested, giving her arm a nudge. "Maybe he's a traveling man and you'll get to see the world."

"Ask if he's single," Rosie added, waggling her drawn-on brows.

"Ladies," Sarah scolded them. "Didn't I just remind you of the reasons why I don't care if he's single or not? Still, as the planner, I should see why he's here."

She started to stand, but another volunteer positioned closer to the door walked up to talk to the newcomer. With the music and the chatter around the room that had resumed, Sarah couldn't hear what he said, but Carrie turned and was pointing toward Sarah's table.

Sarah's belly did a flip-flop.

"Do you know him?" she asked the woman sitting next to her, wondering if this handsome stranger was some long-lost son.

Maybelle squinted her eyes toward the man, then shook her head. "Can't say as I do, but looks like we're about to find out. He's headed this way. Rosie, you'd best behave."

Rosie pursed her lips at Maybelle. "I'm not making any promises. He offers to whisk me off my feet and carry me to his castle, I'm out of here."

"He offers to whisk you off your feet and carry you

off to his castle, then somebody had better call 911, because I'd have a heart attack right here and now," Maybelle warned, her tone its usual dry sass.

Still talking to Carrie, the man nodded, then headed toward her table, too, his gaze settling on Maybelle.

"He looks more like a villain trying to storm the castle than the prince inside," Sarah mused, studying the man's intent expression, his broad shoulders that tapered to a narrow waist, and his proud stride.

He definitely had a "you'd better not mess with me" vibe.

"Ma'am," he said when he reached them, his eyes trained on Maybelle, before taking a moment to visually acknowledge each of the women at the table. His gaze lingered a millisecond when it connected with Sarah's, almost as if he was surprised by her presence, perhaps because she was so much younger than the other women. But then his sharp blue eyes moved back to Maybelle.

Sarah gulped, wondering at the tightening in her throat at his perusal. She'd swear she'd just been mentally photographed. That they all had been, to the point where if he was called upon to give every detail of the room and the people in it, he'd be able to do so with vivid detail and perfect accuracy.

"Do I know you, son?" Maybelle never had been one to beat around the bush.

"No, ma'am." His stance was stiff, overly formal. "But I came to Pine Hill to find you."

"Lucky you," Rosie stage-whispered, giving Claudia another elbow to the arm.

It was rare for anyone to surprise Maybelle, but

the woman looked shocked. "Why in the world would you want to find me?"

He glanced around the table again, looking a little uncomfortable. That surprised Sarah. She doubted much got under this man's skin. He came across as a guy who had seen a lot during his lifetime.

"Is there perhaps somewhere we could go talk in private, Ms. Smith?"

Four jaws dropped, but not Maybelle's.

Maybelle arched a brow and gave him a look that had been straightening up naughty Sunday school children for years. "Ms. Smith?"

"The blonde at the door pointed me in this direction. You are Sarah Smith?"

Rosie's shoe delivered a swift nudge against Sarah's foot. Sarah knew that any second now, Rosie would be inviting him to join them for ornament making and pointing out Sarah's ringless finger. With her stomach feeling fluttery, Sarah tucked her feet as far back beneath her chair as they'd comfortably go and attempted to use telepathy to get the woman to hold her tongue.

No doubt fully aware of Rosie's soccer tryouts beneath the crafting table, Maybelle laughed. "Looks like your ad in the paper worked this time, Sarah, and found you a man, after all."

Sarah knew where Maybelle's mind had gone. It wasn't on help-wanted ads or house repairs. *Ugh.*

"This one looks as if he can take anything you dish out at him," Maybelle continued, all innocent-like.

Sarah gave Maybelle her best glare. She hadn't dished anything out to the other handymen. She'd expected them to do their job. Hamilton House deserved better than a messy, thrown-together restoration.

If she was lucky, this guy could finish the needed remodeling to the downstairs suites and the other repairs she needed to get done prior to her Grand Opening of Hamilton House on Christmas.

"Let's hope he isn't afraid to get his hands dirty," Rosie piped up from across the table.

Sarah's gaze dropped to the stranger's hands. They did appear capable of anything she might ask of him. Sturdy, slightly calloused, with bluntly cut clean fingernails. Ringless.

Ringless?

Now why in the world had she noticed that? Because of her friends' earlier suggestions? Or because his blue eyes were fringed with thick lashes and held intelligence and intrigue that made her want to dig deeper? Because his strong chin beneath high cheekbones indicated determination and resolve, while the tiny scar above his left brow hinted he was a man who didn't back down when things got tough?

She didn't need to feel Rosie's shoe nudge hers again to know exactly why she'd noticed his bare finger. Had her friends been nowhere around, she still would've noticed the handsome stranger. He wasn't a man a woman could ignore.

She'd have to be careful not to encourage the Butterflies, or they'd really be playing Cupid.

Even if she'd been interested in meeting someone— which she wasn't—a man who had yet to smile wasn't her type. No matter how handsome he was.

CHAPTER TWO

B ODIE HADN'T BEEN SURPRISED WHEN the old man on Main Street had told him he'd find Sarah Smith at church. She'd talked about church in her note. That the stately woman he'd identified wasn't Sarah did confuse him.

He took in the women at the table, trying to figure out which one was Sarah. All the women were sixty-plus, save one who he'd guess to be in her twenties.

A blue-haired, ruby-red-lipped woman bared her gleaming white dentures in a flirty smile, then waved and batted her lashes at him. Was that Sarah Smith?

"As you can imagine from the ad, Sarah needs a man desperately," a dyed redhead pointed out.

What kind of ad had Sarah put in the paper?

"You have a resume? Any photos of past jobs so we can see your work?" This came from the woman he'd first thought was Sarah Smith. "Just because she's desperate doesn't mean just any man will do."

"She's picky," a petite woman with a grayish white bun and a round face confirmed. Had she not been sitting on the opposite end of the table from where the blond had pointed, he'd have guessed she was Sarah Smith.

"You'll have to have references," Blue-hair said, her face overly friendly. "And be affordable."

"But that doesn't mean you can compromise on the work. Doing the job right is a must."

The older women were enough to make Bodie wonder if he'd made the right decision in coming to Pine Hill. Maybe he should've just written a thank-you note and been done with it.

The young woman watched the others with an expression that spoke of a mix of loving indulgence and an intense desire for them to quit talking. When her gaze met his, she gave a little shrug at the women's rapid-fire comments. Despite the long red-and-green ribbon in her hair and the somewhat ugly Christmas sweater she wore—the first, more appropriate for a teenager, and the second, better suited to a senior citizen—he was sure that he'd been right in his first assessment of her age.

Clearing her throat to silence the older women—surprisingly successfully—the mid-twenties woman stuck out her hand. "Hi. I'm Sarah. I'm the one who placed the help-wanted ad."

Bodie prided himself on rarely being caught off guard, and on not showing it when he was, but he was sure his face displayed his shock. She was Sarah Smith? This smiling young woman had been the one who made his quilt?

"Thank you for responding in person," she continued.

Her wholesome aura hit him deep in the gut with sugary goodness that couldn't be for real in this day and time. Warning bells clanged in his head to get out of Dodge—er, Pine Hill—but they were silenced in an instant when he looked into her warm brown eyes. The intensity of his reaction blared through his whole jaded being.

"Though a phone call would have been fine."

His gaze dropped to her outstretched hand. Those fingers had stitched his quilt? Had lovingly held the material as she created a work of art?

All this time, he'd pictured an elderly woman whiling away time making his quilt. The only person he'd ever known to quilt had been his great-grandmother, and he'd thought hand-quilting a dying art. Never had he considered that a woman younger than him had placed the intricate stitches.

Why would she have spent the hours and hours making his quilt? Did the older women keep her locked in a tower or something? That would certainly explain her wholesome persona and why she'd spend so much time on such a time-consuming task for a complete stranger.

Her smile deepened, lighting her pretty face. "You are here about the ad, aren't you?"

"We hope so. Sarah really does need a man," Blue-hair managed to get out before Red elbowed her.

"Yeah, she's never going to get that big old house fixed up by Christmas if you guys keep quitting on her," Gray-bun said, finally clueing him into what Sarah needed a man for.

"Do her a favor and stick around to finish the job."

Sarah blushed.

It had been a long time since Bodie had seen a woman blush, and he stared at her in continued wonder, questioning again if she was from another day and age.

The world was harsh, cruel—not filled with kind, smiling women who blushed.

Realizing that he should've already acted on Sarah's outstretched hand, Bodie caught her hand just as, her smile fading, she was lowering it.

Opening his mouth, he started to introduce himself by giving his rank, then paused. Whether he liked it or not, he was a civilian now.

Heart heavy, he said, "Bodie Lewis."

Her hand felt small in his, almost fragile. Feminine. He'd worked beside some amazing women in the military, had dated a few. None of them had hands like Sarah's—soft, but capable of creating beautiful things.

"Nice to meet you," she assured, pulling her hand free and looking a little disconcerted. "So you're here about the ad. And since you came in person, I'm guessing you can start right away?"

The desperation as she asked the question pleaded with him to say yes.

She'd spent a lot of time making his quilt, had given without expecting anything in return. Now that he'd met her in person, his first impression was that she was a genuinely kind and generous person.

From what the women had said, she needed house repairs. Having grown up with a stepfather who made his living as a handyman, there wasn't much around the house Bodie couldn't do.

Indecision tore at him. He didn't have to be anywhere for a few weeks.

If the woman who'd made his quilt needed his help,

he should help her. He couldn't walk away and leave her hanging after what she'd unknowingly done for him. Not if he wanted to maintain any sense of pride in himself as a man.

Without knowing what he was getting himself into, Bodie nodded. "Tell me exactly what it is you need me to do."

"I need a favor," Bodie said into his cell phone as he opened his truck door and motioned for Harry to jump in. The dog had patiently waited outside the church on the stoop right where Bodie had left him.

Once the dog was in the passenger seat, Bodie climbed in, shut the door, and gave the dog a scratch behind the ears.

"Okay to list you as a reference?" he asked the man on the phone.

"For a job?" Lukas Watts sounded almost as surprised at the request as Bodie was that he was making it. It was no wonder his best friend sounded shocked. A job in Kentucky certainly wasn't in the cards when he'd left Lukas's house early that morning.

Bodie had planned to thank Sarah, then hit the road to Texas, not go to work for her. But this wouldn't require a major change in his plans. From the sound of things, he'd only be here for a few weeks. No problem. He had the time to spare before starting the next phase of his life.

"You're still coming to work for iSecure?" Lukas continued. Lukas had served in the Army with Bodie for six years and had quickly become Bodie's best friend. Lukas had opted out rather than reenlisting a few years back and had started the protective services business. They'd stayed in touch on the rare occasion when Bodie had access to communication with the outside world. Lukas and his wife had come to visit him not long after he'd been transferred to a hospital in the states. While he'd been grateful for his friend's loyalty, he'd still hated anyone seeing him so helpless and dependent upon the nurses and therapists.

His leg and hip still ached and he had some nasty scarring, but he was slowly getting his strength and agility back. To see him now, few would guess that earlier that year he'd been told he'd never walk again. As Lukas and Kelly had taken him in after his discharge from the rehabilitation facility, they'd witnessed how far he'd come, how he'd gone from self-loathing that he'd been the sole survivor of his unit to determination to live again—thanks to a quilt reminding him of the world beyond his harsh experiences in the Middle East and various medical facilities.

"For some reason, iSecure's owner doesn't want me to start until the new year," he drawled.

"Yeah, for some reason." Lukas laughed. "Like that busted-up hip and leg of yours and him wanting you to take some time to recharge."

"My hip and leg are fine." They both knew that the continued time off Lukas insisted upon had more to do with the things Bodie had seen and felt, rather than his physical injuries. The pain in his left leg and hip was nothing compared to the one in his heart at the far-too-early end to his military career, not to mention the anger that burned at the senseless death of his comrades. "The reference is for a small job I'm taking in the interim."

"Why take an interim job at all? A few more weeks to recuperate before starting at iSecure will be good for you," Lukas said. "Besides, you can't start at iSecure until your official background check is approved."

Bodie snorted. Lukas knew more about his background than a computer search would reveal. His friend knew what a bad mental place he'd been in, so it was no wonder Lukas was hesitant to put him in a possibly high-stress situation.

But if by "recuperate," his friend meant "forget what happened," well, that wasn't ever going to occur. To the day Bodie died, he'd be reliving that nightmare.

He owed it to his friends not to forget.

"Should I be concerned that one of my competitors is trying to steal you away?" Lukas asked.

How could he explain the position he'd be taking? He hadn't mentioned the detour to Pine Hill when he'd left Lukas's that morning. How much did he tell his friend? That he'd gone to tell his quilt maker thank you and he'd gotten sucked into applying for a handyman job?

"This isn't for a bodyguard position." Bodie glanced down at Harry as the dog laid his head over Bodie's thigh. Bodie swapped hands holding the phone and put his hand on the dog's back. "I'm doing some house repairs and was asked for references. Just keep information minimal."

"What? Listen, man, if you need money—"

"This isn't about money." He'd been in the military since he was eighteen and the Army had covered almost all his expenses. His salary had been auto-deposited, and the money in the account had done nothing but grow over the years, especially thanks to bonuses with each active combat deployment, and his minimalist living. It wasn't as if he'd had a lot of opportunity to spend where he'd often been.

"Speaking of money, Kelly found what you left on the coffee table. You shouldn't have."

"Room and board for the past few months. No big deal." Scratching Harry, Bodie shrugged, despite the fact that his friend couldn't see him.

"You didn't need to do that. iSecure is doing great and even if it wasn't, you're always welcome here. You know that."

"Yeah, well, put it toward the kid's college fund." Kelly was due to deliver their first child in a couple of months. Which was the main reason Bodie had headed out that morning. He'd been going to Texas so the couple could have some time to themselves them before their baby arrived.

"A gift from Uncle Bodie?"

Bodie heard a chair squeak and could picture his friend sitting at his desk. Lukas had transitioned into civilian life without issues. Bodie was glad, and hoped he'd be able to find the same sense of peace in the civilian world. At iSecure, he'd start with smaller jobs, mostly guarding celebrities or politicians, as he continued to recover. When Lukas felt he was ready, he'd move to the more secretive jobs the company didn't advertise. Governments and the mega-wealthy came to them seeking their services for high-risk situations. Bodie could do babysitting bodyguard jobs while he honed his body back to full capacity and placated Lukas. What a joke, when his friend knew the things he'd done and was capable of.

"On the reference you're needing, this an under-cover job?"

Since he hadn't told Sarah why he was there in case she refused his help under those circumstances, he supposed he was undercover.

"Yes." His tone warned Lukas not to push. He'd rather his friend not know he'd gone soft and was helping Sarah because she'd once made him a quilt. Lukas had already teased him about the quilt having super healing powers as his friend had witnessed the change in Bodie after its arrival.

Maybe the quilt did have something special in its stitches. Beneath the fabric, he'd felt comfort. No, that wasn't right. He'd felt the need to do something, to be something. For the first time since his injury, he'd felt he had a reason to heal, spurred by the idea that there was something out there waiting on him.

Seeing the quilt, he'd had flashbacks to when he'd been five years old and taken his only out-of-state trip with his mother. He'd stared out the window in awe at picturesque barns with painted quilts on them surrounded by lush green fields as she'd driven them through Georgia for his grandmother's funeral. They'd packed a few of his grandmother's belongings to bring back to Texas, including a raggedy old quilt that Bodie had slept beneath on the drive and countless times thereafter.

Touching the quilt from Sarah had taken him back to when, wrapped in that tattered quilt, he'd watched old war movies while downing a bowl of cereal and dreaming of being a soldier to fight for justice for all.

Sarah's quilt had reminded him of who he'd been,

of who he'd wanted to be, and why he'd needed to quit wallowing in gloom.

Like a magic cloak, he'd wrapped it around him to ward off darkness and it had worked.

"Fine," Lukas agreed, interrupting Bodie's trip down memory lane. "You got it. You know there's no one I'd trust more. How's my dog?"

"You mean *my* dog, and he's good."

Lukas laughed. "A good traitor. Must have sensed our family was expanding yet again and decided he wanted to keep to the bachelor life."

"Must have." Bodie scratched Harry's scruff while the dog looked up at him with his one blue eye and one green eye. Harry's expression was one of pure adoration.

Bodie had owned pets over the years, but he'd never had a dog as smart or as loyal as Harry. From the moment he'd arrived at Lukas and Kelly's place, Harry had taken to him so intently it was impossible not to notice the dog's attachment. Sarah's gift had helped him to push through the physical and emotional pain and refocus on why he'd done the things he had. But he hadn't been ready for a dog to want his attention and affection twenty-four seven. Harry hadn't cared if he was ready or not. If Bodie wasn't gone for his physical therapy, or to a doctor's appointment, the dog refused to leave his side.

Lukas had insisted Harry go with him when Bodie left that morning, stating he'd gladly take the dog for extended visits when Bodie left on iSecure jobs so the dog didn't have to be boarded.

Bodie talked with Lukas a few more minutes, then dialed his stepfather.

Leaning his head back against the truck's headrest, he scratched Harry's neck.

"Thought you planned to go back to high-stakes, behind-the-scenes adventures," his stepfather mused after Bodie explained his new plans. "You know, if you want to do this handyman kind of thing, I'll hire you in a heartbeat. You were the best help I ever had. Your mother wasn't the only one who was disappointed when you joined the military. I'd always hoped you'd join me."

His stepfather was a good man and had taught Bodie everything he could to prepare him for life from the time Bodie had met him at age ten. Bodie had been lucky in that regard. Steve had treated him well, like his own son. Thanks to the man's patience and guiding hand to a kid whose real father had long since stepped out of the picture, there wasn't much Bodie couldn't do around a house.

"I'll keep it in mind, Steve. I appreciate the offer and the reference."

Hanging up the phone, he glanced down at Harry.

"Now what?" he asked the dog, who just cocked his head as if to say, *You tell me.*

He punched the address Sarah had given him into his phone's map app. She lived less than ten minutes away, which meant he had a couple of hours to kill.

For now, he and Harry needed sustenance and time out of the truck cab.

Thinking back over what he'd passed on his drive into town, he recalled a diner with several cars out front and wondered if they were pet-friendly.

It occurred to him that he hadn't eaten since early that morning during one of many pitstops made to stretch the stiffness out of his hip and leg from the long drive. He hated having to take such mundane things into consideration, but he'd do whatever was necessary to heal back into tip-top shape.

He'd been told by multiple health professionals that had he not been in such good physical condition, he'd never have survived the IED.

There had been a time when he wished he hadn't survived.

He glanced over at the folded patriotic quilt sitting on top of a duffel bag in his passenger floorboard and was reminded of exactly why he was in Pine Hill.

Sarah had meant to get to Hamilton House and straighten up any extra mess before her new handyman arrived. No such luck. It had taken longer to clean the church community room from their Christmas crafting than she'd intended, which was why she was feeling anxious as she drove the short distance home.

Her nervousness had nothing to do with the man she was meeting.

Just that she was running late and keeping an eye on her speedometer to make sure she kept it at the speed limit. Silly Donnie Jones had written her a ticket last week.

When she got to Hamilton House's driveway, a late-model pickup she didn't recognize was already there. She pulled up beside it and saw the cab was empty.

She looked around and spotted Bodie in her yard. What was he doing? Surprised, she realized he was petting a black and white speckled dog.

"Sorry I'm late," Sarah apologized as she got out of the car, putting on her hat and scarf as she eyed the unfamiliar animal. He looked like a Blue Heeler mix, but she'd never been great on telling one breed from another. Where had he come from? He looked friendly enough and seemed to be eating up the attention Bodie was giving him, but who knew what the forty-or-so-pound dog was capable of?

"Be careful. That's not my dog. I've never seen him before," she warned, pulling her jacket tighter around her to block the chilly wind as she walked toward Bodie.

Straightening, Bodie stuck his hands in his jean pockets. "Harry's mine."

As if to second the notion, the dog, Harry, ruffed and took a sitting-but-on-guard post at Bodie's feet, watching Sarah's every move as she stepped closer.

As she approached, using caution in case the dog decided he didn't like her getting near, Sarah's eyes widened. "You have a dog?"

"I have a dog. You sound as if you thought I'd be more likely to have a dragon or something." He reached down to scratch the dog's head again.

The dog watched her with great curiosity, as if trying to decide if she were friend or foe, and waiting for his owner to clue him in.

Heat infused her cheeks at her rudeness. "Sorry. You just didn't come across as a dog person."

Harry licked Bodie's fingers in appreciation of the scratch.

"No? What type of person did I come across as?" Flecks in his eyes caught the light, almost giving the impression he was teasing her.

"Surely not as a cat person," he continued, his lips edging upward ever so slightly.

"No," she assured, thinking for a second Bodie was going to smile.

Hoping he was going to smile.

Come on, she wanted to encourage. *Smile for me.*

Which made no sense.

It did not matter to her whether he smiled or not. He was here for a job. Not a friendship.

Then again, didn't she pride herself on being friendly to everyone? If Bodie was going to work at Hamilton House, of course she'd want to be friends.

"Not that there's anything wrong with cats," he continued, his blue eyes still looking a bit mischievous. "I grew up with a houseful. But since meeting Harry, I've discovered I'm a dog guy."

Harry nudged up against him as if to say that he was a Bodie Lewis kind of dog. The love the animal had for his owner was obvious, and had Sarah softening even if Bodie hadn't smiled. Animals were good judges of character, right? Maybe Sarah's first impression had been all wrong. After all, anyone who had a dog had to smile from time to time. How could they not?

"May I?" She looked to Bodie for permission to pet Harry.

Interestingly, the dog seemed to also be waiting for Bodie's permission as he cocked his head and looked expectantly up at his owner.

Having witnessed Bodie's nod of approval, Harry was happy for more attention and hunkered into a somewhat submissive position. He rolled onto his back so Sarah could scratch his belly, then back onto his feet to nudge her hand with his nose.

Laughing at the dog's antics, she glanced up at Bodie. "I'll admit, I didn't see you as a pet person, in general, but I can see how Harry would win a person over."

Hands back in his jean's pockets, he eyed her petting Harry. "You just met me, so I'm not sure what to say to that."

True enough. She didn't know what to say to that, either.

Knowing she'd stuck her foot in her mouth enough for one conversation, she gave Harry one last stroke behind his ears, then straightened and gestured toward the house. "You want to come inside and see what needs to be done? Or do you want to see the outside of the house first?"

He glanced toward the house. "I took the liberty of walking around and inspecting the outside while I was waiting. It's in good shape, overall. Looks like you recently had it repainted. The trim work is great, especially around the porch. There are a few places that need to be touched up that were missed and a piece of damaged wood that, although covered with fresh paint, really needs replaced to keep in line with the rest of the woodwork. Otherwise, not bad on the outside. It's a beautiful place."

Sarah knew exactly the piece of trim he meant and those missed paint places had driven her crazy. Although they'd done a great job overall, she'd mentioned the spots to the painters several times, but they'd never come back to correct the areas. That Bodie had noticed impressed her. At first glance, the paint job looked good, but she wanted Hamilton House perfect.

Perfection was impossible with a house that was over a hundred years old. She knew this. But still, how much more work would it have been for the painters to have replaced the damaged trim piece rather than to just slap a couple coats of paint onto it? Especially when she'd been willing to pay to have it made right?

Bodie asked, "You've had someone inspect the foundation?"

"Structurally, the house is sound." Or so said the architect she'd consulted prior to her embarking on her dream of turning Hamilton House into a B & B. The gentleman was a local, a friend of her father's, and hadn't charged her a penny even though she'd tried to pay him.

She'd needed all the help she could get since she didn't know anything about foundations, architecture, electrical wiring, or plumbing. She just knew she loved this house, had loved visiting her aunt Jean every afternoon when she'd gotten out of school and staying with her during summer breaks while her father was at work. Aunt Jean had taught her so many things— how to cook, to sew, to quilt—and had encouraged her love of reading, her love of serving others.

Oh, how she missed Aunt Jean.

"I've gotten a lot done over the past year, including an unbelievable amount of paperwork to make sure I have all the right permits and licenses. I've been able to do that end of things myself. On the physical repairs, I've worked on what I can, but it needs a lot more. Much more than I can afford to give, really." The sooner she got it up and running, the better. "My goal is to have the downstairs looking sharp by Christmas, which will be"—hopefully, and depending upon him—"the grand opening of Hamilton House Bed and Breakfast."

She loved saying the name out loud. It made her dream seem more real. Aunt Jean's dream.

"As the bed and breakfast takes off, I'll do renovations to the upstairs rooms and get them rent-ready."

Renovations that would include replacing furniture her aunt had sold off over the years for financial reasons. Sarah had found a ledger in which her aunt had kept records of each piece and who she'd sold it to. An antique store in Louisville had purchased most of the pieces initially, but over the last few years her aunt had sold only to an entry marked as "B."

Sarah's heart ached at the permanent loss of the lovely antique pieces her aunt had once owned. Antiques Sarah had treasured and that had been a part of her childhood. Pretending she was mistress of the house, she would go from room to room imagining that she was hosting elaborate dinner parties and balls. She could vividly recall the grandeur of each room—the lavish decor, the tapestries on the walls, the rich woods of the sturdy furniture.

Once upon a time, Hamilton House, as she'd dubbed it as a child, had been a gorgeous home that could've been snatched straight out of a movie. Unfortunately, Roy Hamilton had gone to serve in the Vietnam War and had never come back. He'd left his teen bride in his family home with his elderly parents, a well-to-do couple who'd lived with Aunt Jean until their passing. He'd left his young widow well-off financially by 1960s standards, to the point where she'd never had to work. But neither one of them could have predicted the twists and turns of the financial market, or how that would impact Jean's situation. As the years had passed, so had the money, apparently.

Sarah hadn't known about her aunt's poor finances in her latter days. How could she have, when it had been years since she'd had reason to go into any of the four second-level bedrooms while visiting her aunt? She'd had no idea her aunt had been emptying one room after another, each slowly stripped of its treasures. How it must have pained Aunt Jean to let each piece go. If Sarah had known, she'd have taken on another job or moved in and paid rent.

Something. Anything.

"The roof looks new, too," Bodie said, calling Sarah's attention back to him.

"I replaced it this past spring." It was the first thing she'd done after getting her loan. "As a matter of necessity. Apparently, there had been a slow leak for years." The memory had her stomach dropping. That the wood beneath the roof was so rotted had been a big blow. "There was so much damage that they had to rip out and replace a section of beams and wood in the attic ceiling, too."

She glanced up at the new roof that topped the mint-green house with its intricate white trim work.

"Fortunately, the interior damage from the leak was limited to a section in the attic."

She'd had to toss a few boxes of old books, receipts, and papers that had been water-damaged. Someday, Sarah planned to go through the remaining boxes and trunks in the attic in hopes of finding things that had belonged to Aunt Jean or to Sarah's grandparents. Once she got the downstairs restored to its former glory and Hamilton House was up and running, then she'd make time for going through taped-up boxes with layers of dust on top.

Sarah pointed to the porch that wrapped around one side of the house. "You ready to have a look inside? There's a lot to be done before I open up the house to visitors."

They made their way up the porch, Harry at Bodie's side.

"If you don't think he'll bother anything, Harry can come in," she offered. It was chilly outside, and Harry was so well-behaved, she couldn't imagine him causing trouble.

Bodie nodded. "He can wait inside the door." After they followed Sarah inside, he paused and looked at the dog. "Stay."

After only a moment's obvious disappointment, Harry laid down on the rug, looking up at his owner with obedient, loving eyes.

Bodie glanced around the foyer of Hamilton House. He took in the curve near the top of the staircase with its beautiful walnut handrail and top-to-bottom antique runner down the center of the wooden steps, the gleaming hardwood floor, and the ornately trimmed ceiling with its decades-old chandelier. His gaze paused at the three photos on the stair wall—a black and white of Uncle Roy's parents at their wedding, a black and white of Aunt Jean and Uncle Roy on their wedding day, and one of Sarah as a snaggle-toothed little girl. Sarah had complained that the photo needed to be updated, but Aunt Jean had insisted she could only replace it with a black and white wedding photo.

That goofy picture would probably be there as long as the house stood.

The foyer was the showpiece of the house. Always had been. Pride filled Sarah as she watched Bodie's eyes fill with appreciation of the room.

An appreciation she hoped each guest would feel when they visited Hamilton House.

"I had the floors redone and the paint freshened," she said, unable to hold in her excitement, "but otherwise, this is how this room has looked since the house was first built."

Even when her aunt's financial situation had worsened, she'd kept this room pristine, knowing that it was the first thing a visitor would see and that it would shape their opinion of the house. It was also the threshold Aunt Jean's beloved groom had once carried her over the first time she'd entered the house as his wife.

"Well, except for the light fixture," she corrected, eying the intricate metal and crystal chandelier. "I know it's old, but I'm not positive it's the original fixture or if it was added at some point. And obviously, the photos are newer additions. But otherwise, this is Hamilton House as it should be." She spread her arms and slowly turned. "This is what I want to restore the rest of the house to."

CHAPTER THREE

FEELING AS IF HE SHOULDN'T touch anything—and maybe that he shouldn't even be inside the house—Bodie took in each room.

No doubt, Hamilton House had been a showplace in its day, and Sarah was intent on returning it to its former glory. Her pride and love for the place oozed from every pore. The fact that she belonged here did, too.

After the terrible places he'd been, this old house, and Sarah's connection to it, seemed an oddity. That anyone could be so caught up in a house, could so obviously belong within its walls, fascinated Bodie.

Or maybe it was Sarah who fascinated him.

She didn't wear a wedding band, or any jewelry save a gold chain around her neck. The attached pendant was hidden under her collar.

"You're doing this by yourself?"

She shook her head. "I've had an architect, contractors, electricians, plumbers, floor people, roof people, pest control people, the Historical Society, painters, and dozens of others giving their input or working. I can't take credit for much of the actual labor. My home restoration skills are minimal at best." She gave him an impish smile. "Mostly, I'm overseeing things."

He'd wanted to know whether or not she had a husband or significant other to help her. Still, she'd answered his question.

"Why?"

Her warm brown gaze met his. "This was my aunt's home. I spent a lot of time here while growing up." A faraway look settled onto her face as she continued. "Later in life, she dreamed of turning the house into a bed and breakfast so it would be filled with love and laughter and people again. When she died, she left me the house and her dream."

Things and places didn't matter too much to Bodie. He'd moved a lot as a kid and had found it easier not to get attached. Just being inside four walls was enough to make him antsy. Sarah Smith didn't seem to suffer from that malady. She was invested in this house and in her aunt's vision.

What did that even feel like? To be so attached to a place?

"Fulfilling that dream is my legacy."

He nodded as if he understood. In truth, he couldn't help but stare at her, wondering at how different their lives had been.

Glancing around the kitchen, she changed the subject. "I've finished this room. Don't you love it? I tried to modernize without taking away the charm from the past."

She'd done a good job. The room looked like something off one of those television home remodel shows he'd watched while laid up in bed month after month.

"All the appliances are new." She looked around the room, delight lighting her pretty face. "Well, most everything in this room is new. I was able to use the cabinets—I just reinforced them so I could replace the countertops with granite and put a coat of paint over them. I had the new sinks put in and the island built with the extra sink, oven, and the commercial dishwasher."

Her pleasure in the room coated every word.

"Someday, I hope to be able to cater to ten guests at a time. Can't you just see them sitting around on the opposite side of the island and in the breakfast nook?" She gestured to a hexagonal area with multiple long windows and a built-in bench that ran the entire length of the outer walls of the nook. Dark gray drawstring curtains topped each window. The table was shaped the same as the room and fit the area perfectly. "They'll fill the space with energy and conversation while I cook them breakfast."

Her voice was so dreamily content, Bodie's gaze cut to her rather than the cozy area she'd created. He couldn't recall having ever met someone so idealistic, so a part of their surroundings, so full of dreams.

"They'll be drinking coffee or hot cocoa, a few reading the paper, catching up on world news. The whole house will smell of whatever is baking in the oven. Christmas music will be playing in the background and there will be a garland with lights over the cabinets. I'll have a big Christmas tree over there."

A soft sigh escaped her mouth. Bodie couldn't keep his gaze from dropping to her pink lips.

Quickly, he looked away.

That was not why he was here. Not even close.

He was there to thank Sarah. Not to complicate her life, or his, by noticing how pretty she was or how being near her made him excited to be a small part of the restoration, to play a small role in making her dream come true.

"This room and the living room are done." She ran her finger along the neutral gray and white granite with its subtle flecks of black. "But, in addition to my room, there are two downstairs suites and neither of them are even close to ready to receive guests."

"That's what you need me to do? Get those suites ready?"

Still lost in her vision of the house, she nodded.

"Let's see them so I can make sure what you need is within my skills."

When they stepped into the first suite, Bodie frowned. "Who started the remodel?"

Sarah's forehead wrinkled. "Which time?"

Bodie gave her a dubious look. "What happened?"

She didn't meet his eyes. "The last one quit."

"Because?"

Pink stained her cheeks. "Because of me."

Her expression was so flustered, Bodie could only imagine what had happened. "He fell for you and you had to let him go?"

Eyes wide, Sarah laughed. "The only falling he did was off the ladder in his hurry to get away from me. He couldn't get out of here fast enough after I yelled at him for dribbling paint all over the newly-refinished hardwood floors."

"There's plastic taped down to protect the floors," Bodie pointed out, not mentioning that she should've had the painting completed prior to getting the floors refinished. Why hadn't someone told her that?

"There is *now*. But on that day, there wasn't anything protecting the floor. It took me several hours to clean up the paint splatter." She closed her eyes as if to erase the memory. "I put the plastic down because I wasn't risking that happening again."

Maybe it was her Christmas sweater and hair ribbon, but the woman personified good cheer and he had a difficult time imaging her being upset with anyone, the painter included.

Thanking whatever fate had put him in the right place at the right time that he could do this for her, he asked, "You have furniture to go in here?"

"I had what's left of my aunt's things moved into my father's garage before the hardwood floors were redone." She gestured to a far wall that had a new, unframed doorway cut into it. "That is going to be a bathroom, as there's only one bathroom in the whole house. Even that was high tech for the time the house was built. However, it won't be enough for a bed and breakfast."

He walked over to the cut-out doorway, then entered the dark room. The room was framed. Plumbing and electric wiring had been started. But that was it. No walls covering the framing two-by-fours, and there was no tub, vanity or sink, and no toilet. Nothing but the ceiling, the exposed walls, and the rough plywood floors.

It was decent-sized for a bathroom. He suspected the bathroom for the other bedroom was on the other side of one of the walls. No doubt a small room had been cut up to make the extra bathrooms.

Bodie tallied how long it would take him, adding in extra time for unexpected things that would likely arise. He should be able to finish what Sarah needed in her time frame.

"I can do the work."

Her eyes brightened. "Really? You can finish everything? The electrical and plumbing, too?"

"Nah," he couldn't resist saying.

Her lips parted. "Oh?"

One side of his mouth hiked up. "I'm kidding, Sarah. Check my references. I haven't done this kind of work in a while, but everything you need is within my capabilities. If you want me, I'm your man."

"I heard your fella had dinner over at Lou's place and then checked into the Pine Hill Motel."

"He's not my fella," Sarah insisted as she, Maybelle, Rosie, Ruby, and Claudia sorted through the ornaments they'd made the day before, checking for any that needed a touch-up, prior to working on that day's batch.

Memories of the afternoon before hit. She hadn't expected Bodie's half-smile or how her heart had thundered at the expression, and at the fact he'd teased her.

At his promise that if she wanted him, he was her man.

"Well, technically, he is," she added, correcting herself. "He started at Hamilton House this morning."

"You left him there alone?" Claudia asked, sounding surprised Sarah wasn't standing over him with an eagle eye.

"I didn't babysit the other handymen. Why would I with him?" she asked. "Besides, there aren't any family jewels for him to take off with. If there ever had been, they'd be long gone by now."

"His references checked out?"

He'd given two and they had both answered her questions about him with enthusiasm and without hesitation. One had been a handyman who'd employed him years ago, and another was the owner of a security company who had hired him to start work in the new year.

"They couldn't sing his praises loudly enough. The owner of Steve's Home Repairs says there's not much he can't do and do well. Actually, he said Bodie was the best help he's ever had, and he'd take him back in a heartbeat." Good. She needed Bodie Lewis to be the world's greatest handyman. "Apparently, he's been military and is just back to civilian life."

At least, that's what the owner of the security company had told her. They'd served in the Army together. Recalling how Brody had looked when he'd entered the community room the day before, she had to admit the military background fit.

"Mr. Lewis seemed like an honest enough fellow, but he's not from around here," Maybelle said.

A big no-no in all the older women's eyes, as they claimed Pine Hill men were built better than others— or maybe it was just Ruby who claimed that last part?

"Just be careful," Maybelle continued. "Don't be too trusting."

"Or loosen the reins to your heart too quick."

Taken aback, Sarah turned toward Ruby. "Pardon?"

"Not every man can be like my Charlie." She giggled, fluffed her dyed red hair, then continued. "Actually, no man can be as good as my Charlie, but be sure this guy is a good one before you give away your heart."

Sarah choked back a laugh. "Not that I'm interested in anyone who can have an entire conversation without a single smile, but I think I'm safe. He didn't seem overly interested, either."

Now why had she said that? She wasn't giving her heart to Bodie Lewis, or any man in the near future. What did it matter if he'd looked interested or not?

Realizing the women were suspiciously quiet, Sarah glanced around the table. The four older women exchanged a look that spelled trouble.

"What?" Sarah asked. "He didn't smile. Not once." But that wasn't quite true. She remembered his half-smile again.

Silence met her as the women were exchanging silent communications that came from decades of friendship.

"Surely you noticed?" Sarah persisted, not liking that she was the subject of those looks. She might not have been around since the inception of the Butterflies, but she'd known these women all her life. She could feel their Cupid pings shooting her way as surely as if they pricked her skin.

Didn't they realize they were wasting their time? Her life experiences served as a pretty good shield. Experiences that included her runaway ex, Hamilton

House, and money woes. The last thing she needed was a man distracting her.

Averting her gaze, she went back to studying a plastic canvas snowflake.

"I was busy noticing other things," Rosie said with a waggle of her drawn-on eyebrows, breaking the silence.

"I noticed—his lack of smile and the things Rosie is referring to." Maybelle held up an ornament and gestured toward Sarah. "I wondered what had dimmed his inner light, because that man has powerhouse potential. It makes me want to know why he isn't a beacon."

Sarah blinked at Maybelle. The woman always saw too much. Sarah would swear that at any point in her life when she was struggling with something, Maybelle had known from one look that something was wrong.

She and Aunt Jean had both read Sarah like a book.

She supposed she should be grateful Maybelle hadn't outright asked Bodie to tell her his life story and then, if she approved, asked if he was single.

But now that Maybelle had brought up the idea, it nagged at Sarah. Had something bad happened to him? Or had he always been someone who didn't have happiness? Not everyone did, unfortunately. Sad when his handsome face appeared to have been made for smiling. Would a full smile reach his blue eyes? Light up his whole being? Calm the storm she'd sensed brewed just beneath the surface?

Why was she obsessing over wanting to see a total stranger smile?

"Maybe he needs you to give him a reason to shine," Claudia added.

"I'll get Charlie to talk to him," Ruby offered. "He can put him on the right path for you, brighten him up a bit."

The thought of seventy-year-old Charlie having "a talk" with Bodie had Sarah shaking her head and staring at the women.

If she wasn't careful, the Butterflies would have Bodie doing more than repairing Hamilton House. They were all Cupid wannabes who needed to have their wings clipped. Good thing she had sense enough to not get caught up in their shenanigans.

"Perhaps y'all are forgetting, or just indulging in wishful thinking, but I placed a help-wanted ad, not a singles ad. Mr. Lewis is looking for work, not someone to put a smile on his face, light his beacon, or make a match for him," Sarah reminded. "I am just thankful he happened through Pine Hill and saw my ad."

"No one just happens through Pine Hill."

Sarah frowned. Ruby was right. Pine Hill was off the beaten path.

"I should ask him how it was he ended up in our tiny neck of the woods," she said.

"You definitely should. He could be a serial killer on the run," Claudia suggested, tucking a loose strand of gray hair behind her ear.

Maybelle rolled her eyes. "He's not."

Something in the way Maybelle said the words so confidently had Sarah asking, "How do you know that?"

"I had Sheriff Roscoe run his tags," Maybelle said matter-of-factly, as if it was no big deal.

"What?"

"You heard me." Maybelle didn't so much as bat an eyelash, just kept on sorting through the ornaments and placing the ones that passed inspection carefully into a box that would be stored until the day of the Christmas festival.

The woman never ceased to amaze Sarah. Outside of doing something illegal, Sarah couldn't imagine Sheriff Roscoe, or anyone, ever telling Maybelle no. When the town matriarch said to jump, most people asked how high.

"Dare I even ask how you got his tag number?"

Maybelle glanced at Rosie who beamed with pride, rather than guilt.

Oh, good grief, what had they done?

She could just see them donning black clothes and ski masks, stalking Bodie. They could probably tell her his shoe size and what he'd had for breakfast, too.

Rosie's chin tilted a little higher than usual as she said, "You might recall Lou had that fancy security system installed at the diner a few years ago. Seems his cameras pick up all kinds of things in his parking lot."

They'd gotten Lou in on their investigative action? The big-hearted restaurateur didn't seem the Sherlock Holmes type. Poor Lou. There was no telling what Rosie had done to get him involved.

Eyebrow arched, she asked, "Things like Bodie's license plate?"

Rosie nodded. "Pulled the recordings right up on his phone and there it was, clear as a bell."

"Why would Lou pay any attention to Bodie's

truck?" Sarah's head spun as she processed what the women had been up to.

"When I mentioned our visitor, Lou told me he'd met him in the diner," Rosie said. "He said he seemed like a nice enough fella, but didn't stay long, just ate and left."

"Lou figured he didn't stick around because he had a dog with him that stayed in his truck while he was in the diner," Ruby added.

"Harry," Sarah filled in. At their confused looks, she clarified, "The dog. His name is Harry. Smartest dog I've ever met."

"Okay, so Harry was in the truck." Rosie looked at Sarah with a touch of annoyance that she'd interrupted for such a trivial detail. "Anyway, I had Lou pull up his security footage because I wanted another look, just wanting to make sure I didn't see anything suspicious about your new handyman, of course."

"Of course," the other three women and Sarah said at the same time, causing all to chuckle.

"Mighty generous of you taking it upon yourself to check Mr. Lewis out further for our Sarah," Maybelle contributed with her usual bit of sass.

"Without me, you wouldn't have gotten to ask Sheriff Roscoe to run his tags, now would you?" Rosie pointed out to her friend, then patted her well-coiffed blue hair. "Now, where was I? Oh yes. Lou's been after me for years. When I mentioned I was worried about you because of this newcomer, he mentioned his cameras. He appreciated the opportunity to do something nice for me. Some people do, you know."

"We know," they all said in unison, eliciting a

round of giggles that better befitted teens than senior citizens.

"I took a picture of Lou's video footage and sent it to the others, so they'd know I was doing my part to keep you safe."

"Sarah didn't need a play by play." Maybelle's eyes went heavenward again. "After that, I zoomed in on the picture Rosie sent, cropped his tag, and texted my photo to the sheriff."

Maybelle's tone brooked no argument on the fact that she'd been well within her rights to do so.

"And to think, I taught you how to use a smartphone," Sarah mused, secretly impressed by the women's sleuth work. Sometimes she wondered if the Butterflies were some former secret society in days gone past.

"That was a useful class you put on," Claudia praised. "Now I can text with my grandkids and wow them with my emoji-sending abilities. It was one of the best classes you've ever put on in the community room."

"You really should consider annual update courses," Rosie added, pulling her phone out and clicking on her camera. She had it in reverse camera mode. It was a distinct possibility that, other than the rare spying photo, Rosie's phone was permanently set that way. "It took me forever to figure out how to add gifs to my messages."

"Didn't take her near as long to figure out how to Photoshop twenty years off her selfies," Maybelle added drily, pulling a snowflake out and putting it in the "needs work" stack. "One click of a button and wrinkles be gone! Of course, so is her nose since it takes so much blurring."

Rosie's mouth dropped open and she tossed an ornament at Maybelle, who just chuckled and added it to her "needs work" pile.

"I do not blur my nose out of photos, Maybelle Kirby," Rosie denied with great indignation, then smiled sweetly as she added, "I understand how you could miss it, though, being as it's not nearly as big as the one on your face."

Staring at them, Sarah slowly shook her head. "I don't know why I thought any of you could be trusted with advanced technology."

Poor Bodie. He had no clue what he'd gotten himself into when he'd agreed to work at Hamilton House.

"His references checked out and I hired him."

From the moment she'd watched him with Harry, she'd liked him. There was an inherent honesty about Bodie. Yes, he had a dark cloud hanging over his head that said *back off*, but just as visible was a sense of honor and morals. She'd barely met him, and yet she trusted him.

"Aren't you curious what the sheriff found out?" Maybelle tempted, the twinkle in her eye saying she knew something Sarah didn't.

"You already told me he wasn't a serial killer," Sarah reminded, feeling a little guilty that they'd essentially done a background check on Bodie. Still, she supposed since he was a stranger to Pine Hill, she understood why the women had. Despite her gut instinct that told her he was a decent person, she should have requested one herself.

She wouldn't tell the spying queens, but knowing

they'd checked Bodie out made her feel less silly for immediately taking him at his word. He'd come across as someone who was dependable, and who lived by high ethics. Time would tell.

"Sheriff Roscoe says he's clean," Maybelle continued in her deadpan voice, letting Sarah know a punch line was about to come.

She wasn't disappointed.

"Not even a speeding ticket on his record."

Sarah fought sticking her tongue out at Maybelle. She was way too old to do so, but sometimes, the Butterflies made her feel as if she were back in grade school, hanging with Aunt Jean and them as they worked on some project. They'd always included her, always treated her as if she belonged to them all rather than just Aunt Jean.

"If that was a jab at me," Sarah said, ignoring the laughter in Maybelle's eyes, "You should know that I was running late to meet with the school board about our back-to-school backpack program and wasn't driving that fast."

She'd only been going four miles over the speed limit and there hadn't been another car on the road for miles, for goodness' sake. She'd barely crossed into the lowered speed zone when the blue lights came on.

"Donnie should have given me a warning, not an actual ticket."

"He gave you a warning the time before," Claudia reminded in her most grandmotherly tone.

Sarah wrinkled her nose. Well, yeah, there was that time last month when she'd been going a whole two miles over the posted speed limit when Donnie had gotten blue-light happy, too.

"Well, it's good to know Bodie hasn't run into Donnie since he's been in town," she pointed out, then gestured to their ornaments. "That's the last of these. Ready to cut out more snowflakes before it's time to deliver meals to shut-ins?"

There were lots of little odds and ends needing addressed or touching up, but Bodie had decided to start with the first bedroom Sarah had shown him. It was the bigger of the two downstairs rooms she wanted done and had been her aunt's. The other had belonged to her aunt's in-laws.

Sarah had told Bodie he could go anywhere in the house and Harry could come inside if he kept an eye on him. No worries on that account. If he moved, Harry moved. The dog apparently thought Bodie couldn't inspect the house unless he accompanied him.

Still feeling as if he didn't belong inside the sprawling old mansion, Bodie pushed the uneasiness aside by focusing on his work. He did a full check starting at the bottom by crawling under the floor space. After making sure to clean off any stray dirt, he then checked the attic to identify any problems Sarah might be unaware of before heading downstairs.

One by one, he inspected the rooms, making written notes.

When he'd gone through the door to the room where Sarah slept, his throat had tightened.

With its sunny yellow walls and intricate blue and yellow quilt covering a full-sized bed, the room fit Sarah. Next to her bed was a walnut nightstand with a well-read Bible and lamp on it. There was a matching walnut wardrobe and dresser. But what drew him was across from Sarah's bed.

He walked over to the table where the antiquated sewing machine was set up and ran his finger over the sleek line of the black and gold machine. The quilting in Sarah's creation had been done by hand, but most likely she'd sewn the quilt top pieces together while sitting here.

Even now, with everything she had going on, there were sewn pieces of fabric neatly stacked in a basket where she worked on a new quilt top.

Red, white, and blue fabric.

She was making another Quilt of Valor, a precious gift to another soldier. Would that recipient appreciate Sarah's generosity the way Bodie had? Would this quilt offer hope the way his had to him?

Would that person go from the bleakest black to seeing a flicker of light as he or she read the note Sarah would no doubt attach to the quilt?

Closing his eyes, he took a deep breath.

He shouldn't be here. Not in Sarah's room. Not in Hamilton House. Not in Pine Hill. He didn't belong.

But he would do this, would make the repairs for Sarah, would pretend he fit into her shiny world when he'd only ever belonged as an Army Ranger serving his country in a desert half a world away.

When the repairs were done, he'd move on, having repaid her kindness. She need never know why he'd come to Pine Hill or why he'd been willing to linger in the town she'd painted so vividly in his mind but that made him starkly aware of how much he was an outsider.

She'd told him to go wherever, but being here, in

her private space, in the room where she'd likely made his quilt, felt wrong. He exited the room, closing the door behind him even though she'd left it open that morning. He didn't want to see into her room when he walked down the hallway.

Bodie continued his inspection, taking measurements and making notes. When finished, he sat down at Sarah's kitchen island with a pen and paper and began making lists. He was still sitting there working when Harry's ears perked up at about the same time as Bodie heard a car in the driveway.

Barking, Harry took off toward the noise. He sounded ferocious, but the second he reached the front door and realized it was Sarah, the dog quieted.

"Bodie?" Sarah called from the foyer. "Hey, boy," she baby-talked his dog. "Yes, I know you want this, but this is lunch for Bodie and me. Next time I'll bring something for you, too."

"In here," he called, glancing toward his wrist. He was surprised at how much time had passed—and even more surprised that Sarah had brought him food.

"Oh," she gasped when she stepped into the kitchen, bags in hand, and caught sight of him sitting at the bar. "I didn't realize you were in here."

He stood up from the barstool and reached to take some of her bags. "Let me help you."

"Thanks," she said, placing the remaining bags next to the legal pad he'd been scribbling on. "I wasn't sure if you'd brought anything for lunch, or if you planned to go get something, or what. When I picked up my lunch from Lou's, he sent some for you, too."

Whatever was in the sack was making his stomach

rumble with the same hungry longing he saw in Harry's eyes.

He'd eaten at Lou's twice the day before and had met the owner. Nice guy—mid-sixties to maybe seventy. Crinkled eyes and forehead; calloused, scarred hands that implied he'd worked hard his entire life; and a friendly hello to everyone who came into his restaurant.

"Why would he do that?" The man had been nice enough, but restaurant owners didn't usually give away their wares to strangers.

As she was pulling items from the bag, Sarah looked at him and she shrugged. "I think he felt guilty."

Bodie frowned. His lunch and his dinner the night before had been excellent. What did the guy have to feel guilty about?

"Why?" Had the man felt bad that he had a "no animals inside the restaurant" policy? It hadn't been that big of a deal. Lots of places didn't allow pets.

Sarah tilted her head and gave a little shrug as she continued to pull items from her bag. "Let's just say Lou may or may not have played a role in a background check being run on you."

Bodie's brows rose. "Why would a restaurant owner run a background check on me?" He'd paid with cash, but even if he'd paid with a credit card, not that he had one, that would've been a bit excessive.

Not that anyone would find anything problematic. He'd done some nasty jobs, but everything he'd done had come from official orders and he had a pristine service record. He'd been a good soldier.

"Don't be upset," Sarah urged, pausing in what she was doing to give him a pleading look. "Lou was watching out for me." She paused, then started over. "Well, he might have been trying to win points with Rosie, too." Sarah gave an indulgent smile at the woman's name. "To hear her tell it, that was his motivation, anyway. Regardless, Lou's intentions weren't bad."

Still confused but not wanting to make a big deal out of it, Bodie shrugged. "No problem. I've got nothing to hide."

Except a quilt he'd folded and packed away inside the large duffel bag in his truck so Sarah wouldn't see it.

"That's what I was told," she admitted, walking over to remove two glasses from a cabinet and flashing another smile that added a sparkle to her eyes. "Water?"

Quietly wondering if anyone had ever been blinded by the dazzle in a smile, Bodie nodded.

When she'd poured them both glasses, she put one of them in front of him and the other in front of a stool one place down from his. Having given him a burger and a box of fries, she sat down and unwrapped her own burger.

"I hear you're so squeaky-clean that you've never even had a speeding ticket," she said before taking a generous bite. "Mmmm, this is good."

It was true—he didn't have any traffic tickets. Possibly because since he'd turned eighteen, he hadn't been in the country for more than a week or two at a time until earlier this year. And even then, it had been months before he'd been released to drive.

Fighting the heaviness that settled onto his shoulders at the memory of why he'd returned stateside, Bodie met Sarah's gaze. He'd just met her in person the day before, but there was something about her that made it easier to pull himself out of the dark pit he'd wallowed in for too long. Maybe it was the quilt, or the joy-filled note she'd attached to it describing a life he'd barely been able to imagine. Having met Sarah, seen Pine Hill first hand, he knew her joy was real. Sarah Smith loved life and that love flowed from her.

She said, "I didn't have you pegged as someone who so closely adhered to the laws of the land."

Her tone was almost disappointed, as if she sort of liked the thought that he might have bad-boy tendencies. Interesting. He eyed her with renewed curiosity.

"Maybe I'm just good enough to not get caught."

Her full lips curved. "I can see how that would be the more likely scenario."

Whoa. Sarah looked at him with a light in her eyes that drew him in like a moth to a flame, making him want to know more, to learn what was beneath the surface, what she thought of him. Maybe someone really could be blinded by a dazzling smile. "Explain."

Her big brown depths shining with something warm and inviting and full of interest, she eyed him as she slowly chewed the bite she'd just taken. "I'm not sure I can without sounding judgmental."

Giving in to his hunger, he took a bite of his burger. It was so good that he would've forgiven Lou on the spot if there'd been anything to forgive. He didn't blame Sarah's friends for checking him out. For that matter, she'd been too trusting to let him into her home unsupervised without looking into his background first. Just because she was full of goodness, she seemed to expect that the rest of the world was, too. Bodie knew better. He'd rarely dealt with goodness over the past decade.

"Try."

She ate a couple of bites, then lowered her dark lashes as she said, "It's just, well, I get the impression that you're smarter than the average bear."

Her explanation wasn't what he'd been expecting. Not that he was sure exactly what he'd been expecting her to say. Then again, she'd just agreed that it was much more likely that he'd just not gotten caught rather than that he was a rule-follower. Whatever it was, he found her answer humorous and he grinned. "You think?"

She went from looking at him, to her eyes widening, to her choking on her burger. When she kept coughing and sputtering, he worried. He stood from his stool and slapped her across the back. Not hard, but enough that if she had food stuck, it would hopefully be dislodged.

Apparently, Harry was ready to act, too—the dog jumped to his feet and gave a loud ruff of concern.

Eyes watering, Sarah sputtered. "You didn't have to do that. I was okay."

"Sure you were. I could tell by the gasping sounds as you tried to breathe."

"See?" She put her hand over her mouth and cleared her throat. "There you go showing how smart you are again."

"Doesn't take a genius to recognize the universal sign for choking."

Wiping at her watery eyes, she said, "I wasn't clutching my throat."

"Much," he corrected, amused at her prideful denials.

Her eyes wide, she asked, "Was I really?"

He nodded.

"I didn't realize," she admitted, staring at her burger. "I, um, was distracted, and, well, my food just went down the wrong direction and then I couldn't breathe, but I was okay."

Thinking back over their conversation, he wondered which part had distracted her. Nothing had seemed out of the ordinary about their conversation other than that they'd been teasing each other a little. Surely that hadn't caused her to swallow her food wrong?

"Glad you're okay," he told her, truthfully. His own ability to breathe had gone on hiatus when Sarah had been coughing and sputtering. Knowing she really was fine, he added, "Now that I saved you."

She arched a brow. "Hero complex much?"

She had no idea. "Just calling things as I see them."

"Yeah, yeah," she teased, then met his gaze. Her eyes crinkled at the corners. "But thank you for saving me." Taking a much smaller bite, she chewed it carefully. "So, Oh Smart One, tell me what you got done today."

Her gaze dropped to the notepad he'd pushed to the side when she'd come in with food. Still chuckling, he finished off his burger, wadded up the foil wrapper, and tossed it into the paper bag it had come out of.

"Those are my recommendations on what needs to be done and what I need to do to accomplish each task. I'm going to pick up tools, supplies, and so on.

Strategizing a game plan, figuring out the variables, is the best way to get the job done right and meet your Christmas deadline." Feet propped on a barstool rung, he leaned back a little to better look at her. "You want to see?"

Excitement lighting her eyes, she nodded. "I'd love to."

CHAPTER FOUR

S ARAH PICKED UP THE NOTEPAD and began flipping through the pages to see what Bodie had come up with. What she saw had her glancing at him in new appreciation. He'd done schematic drawings of the two bedrooms and their new adjoining baths, and had apparently measured every nook and cranny as all the data was there. On each page, he'd made lists of needed supplies.

The pages were quite impressive, as were his drawings. Some of his suggestions didn't fit with her vision, though.

"I should have told you, but I mean to put claw-foot tubs into the baths." She'd bought one at an estate sale and been over the moon when the previous owner had delivered. She was still searching to find another.

He shrugged. "Up to you, but you need at least one walk-in shower, too."

"Why?"

His gaze dropped from hers to stare at the notepad, then he shrugged.

"Not everyone can climb in and out of a tub," he said, as if it was obvious.

And it should have been—yet she hadn't considered it, despite all the hours she'd put into dreaming up the bed and breakfast.

"You want to be able to accommodate disabled or elderly guests that might not be able to or want to step up into one."

With growing respect, Sarah stared at him.

"I think you should put a walk-in, tiled shower in at least one of the baths. That way, you're accessible and just making it easier on anyone with mobility problems whether from age, injury, or health concerns."

What he said made sense, but she had that beautiful old cast-iron claw-foot tub and it fit with the vibe she wanted for the house.

"If you want to use the claw-foot tub, too, we could make it work." He studied his drawing of the room. "But the room will be a little crowded."

"I don't want crowded or cluttered. That's not the feel I want for Hamilton House." But he made valid points. She would have to accept not having the claw-foot tubs in both of the downstairs rooms.

"Or we could just use a tub in the larger of the bathrooms." Had he read her mind or what? "We'd still need to install a shower unit with the tub if it's the only means of bathing for that room, because most people take showers, not baths."

Sarah stared at him, feeling a little awed and a whole lot impressed. She felt foolish for not having thought of the things he was saying. She'd been trying so hard to make sure she covered all her bases and yet what he said was so simple, so sensible, so important for her to have available for her guests.

How could she have missed that? Why hadn't any of the other dozen or so people who'd been in and out of the house made a similar suggestion? Especially the contractor who had framed the bathrooms.

"Okay." She added at least one tiled shower to her mental list of necessities. She'd have to see cost and possible layouts before she made a final decision on whether both suites would have them. "What else?"

She listened carefully as he rattled off item after item. She couldn't disagree with a single suggestion he made. Fortunately, most of his suggestions were small fixes.

"Everything you've said sounds great, but I'm not sure it's all in my budget." She sighed. "Looks like the plumbing issues are a must."

He nodded.

"On the rest of the items, I'll need to prioritize, run the numbers, and see what will have to wait until I get Hamilton House up and running."

"I can do most of the labor by myself, Sarah. That should save you quite a bit, since you'd only have to pay for supplies."

He sounded so sincere, as if paying him was no big thing, that a smile tugged at her lips. "Sounds great, but I have to be able to pay you, too, Bodie."

His mouth opened and for a moment she thought he was going to say she didn't have to pay him. The sentiment was so strong between them, she'd swear that was what had almost come out of his mouth. Which made zero sense. He was a complete stranger, even if sitting here with him at her kitchen island didn't feel strange at all.

It felt... natural. As if she'd known him her whole life. Yet, he really was a stranger whom she knew very little about.

"I'm in no hurry to be paid. You can give me an IOU and pay me after Hamilton House starts showing a profit."

Assuming it ever showed a profit.

She shook her head. "You have to eat and pay for a place to live while you're in town. Besides, how can you trust that I'll ever get around to paying you if you let me decide when I can spare it?"

"I won't starve or have to sleep in my truck if you wait to pay me. I know you'll pay me eventually. I trust you."

Sarah's insides warmed at his claim. Bodie trusted her. Which fit with her feeling that they'd known each other much longer than a day. He had no more reason to trust her than she did him. But she wouldn't let him work without pay.

She would pay him. Once a week, as they'd agreed to the day before when she'd hired him.

If she reached the point where she couldn't pay him, she wouldn't let him work. She didn't and wouldn't take handouts.

Her father and aunt raised her to be a giver, not a taker.

As much as Bodie made her feel as if they'd known each other much longer than a day, they hadn't. This was the beginning a business relationship, nothing more, and she'd do well to remember that.

A week had passed. A week in which Bodie worked at
Hamilton House every day. She'd tried to get him to
take the weekend off, but he'd refused, stating that he
didn't have anything else to do and wanted to get the
job done. He showed up early in the morning and left
late each evening.

Sarah had gotten used to coming home from work
to find him busily working. She'd gone with him to
pick out tile and supplies for the showers. She'd
selected toilets, mirrors, light fixtures, and vanities
that had an antique look to them to fit with the rest
of the house. Bodie had gone behind her, picking up
needed supplies to install her choices, and had made
suggestions—good suggestions—when she'd asked
his advice.

His knowledge and insight impressed her as
much as his efficiency and how much he had already
accomplished. He'd installed the plumbing and
insulation for sound reduction and hung sheetrock
in the two bathrooms. He'd finished painting the
bedroom walls, and they'd done Aunt Jean's bedroom's
trim together the night before. Sarah had painted the
baseboard trim and Bodie had painted the ceiling's
crown-molding, the doors and their trim, and around
the fireplace, taking great care to protect the tile and
fixtures.

Sarah liked Bodie's attention to detail. A lot.

Harry met her at the door each day, probably
because she continued to bring food home each
night, now always including something for the dog.
Not the juicy cheeseburgers Lou had sent that first

day, though. Her cholesterol levels would've put up a protest.

She'd started stopping by the grocery store and picking up items to cook for them. She told herself it was good practice, since she needed to come up with a few staple recipes to use when the bed and breakfast opened. Bodie was fun to cook for, and she enjoyed watching him eat and listening to him give "reviews" of her meals. Tonight, she planned to keep their meal simple because she had other things on her agenda.

"I should have known the minute Harry disappeared that you were here." Bodie walked into the kitchen. He must have been crouched down on the floor or in some awkward position because he moved a little stiffly.

Sarah laughed, bending to talk to the dog at her feet who had totally won her heart this past week. She'd grown fond of Harry's welcome home.

"Harry is a good boy," she said, more to the dog than to Bodie.

Bodie shook his head. "Sweet-talking my dog."

"'Cause he's so sweet." Sarah grinned, straightened, then washed her hands.

"What's that?" He glanced toward the box she'd put on the countertop along with the grocery bags she'd carried in on her first trip inside the house.

"The On-The-Square Christmas Festival is in barely over two weeks," she reminded him—not that he could have forgotten, with the way she constantly talked about the event. Well, when she wasn't going on and on about Hamilton House and how excited she was at their progress.

He didn't say a lot, unless it was about the house.

Come to think of it, she didn't give him many openings. He probably thought she never shut up.

"Despite starting earlier this year," she continued, "we still don't have enough ornaments to sell. I'm going to take a night off from working on the house to cut more plastic canvas pieces so we can move faster at tomorrow's session. With this weekend being Thanksgiving, tomorrow's our last official meeting. We need to get lots of ornaments made."

He eyed the box. "How many more do you need?"

"As many as we can muster. We have volunteers working on other ornaments, but the Butterflies and I usually make the snowflakes." She began unpacking the bagged items for the soup she was going to throw together before settling in to cut canvas. "You want to help?"

"Make ornaments?" His expression suggested she might have sniffed too many paint fumes the night before.

She hadn't expected him to say yes, but him looking like she'd asked him to do something impossible was too funny to let go. "What? Don't tell me you aren't as handy with a pair of scissors as you are with a hammer."

He gave her a skeptical look. "You've never seen me use a hammer."

"I've seen the changes taking place in my house, so you must be doing something right."

Like how at times, he seemed to relax.

He still didn't smile much, but he did smile. Mostly when talking to Harry, but she managed to get a smile out of him here and there.

Bodie smiling was a beautiful thing. He really should consider doing so more often.

"You're quiet," he pointed out a little later as he walked to the island sink and washed his hands.

"Just making dinner. I'm glad you don't mind being my guinea pig on all these recipes."

"Being fed home-cooked meals? I'll risk being your guinea pig." He turned, eyed her with blue eyes that saw straight into her. "You're not usually quiet while you cook."

Yep, he thought she talked too much.

"You're not usually in here with me while I cook," she countered, looking away from his intent gaze. He'd only been there a week, but having him in the house felt right. She hadn't admitted it to herself, but from the point she'd moved out of her dad's home and into Hamilton House, the house had felt lonely. Probably because Aunt Jean wasn't there. Soon enough, she'd fill the walls with paying guests, with love and laughter.

"Maybe not, but I hear you singing."

"You got something against Christmas carols?" Glancing Bodie's way, she wrinkled her nose. She did sing while she cooked. While she did a lot of things.

He shook his head.

"Good. We need more carolers for Christmas Eve. I'll add your name to my list."

"That escalated fast. I'm not going Christmas caroling, Sarah. If all goes well, I won't be in Pine Hill at that point."

Because he'd have finished his work—which meant he would be gone. That shouldn't bother her.

She wanted him to finish... but having him around was nice.

She turned and gave him a smile. "Since you never said you weren't helping with the ornaments, does that mean you're going to keep me from being up all night doing them by myself?"

His expression was dubious. "You'd be better off putting a hammer in my hand rather than putting me to work crafting."

"But you're willing to learn?" she pushed, wanting him to help, although not sure if it was the prospect of his company or an extra set of hands that motivated her.

"I may or may not have failed art class in school."

Smiling at his answer, she shook her head. "I don't believe you."

His brow arched. "Why not?"

After first wiping her hands over her apron, she put them on her hips. "I've seen your drawings. Besides, you, Bodie Lewis, don't do anything halfway. Which is why I'm counting on you to help me have lots of snowflake pieces cut for tomorrow's session with the Butterflies."

"I'm not really going to be wielding scissors?"

She shrugged. "If you'll cut the canvas, that'll be a huge help, but we could just as easily cut pieces and decorate them ourselves if you prefer. Either way will end up with the same result—our having more snowflakes to sell at our booth."

Although he didn't look like he wanted to say yes, he only hesitated another moment before he nodded. "If you need me to help cut snowflakes, I'll cut snowflakes. I'm here to help you, Sarah."

Her gaze met his and it struck her just how much Bodie had helped already.

It would be easy to get used to him being around, to leaning on him. She couldn't let that happen. Not beyond what she'd hired him to do. Eventually, he'd leave. He was just passing through Pine Hill, not there to stay.

Still, he was there now, and she enjoyed his being there.

"You know, if I can't rustle up more volunteers for our caroling, I'm going to remind you how much I need your help with that, too," she teased, ignoring that he'd already said he wouldn't be in town.

"You'd regret it. I'm worse at singing than I am at crafting," he assured, not reminding her of his earlier comment. He leaned against the kitchen island and watched her wash off zucchini. He gestured to what she was doing. "Need me to help do that or chop something?"

"Will I regret it if I say yes?" she teased, tossing his words back at him.

His lips twitching, he shrugged. "One way to find out."

Wielding the scissors for cutting plastic crafts felt strange—frivolous, even. But once he got the pattern in his head, Bodie cut canvas. It didn't take a genius, just attention to detail. He could handle that. Attention to detail had been key to being good at his job for years.

And yet, crafting in a homey kitchen with the most upbeat woman he'd ever met wasn't something he'd ever seen himself doing. This saying thank-you for his quilt had him slipping down a rabbit's hole into so many things he'd never expected.

"How is it you can cut two to my one and I've done this dozens of times?" Sarah complained, eyeing his stack that towered above hers.

"Fast learner?"

"Apparently." Sarah laughed. "I always have to stop between every few cuts to count to make sure I have the right number of block spaces."

Bodie made one last snip, then stacked the perfectly shaped piece on top of the ones she'd cut, upping her stack. "Each side is the same, so it's just a matter of getting a plan in your head, then executing it."

"You're definitely a planner."

"If I didn't know you were a planner for a living, I'd think you sounded disapproving," he accused.

She shook her head. "Just trying to figure you out."

He paused in his cutting. "Why?"

"Do you always have to ask the reason for things?"

He shrugged. "Asking is the best way of learning the answer."

"You have to have an answer for everything?" she pressed, though her tone was teasing.

"Not really." In the military, he'd followed orders without questioning most of them. It was his job, and he'd done it whole-heartedly—right up to that last mission.

He should be overseas, not cutting out plastic snowflakes at a kitchen counter. He'd dealt in life and death for so long that sitting there felt foolish. He should be doing something more...something that mattered more.

"I'm sorry." Her voice was soft, sad almost.

Closing his mind to the past, he looked at the woman across from him cutting plastic, letting her fill his mind and light up the threatening shadows. "For?"

"For whatever put that look on your face."

He winced. "You didn't do that."

"I'm the only one here."

As if he understood everything being said, Harry whimpered, and Sarah glanced over at where he lay in the floor, his head resting on his paws as he watched them work.

"Sorry, Harry," she apologized. "No offense meant." She met Bodie's gaze. "Sometimes I wonder about that dog. He's either quite brilliant or has really good timing."

"Probably both." He nodded toward the piece she was cutting. "Hate to tell you, but you just cut one square too many."

Staring at the piece, she frowned.

"I'm supposed to be the one teaching you to do this." She put down her scissors. "I need a break from cutting. Want to decorate?"

Sticking to cutting might be a better idea. But her smile slipping from her face did funny things to his insides and he went against his better judgment.

"Only if I get to use the glue gun."

When her eyes met his, her smile was back and Bodie was glad he'd agreed.

"Typical man," she accused, pulling glitter, sequins, yarn, and a bunch of other shiny things from a box, "wanting to use the tools."

"Stick with what you know. That's my motto."

"What you know is impressive." She threaded a large needle with white yarn and picked up one of the plastic pieces.

"Don't let first impressions fool you."

She looked up from where she was sewing the yarn into the canvas. "I shouldn't be impressed?"

He hesitated a moment before answering, "Not by me."

"We have a problem then, because I am impressed. I've never known someone to cut out that many canvas pieces without messing up a single one."

She'd meant the ornaments. He'd meant...what had he meant? That he'd thought he was a good soldier, but if he'd really been that good his comrades would still be alive?

As if sensing Bodie's mind was going where it shouldn't, Harry raised his head from his paws and made a sound that was somewhere between a whimper and a bark.

Yeah, boy, I know. I'm having way too good a time to go down that mental highway.

So, Bodie focused on the pretty woman smiling at him, embracing her goodness. Her big brown eyes were full of merriment as she hummed along with the Christmas music she'd insisted had to be playing while they cut.

He leaned back, eyes locked with hers as he challenged, "That's all it takes to impress you? Perfectly shaped snowflakes?"

She held up the snowflake piece she was working on and waved it in front of him. "Don't underestimate the power of a perfectly shaped snowflake."

"I thought snowflakes were supposed to be unique, each one different."

"They are. That's where all this comes in." She gestured to the decorating bits. "But as unique as they are, all snowflakes are made up of the same basic ingredient."

"Snow?"

"Only with our snowflakes, our basic ingredient is plastic."

Bodie laughed. "Not nearly as eco-friendly."

"But it lasts longer. I still have snowflakes Aunt Jean and I made when I was a little girl."

Bodie's brow lifted. "You've been making these that long?"

She nodded. "Aunt Jean loved to make things. Clothes for me, quilts, crafts of all kinds—you name it. Had she not gotten pneumonia, she'd be right here with us making these ornaments."

Had her aunt been alive when Sarah had made his quilt? Had she helped?

"Is that what she died from? Pneumonia?"

She nodded. "Influenza that turned into pneumonia that turned into respiratory failure that turned into me losing her."

Bodie reached out, placed his hand over Sarah's much smaller one and gave a gentle squeeze. "I'm sorry."

Their gazes met, held. Sarah's eyes held surprise.

No wonder. Bodie was surprised at what he'd done, too. He wasn't usually a touchy-feely person. He pulled his hand away, picking up another piece of plastic canvas.

He shouldn't have touched her, had no right to

touch her. And yet he'd taken her hand instinctively, wanting to comfort her in her loss.

What made him think he could ease her grief when he couldn't even console himself?

"You talk about your aunt a lot." He wanted to move past the awkwardness he'd created. "You've mentioned your father plenty of times, but never your mother. Why?"

Seeming to know what he was doing, she searched his eyes a moment, then gave a small smile as she accused, "There you go with the questions again."

Rather than immediately answering, she started sewing again. When she came to the end of where she meant to sew the yarn, she tied a knot in the string, then cut the needle free.

Without looking up from what she was doing, she said, "It's not a secret or anything, just not something I talk about."

She threaded the large needle with a new piece of yarn and sewed along the outside border of another canvas piece. Feeling like a slacker, Bodie went back to cutting canvas, but his gaze kept returning to Sarah. She seemed to be concentrating on the snowflake, but he could tell her mind was far away.

"I have no memory of my mother other than stories other people have shared," she confessed. "She died when I was born."

Bodie winced. "I'm sorry."

"Me, too." She sighed. "I wish I'd known her, had memories of her that were my own. I wish I could have known what she thought, what she felt, what her dreams were. Those kind of things, you know?"

He'd spent his first eighteen years with his mother. She'd worked hard, providing as best as she could for them, but she'd never been an affectionate person. Possibly because between her two jobs, she'd been too tired to do more than the basics when at home. She'd softened when she'd met and married Steve, but despite his young age, Bodie hadn't softened with her. He'd gotten along well enough with his newfound family. He'd been Steve's shadow as the man had paid him for his work, but Bodie had always known he'd leave Houston, would travel the world and serve his country. It hadn't been hard to leave them behind when the house there had never truly felt like home.

Sarah's emotional strings that bound her to her family, to this house, were so different from anything he'd experienced.

"Your aunt was your dad's sister?"

Sarah nodded. "Aunt Jean was almost twenty years old when my dad was born. Apparently, he was an unexpected surprise to my grandparents and they all, Aunt Jean included, doted on him." Sarah laughed at whatever was dancing through her mind. "Despite the big age gap, she and my dad were close. She was like a second mother to him. She certainly was to me, possibly because she and Uncle Roy never had children. You've seen the photo of them in the foyer."

He knew the one she meant. A black-and-white wedding picture with a pretty dark-haired woman and a young man with slicked-back hair and strong features.

"You're a lot like your Aunt Jean?"

She smiled. "I hope so. I couldn't imagine a better

person to emulate. This house isn't just a beautiful building—it's such a part of her that I couldn't help but love it." Her eyes grew glassy. "I want the same things for this house that she did. Love, laughter, warmth, family filling it. It's been years since Hamilton House had those things."

"You're wrong."

She looked up from where she sewed. "Excuse me?"

Now why had he said anything? He should have just kept cutting canvas. Only where Sarah was concerned, he kept doing things that put him on the spot.

He tried to shrug the question away, but her gaze pinned him. "Now it's my turn to want to know the reason why. Why am I wrong?"

"If you were here with your aunt, in this house, then Hamilton House had all those things you say you want for it."

Her hands pausing from their crafting, she stared at him. Her eyes filled with disbelief, then awe. "That, Bodie Lewis, very well may be the nicest thing anyone has ever said to me."

Bodie's insides melted. Or did something. Melt was the best way he could describe the thawing, cracking-open sensation in his chest.

Plus, melting justified the heat in his face.

Then, as if to give her a moment to get her emotions in check, she said, "But don't think compliments are going to get you out of helping. Cut more or get busy sewing until we have a few ready for you to demonstrate your hot glue gun skills."

Grateful for the reprieve from questioning what she did to his insides, Bodie picked his scissors back up. "Yes, ma'am."

CHAPTER FIVE

THANKSGIVING LUNCH WITH SARAH'S FATHER went well. She visited with him for several hours and helped him put up his Christmas tree, all the while thinking she needed to get started decorating Hamilton House for its grand opening. Then, she snuggled under a quilt her mother had made and they watched *How the Grinch Stole Christmas*, as was their father-daughter tradition.

It was late when she got home, so she was surprised to see Bodie's truck still in her driveway. She'd tried to get him to take the day off, but he'd refused.

As he always did, Harry greeted her at the front door.

"Hey, boy. I have a habit of coming in with food, don't I?" she told the dog, laughing as Harry excitedly bounced around her, no doubt thinking she'd brought something for him, too. "You'd like leftover turkey and dressing, wouldn't you? I'd bet money it came from Maybelle's kitchen, but shhhhh, I'm not supposed to know that."

She carried the goodies her father had sent home

with her to the kitchen island, along with her purse, then went to find Bodie. She found him in the larger suite's bathroom, working on the tile.

"Wow. That looks great."

"Just doing my job." He finished setting a piece, then straightened. "You did a good job picking out the tile."

"And you're doing a fabulous job installing everything. On Thanksgiving." She met his gaze. "I feel so guilty."

He snorted. "I've worked on Thanksgiving for over ten years. It's just another day."

It was sad he felt that way, but given his military background, she understood. Still...

"I wish you had come with me to my dad's."

Glancing at her from where he worked, he shrugged. "I didn't want to intrude. Besides, how would you have explained that?"

Confused, she stared at him. Did he know about the Butterflies and how they had him all picked out as her next big romance? She'd threatened them with bodily harm if they bothered him at Hamilton House, but she wouldn't put it past them to have found a way. They were sneaky like that.

"Me going to Thanksgiving dinner with you." He shook his head as if the idea was inconceivable. "Everyone would have made incorrect assumptions."

The Butterflies would have, because that's what they did. But other people would have seen it for what it was. Friendship. Nothing more.

Right?

"Friends go to dinners with each other," she reminded.

"Maybe," he conceded, but didn't look convinced. "Everything go okay?"

She nodded. "It went great, except I don't think Dad wanted me to leave. This is the first Thanksgiving without Aunt Jean, which is difficult enough, but also the first Thanksgiving I've not lived at home."

Her father had let that little tidbit slip out in his conversation over dinner. She'd been so busy focusing on the positive, on getting ready for the festival, on preparing for the grand opening, she hadn't thought about her dad missing having her there.

"He's taking my moving out harder than I thought he would," she said.

"It's just been the two of you for years?"

She nodded. "Since Mom passed. I think he feels closer to her when I'm around."

Still, she was twenty-five. She should've moved out long ago. But none of that changed how guilty she'd felt when he'd asked if she had to head back to Hamilton House so soon, even though she knew he wanted her to live her own life and just missed her.

Bodie stared a moment, then glanced at the shower. "I better get back to work. I have a drill sergeant of a boss."

"Yeah, right. She's the worst," Sarah agreed with a smile. Then she remembered the food her dad had sent with her. "Have you eaten?"

He stopped to think a moment, then shrugged. "Lunch."

She frowned. "Lunch was hours ago. You need to eat. I brought leftovers."

"I'm not eating the leftovers, Sarah." At her look of

disbelief, he continued. "I mean, I don't want to eat food intended for you."

"Seriously, you should. There's no way I'll eat it all. I'll barely even be home for the next few days. Starting tomorrow, I'll be swamped with revamps to the church's website and getting Christmas event schedules printed. Then, I have a ton of things to do for the Christmas festival." Excitement filled her. She loved the Christmas festival. The event was always magical. "I can't believe it's almost here. Hopefully, the booth will do well again this year."

"I don't see how it couldn't do well with all the snowflakes you've made." He didn't look up from where he'd gone back to working on the shower tiles.

"What if no one wants snowflakes this year? What if they are snowflaked out?"

Turning, he cocked a brow. "Has it been a problem in the past?"

She shook her head. "But I've only been in charge of the booth since Maybelle retired. She's the lady you thought was me that first day," she added when she realized that although she talked about the Butterflies, he'd only met them on the one occasion, so he didn't know to which one she referred. "I only took over two years ago."

"I'm sure you'll be fine. And if not, you can focus on new ornaments for next year's sale, or some other Christmas thing, and use the snowflakes as backup items."

What he said made sense.

"I guess that's what we'd do. We do sell other handmade ornaments besides the snowflakes. Plus, we have the baked goods and the Present Pick that's always a hit. But the snowflakes are special."

Because it's what she'd done with Aunt Jean.

He stepped back, inspected the tiles he'd just put up. "What's the Present Pick?"

"Ever see the pick-up duck game at fairs or fundraisers? You know, where kids pick a duck floating in the water and on the bottom there's a number coordinating with a prize?"

He nodded.

"That's the idea behind Present Pick. There are lots of presents that are ring-box sized with lids that lift off. Kids pay to pick a box. When they open it up, inside is a number associated with a prize." Just remembering all the fun they'd had with the booth last year had her smiling.

"I'm sure it will be a big success this year, too," he assured her, looking amused.

Sarah wasn't sure if it was her or the description of the games that had him smiling. Either way, she loved that he smiled. She'd seen him smile several times, but the beauty of it still hit her in smack-dab the center of her chest.

"Now, let's see about getting some food in you," she reminded. "Because if you don't take me up on my offer, I'm positive Harry will."

"You know," he leaned against the bathroom stall, "it slows down my finishing your house when you have me do all these other things."

"Other things such as eating?" she teased. "Don't fool yourself that it's not self-serving. I'm saving myself from you passing out from lack of food."

He shook his head. "Wouldn't happen."

"Listen, I don't think it's going to slow you down that much to eat. Besides, it's Thanksgiving. Live a little. Have leftovers."

"I'll eat, but Thanksgiving is just another day on the calendar."

"Just another day? Bite your tongue."

He'd said as much before, and she'd let it pass without commenting. But today was the day and she wanted to share this little piece of it with him. To give him a taste of her traditions even if that only meant leftover turkey and dressing while sitting at her kitchen island with her for company. "Next thing you know, you'll be saying Christmas is just another day," she teased, expecting him to deny it.

He looked guilty as charged.

"No." She grabbed her heart in an overly dramatic move. "Say it isn't so."

"Check out this fancy tile work," he said instead, gesturing to what he'd worked on all day. He'd built the frames for the shower stalls several days previously, had them plumbed and boxed in. He really was a jack of all trades.

"Saw it when I came in," she reminded him. "You don't really believe Christmas is just another day, do you?"

"Man, I'm starving. Did you say something about food?"

"Chicken," she accused.

"That would be turkey," he corrected, his eyes twinkling.

A laugh slipped from her at his joke. "Don't think we're done with this conversation. But before you faint from starvation, come on. I'll heat you a plate while you clean up and let Harry outside."

"Anyone ever tell you how bossy you are?"

Her cheeks heated. She didn't think of herself as bossy. Quite the opposite. She lived to serve others. Still, she lifted her chin and gave him her bossiest look.

"I'm a Special Projects director. I direct. It's what I do. That's not being bossy. It's directing." Okay, that was a different spin to her job.

"Keep telling yourself that." Bodie glanced around the bathroom. "I'll clean up a little in here, let Harry out, and then I'll take you up on those leftovers."

"You never talk about your time in the military. Why is that?"

Bodie looked up from where he was cutting the corners of the bathroom wall with paint. Sarah had come into the room to ask his opinion on a couple of recipes. Within minutes, she had a brush in her hands and was helping him paint the bathroom walls just as she'd done with the bedroom trim.

"Not everyone talks about everything that ever happened to them."

Holding up her paintbrush in a mock warning, she veed her brows at him. "Was that a jab at me? I'll have you know I don't talk about everything that ever happened to me. I just—"

"I was teasing, Sarah." It surprised him how much he enjoyed teasing her.

"Good thing you explained." Lips twitching, she

lowered her paintbrush. "So, tell me about your time in the military."

"Some things don't need to be talked about."

"Sometimes it helps to talk about things that don't need to be talked about."

She had no idea what she was saying. He sure didn't want to put the grim images in his head into her mind. No one should see the things he'd seen.

"Not these things," he promised.

She seemed to be considering what he said, then asked, "Do you see yourself going back into the military?"

If only.

"No."

"With what little you've said, I sense you liked being in the Army and have the utmost respect for the military." She pinned him with her gaze. "Why aren't you there now?"

"Things."

"You aren't going to tell me, are you?"

Talking with Sarah was easy. Too easy. Easier than talking to the therapist the Army had made him work with for months after coming back to the States. But no matter who was listening, some things were better left unsaid.

Not looking up from where he worked, he shook his head. "No."

"Because what you did was top secret and you'd have to take me into custody if you did?" she teased, obviously wanting to lighten the tone.

"I think you have me confused with a federal agent. I was an Army Ranger. Totally different."

"And before that you were a carpenter."

"My stepfather is a carpenter." He glanced toward her, saw that she was studying him with big, curious brown eyes. "You spoke with him when you checked my references. But, yes, I worked as a carpenter prior to joining the Army."

"I didn't realize your reference was your stepfather. He never said anything to that effect."

Dipping his brush into the paint, Bodie eyed her. "Does it matter that he was one of my references?"

"I suppose not." She shook her head. "You told me you'd only be in Pine Hill for a few weeks because of another job. Is that a carpentry job, too?"

He chuckled. "Not hardly."

"Then what?"

"I'll be working for a security company."

"That's right. Your other reference told me you'd be working with him. Will you be a security guard?"

He supposed she could call it that, so he nodded. iSecure had a lot of different levels. On the surface, they provided security to bigwigs. That was all Sarah needed to know.

"The company will give me the opportunity to travel and do what I love."

"Which is?"

What was it that drew him to iSecure other than Lukas? Of all the options he'd considered, iSecure was the one that had held his interest. He hadn't really questioned why. Not until Sarah asked.

"Protecting people." It was true. He liked to protect people. He wasn't sure that was what had appealed most about the Army, but it was an aspect he had enjoyed.

"Hmmm," she said, wiping her paintbrush back and forth as she helped cut the corners in.

"Hmmm, what?"

"I was thinking we're a lot more alike than I would have guessed."

"How's that?" He didn't see it. She was sugar cookies on Christmas morning, and he was coal in a stocking. Not alike at all.

"We both like taking care of and helping others. Only, I want to do that in Pine Hill, and you want to do it wherever you're ordered to go."

That about summed it up.

He turned to tell her so, but she'd moved close, presumably to dip her paintbrush into the paint, but instead stood waiting for him to turn.

Because the moment he faced her, she dabbed her paintbrush toward him.

His instinct was to grab her wrist and stop her, but he allowed her to proceed, and was thankful he prevented himself from hurting her at the unexpected paint smeared across his cheek.

Delight shone in her eyes at what she'd done.

Bodie touched his wet cheek. "What was that for?"

Rather than answer, she dabbed her brush toward him again.

Again, he forced himself to let her. Her tickled smile was worth it.

Staring at her dancing eyes, her challenging smile, her poised paintbrush, that melting, cracking sensation hit him again.

Looking at her, he felt young, unjaded, unscarred. As if nothing bad had ever happened to him or ever could. Her barely-contained joy served as a balm to everything raw inside him.

"You know this means war, right?"

Her lips twitched. "Because you're a soldier?"

"Because you deserve to pay for getting paint on me."

"Oops." She gestured to the smudges of paint on his cheek. "Did I do that?"

He rolled his eyes. "You church girls. Always playing innocent."

"Sometimes we are innocent," she defended, her eyes full of challenge.

"Not this time." The brush in Bodie's hand begged to retaliate, to dab a big glob of paint right across Sarah's pert little nose, to start a playful paint war with her as he'd threatened.

Then he reminded himself he wasn't here to play with Sarah or to dabble in whatever this feeling was that he experienced when she was near. He was here to help her do a job.

Not play in paint.

"You're chicken, aren't you?"

Her taunt had Bodie laughing out loud. Seriously? They were back to that?

"You think I'm afraid of you?"

"Terrified," she teased, waving her brush at him. "You know if you come closer, I'll have you wearing Seafoam Green all over."

He shouldn't have done what he did next. Lord knew he'd been taunted in the past with lots worse than wearing a shade of paint. Taunts he hadn't given in to.

But he gave in to Sarah and grabbed hold of her

arms, gently removing her paint brush from her hands while she squirmed, squealed, and tried to keep him from doing so.

Amidst laughter, hers and his, he got the brush from her.

"You wouldn't," she accused when he wielded the brush toward her.

"I'm going to."

She backed up, bumping against the bare wall they were supposed to be painting. Her eyes were big, but not with fear. Excitement shone brightly in them.

Her lips parted. "I have really sensitive skin. I'll probably break out if you do and then be all rashy during Christmas. Please don't."

Bodie hesitated, studying her. Was she telling him the truth?

Just as he was deciding she might be, she grabbed the brush out of his hand.

"Ha. Gotcha," she claimed, doing a little happy dance while hiding the brush behind her back.

"I guess you did." He laughed, acknowledging that he'd been played. "You know, I'm not sure you helping paint is getting me closer to being done."

"Yeah, yeah, but it's a lot more fun this way."

"That it is."

Chapter Six

"**O**H, CHRISTMAS CANDY CANES!"
At Sarah's good-girl substitute for swearing coming from somewhere else in the house, Bodie glanced up from where he was sealing the tile in Aunt Jean's suite.

Grateful his hip and leg held up after his extended time squatted on the shower floor, and that his body was getting stronger and stronger each day, he straightened to check out his work. When he had made sure everything was up to par, he went to see what had frustrated her.

"Please answer," she said, while flipping through a stack of mail on the kitchen island countertop. Was she talking to him? To Harry?

The dog might have stayed constantly at his side at Lukas and Kelly's, but Harry had a thing for Sarah. These days, the dog was as likely to be found lying at her feet as at Bodie's.

He didn't blame him. Sarah was entertaining.

Like her jolly expletive moments before.

Cellphone to her ear, she turned toward him as he

entered the kitchen, which was where she spent most of her time. Whether cooking or crafting, working on her special projects or poring over the internet for bed and breakfast ideas, she preferred the room she'd made into her dream kitchen.

No wonder. The room was an extension of her. Warm, cozy, inviting, functional, productive, happy.

He wasn't exactly sure how a room could be happy, but this one was. Although he found the room uplifting, it was also a stark reminder of just how much he contrasted with everything about Sarah.

"Oh, sorry," she lowered the cellphone and pushed a button to hang up on whomever she'd been trying to reach. She set the phone down on the kitchen island. "You heard that?"

He nodded.

"I forget how good your hearing is."

Not as good as it had once been, thanks to the IED.

Pushing the thought from his mind, Bodie swallowed and focused on the woman leaned against the island. She looked like a pretty Christmas package with her red and green outfit with its gold buttons, not to mention the gold ribbon tied in her dark hair and hanging near her earlobes.

"You didn't want me to hear your Christmas cursing?"

Her eyes widened. "I wasn't. I just—"

"Calm down, Snowflake. I'm just teasing."

Eyes still wide, she gave him an odd look. "What did you call me?"

"Snowflake." He hadn't really thought about his use of the word, but it fit her in ways that went beyond the ornaments that meant so much to her. She was special. Beautiful. One of a kind. Pristine.

But she wasn't icy. Not cold or even tepid.

Sarah was warm. Everything about her welcoming and kind and heating one's insides.

"Like hot chocolate."

That was Sarah. As unique as a snowflake. As warmly welcoming as hot chocolate on a cold winter's night.

"Snowflake like hot chocolate?"

Her confusion had grown tenfold. No wonder. He was confusing himself.

At the thought of trying to explain himself, Bodie came as close to blushing as he'd done in decades.

"That some wild concoction you've come up with?" she teased, her expression full of delight as she regarded him from across the kitchen island.

"Just a nickname."

"Snowflake like hot chocolate," she repeated, amusement evident. "That's certainly different."

"You want to be called the same thing as everyone else?"

"Sarah is a common name, so something with more pizzazz for a while would be nice."

"Maybe I'll just stick with my initial impression."

"Which was?"

"Drill Sergeant."

She burst out laughing. "Yeah, right."

Deciding he'd dilly-dallied long enough, Bodie walked to a cabinet and took out a glass under the guise of getting a drink.

"You know," she mused, her voice pulling him back to her, "I misjudged you."

He walked to the faucet and filled his glass half full. "How's that?"

"When I first met you, I thought you had a smiling problem."

He did have a smiling problem.

"I was wrong. About that," she continued. "But I was right about how your smile reaches your eyes and lights up your face. I really like when you smile."

Her admission had his lips curving upward. Not because he thought his smile reached his eyes and lit up his face, but because not smiling around Sarah seemed impossible. He should have nicknamed her the Smile Whisperer.

Leaning against the counter, he took a drink of his water and regarded her. "You thought all that when we met?"

Her cheeks a little pink, she nodded. "You have a beautiful smile, Bodie. You should wear it all the time."

"Kind of like the one you were wearing when I came in here?" he teased, ignoring what she'd said about him.

Shoulders dropping, she gave a frustrated huff. "Yeah, well, I was trying to call the man who promised to help me load the ornaments for the Great Christmas Ornament Hunt. He texted to cancel."

"The what?" The name made it sound like she was talking about some kind of big, international event. One he'd never heard of.

"Last year when I took over Special Projects, I started a new tradition at the On-The-Square Christmas Festival." She looked quite pleased with herself. "A Christmas ornament hunt for the good boys and girls of Pine Hill."

"Like an Easter egg hunt?"

Looking as excited as a kid, she clasped her hands together. "Yes, only with ornaments that open and have prizes hidden inside them. Isn't it wonderful?"

"I've never heard of such a thing."

"Because I started the tradition last year." Smiling, she gave him a *duh* look. "I wanted something fun to do at the festival during the afternoon before the parade and tree lighting. There are photos with Santa but not a lot of other things for kids to do. The town is working to make the Christmas festival an all-day event in hopes of reviving the town square and increasing business there. The ornament prizes range from candy to items donated by church members to things donated by local businesses. Any kind of toy, game, gift card, and whatever that can fit inside something this big." She held her hands out just so.

Bodie stared at her, wondering if she was for real or pulling his leg. He'd known she got into the season and all that, but an ornament hunt? He supposed if she had a Present Pick game, she could have an ornament hunt.

"I found the idea online and thought it seemed great."

"It sounds like something you'd like."

Her hands went to her hips. "It was a big hit."

"I'm sure it was." Amusement laced his words.

"You'll see."

At her words, her eyes brightened, and she got a look that set warning bells off in his head.

"You will see." She looked proud of herself.

"Because you, Bodie Lewis, are going to attend your first ornament hunt."

Bodie shook his head. "I don't do ornament hunts or holidays, remember?"

"Yeah, well, it's time you started."

He continued to shake his head.

"You'll have fun."

"At an ornament hunt? I'm a little out of the appropriate age range."

Her chin lifted. "That's never stopped me from enjoying something fun."

"Your point is?"

She laughed. "Okay, so I'm a kid at heart, but what's wrong with that?"

Not one thing. But everything childish in him had died long ago.

"What are your plans for the rest of the evening?"

Incoming. Take cover. That's what all his training warned.

So when he heard himself ask, "What is it you want me to do for the rest of the evening, Sarah?" he could only blame himself for whatever came next.

He knew better. He deserved whatever she served.

"Well..." She got a hopeful look in her big brown eyes. "If you were free, I'd love help carrying Aunt Jean's Christmas decorations down from the attic."

"What's the rush? Thanksgiving was just two days ago," he reminded in case she'd forgotten.

"That's right. And today is the day I start decorating for Christmas."

"Isn't it too soon?"

But he knew better. This wasn't too early for the town of Pine Hill. There had already been decorations when he'd arrived in town and he'd noticed more going up each morning and night as he made his way to and from his hotel.

Nor was it too early for Sarah, apparently, because she was headed toward the stairs and on up to the attic, no doubt.

She turned and smiled at him in a way that had him knowing he'd be following her up those stairs and doing her bidding.

"I don't know whatever possessed you to come to Pine Hill," she said, her eyes full of gratitude and something Bodie couldn't quite label, but that made him feel like his brain was in a vise, preventing logical thought. "But you've been a lifesaver, Bodie. What would I have done without you chancing upon our little town this Christmas season?"

Her question made him uncomfortable as he wondered if he should tell her about what had truly brought him to Pine Hill. But telling her now felt awkward and out of place. And he couldn't regret his decision not to tell her back at the start, when she'd first mentioned the job. If she'd known his sole purpose in accepting her job offer was to repay her kindness, she might not have let him.

Without him, Hamilton House wouldn't be ready for an open house on Christmas, and that would have been horrible. It meant so much to Sarah, and he wanted to give her that piece of her dream.

"You'd have carried your own Christmas decorations down?" he suggested, following her up the stairs and wondering what he'd gotten himself into, when all he'd meant to do when he came to Pine Hill was to tell Sarah thank you and leave.

But now, when he left—as he'd have to do, sooner or later—how much would he be leaving behind?

Sarah had been both looking forward to and dreading pulling out Aunt Jean's decorations. She loved Christmas, loved seeing the house decked in garland and bows, loved seeing the twinkling lights.

Loved seeing the ornaments they'd made together over the years.

But the last time she'd seen these decorations had been after she'd taken them down from her aunt's tree and packed them. She'd helped do so for the past several years, but never with a heavy heart.

Last year, she hadn't known what would happen to Hamilton House, to Aunt Jean's things, with her passing.

Aunt Jean had willed everything to her. There had been just enough left in her aunt's accounts that when it was settled, Sarah had inherited the house and its contents free and clear.

Contents that included her aunt's precious decorations.

The idea of decorating without Aunt Jean had been weighing on her heart, but unpacking the decorations with Bodie didn't seem nearly as daunting.

Was that why she'd asked him to help her? As a distraction?

She tried telling herself it was, but couldn't convince herself. He was a great distraction, but that hadn't been her motivation.

Being with Bodie had. Which came with its own set

of problems, but tonight Aunt Jean's decorations took precedence.

"You should consider using one of the suites for storage, so you don't have to traipse up and down two flights of stairs to get to your decorations," Bodie suggested wryly after they'd made a dozen or so trips.

"What's wrong? Too out of shape to help me carry the rest down?" she teased, grabbing another box to carry down the two flights.

Okay, so her calves were burning and she had no doubt she'd be sore in the morning, but Bodie appeared to be in peak physical condition. The Butterflies had told her he jogged every morning before coming to work at Hamilton House. No doubt they knew that from their spying. She'd ordered them to quit, but they kept ignoring all her protests. Poor Bodie.

She turned to see if he was behind her, but he hadn't picked up his box yet. He just stood there, watching her.

"Bodie?" she asked, not sure why he wasn't right behind her.

His gaze narrowed, and he motioned for her to go ahead. "Nothing. Go on. I'll be right behind you."

Doing so, Sarah set down the box she carried, glanced around the living room. It looked like Christmas had exploded in the room. Unable to resist adding to the mounting chaos, she opened the box she'd just carried to pull its contents out.

One by one, she removed the precious ornamental snowmen her aunt had collected and removed them from their protective bubble wrap.

"There you are," she said when Bodie came back

into the room with a box. "I was about to send a rescue party after you."

Stairs, Bodie thought with disgust. He could breeze through most of the physical therapy exercises the doctor had told him to keep doing as he healed. But stairs? With working on the main floor of the house, he hadn't had a lot of reason to go up and down the stairs. When the need had arisen, he hadn't had issues, but multiple trips had him gritting his teeth as sharp pain shot through his pinned-together hip.

Maybe he shouldn't have been so eager to do Sarah's bidding.

Not if he wanted to keep her from figuring out he wasn't as tough as she thought he was.

He knew he wasn't. But he liked the way she looked at him, as if she thought him capable of doing anything. Being with her made him feel as if he could.

Except stairs.

He was finding out the hard way that going up and down stairs repeatedly was torture on his hip and leg. And his teeth may be permanently damaged from the grinding he'd done that last trip down.

"Would you mind if, rather than bring down more boxes right away, we put these decorations out first?" Her eyes were full of pleading. "I'd like to unpack these, and then we can carry the empty boxes back upstairs to keep from having such a cluttered mess."

Despite his lack of Christmas spirit, he jumped on the offer to decorate if it meant he could give his body a break from the steps.

"Sounds like a great idea."

Getting Sarah's claw-foot tub into the bathroom had been a major pain, but with the help of some of Sarah's church friends that morning, Bodie had gotten it in, and was working on getting it hooked up. The tub made the room a bit tight, but with the right lighting, the finished product was going to look good.

She'd opted to go with the tiled showers in both downstairs suite bathrooms, just a much smaller one in the room with the tub. He'd almost finished Aunt Jean's en suite and was making great progress in the other.

"Bodie and I carried Aunt Jean's ornaments down last night."

Trying not to listen in on Sarah's phone conversation, Bodie focused on his work. Unfortunately, Sarah had a tendency to talk loudly when she was excited, so not hearing her conversation proved impossible.

"I'm going to go pick out a Christmas tree at Harvey Farms later this morning, but I still have to make arrangements for delivery," she continued.

Earlier, she had been in the living area going through the remainder of the boxes they'd carried down the night before. Now, he could hear her moving around, cell phone to her ear, as she decorated the room while talking to her friend Maybelle.

"I need a truck." She laughed. "Maybe I can get Rosie to convince Lou to get it for me."

From where he worked on the tub, Bodie struggled to turn off years' worth of paying attention to every detail in his environment and his need to do whatever he could for Sarah.

"Why is Lou short-handed?" She groaned to Maybelle. "Guess I won't be getting my tree today, after all."

Her disappointment was so heavy Bodie stared at the ceiling and counted to ten.

He didn't have to do this. He shouldn't do this. The absolute last thing he wanted to do was be involved in getting a Christmas tree.

He needed to finish Sarah's job, get to Texas for a short visit, then make a new life for himself at iSecure. Although his body still had its limits—as going up and down the stairs had made painfully clear—he was getting his strength back.

He had been stiff that morning but had pushed through his physical therapy stretches. After moving around all day, he didn't feel much worse for the wear.

Thank goodness. He'd worried about the aftereffects of having overdone it. He'd known better and should have come up with some excuse as to why he couldn't carry down the boxes after his hip had started protesting.

Only that would have left Sarah doing it all by herself. And thinking less of him for not contributing. That didn't work for him.

He was here to help her. First because of the quilt and now... now, because he wanted to help the bubbly do-gooder who was affecting his life in so many positive ways.

Like making him smile.

"I know there's plenty of time between now and Christmas, Maybelle, but if I don't go soon all the good trees will be gone and I'll have to settle for what's left. Who wants to settle for a shabby Christmas tree at their business's grand opening? What kind of start would that be for Hamilton House B & B?"

Bodie closed his eyes.

"This year's tree has to be extra special. Everything has to be perfect."

Why was he still squatted on the bathroom floor? Sarah needed a truck so she could get a tree. Wasn't his purpose for being in Pine Hill to help Sarah?

Gritting his teeth from the discomfort in his hip, he stood, and then marched forward, just the way he used to march into battle.

He found Sarah in the kitchen, having just placed an antique candelabra with red candles on the island. Thick green garlands with red ribbons adorned the piece.

She was just as he'd imaged, phone to ear, pretty in her Christmas green sweater and jeans. Her hair was pulled up and tied with a red ribbon patterned with strings of colorful lights. Around her neck, she wore a necklace made up of more Christmas lights. He'd bet anything that there was a button that made them twinkle.

Sarah liked things that twinkled.

Seeing him come in, she smiled.

The inside of his chest did the little fluttery thing it had started doing when Sarah was around. He should probably see a doctor in case they'd missed something in the scans he'd had that year. He wouldn't say the flutter felt like shrapnel moving, but there was definitely something up in there.

When she smiled at him like that, something inside of him twinkled like he was a string of lights going off in multiple bursts of color.

Him. Bodie Lewis. Twinkling.

It was enough to make him want to slap his hand across his forehead and see if he could knock his brain back into gear because apparently his injuries had extended to his head, after all.

Tough soldiers didn't twinkle.

He winced. He might not be a tough soldier anymore, but he wasn't embracing twinkling, either. The sooner he finished this job, the better.

Her gaze holding his, she held up a finger as if to say to hold on and she'd be off the phone in a few. Rather than wait for her to finish, Bodie pulled his truck key from his pocket and tossed it to her.

Catching it, she looked at the key, then back at him.

Putting her hand over the mouthpiece of her phone, she asked, "What's this?"

"My truck key."

Keeping her hand pressed over the mouthpiece, she veed her brows in question. "I know that, but what am I supposed to do with this?"

"Get your tree."

Her jaw dropped a little as she realized what he meant. "You want me to drive your truck to Harvey's Farm?"

"If it makes you happy."

Because, more and more that seemed to be what motivated his every move. Making Sarah smile.

Sarah stared at Bodie in disbelief. They'd only known each other a short time. That he trusted her enough to let her borrow his truck had her insides filled with warm fuzzies.

"You going with me to get my Christmas tree would make me happy," she admitted, hearing the bit of longing in her voice and not really caring if Bodie heard it, too.

"Well, if you want me to go, I will," Maybelle said over the cellphone.

Oops. She'd forgotten about her conversation with Maybelle and had neglected to keep her hand over the mouthpiece to block out her conversation with Bodie.

"Not you," she clarified, then winced as she realized how that sounded. She should have muted her phone or ended the call. *Something.*

She took a big breath and tried to dig herself out of the hole without ending up in a deeper mess.

"I mean, of course, you going with me would make me happy, Maybelle. But I was talking to Bodie. He just came into the kitchen and—"

"Bodie going with you to get a Christmas tree would make you happy?" Maybelle interrupted, her voice full of curiosity.

Sarah could feel Maybelle's matchmaking instinct going into full-fledged overdrive from over the phone line. Not good. She'd been fighting tooth and nail to keep the Butterflies away from Hamilton House so Bodie could work in peace. So far, she'd succeeded. Any more slip-ups like that one and they'd be camped out on her doorstep wanting to know more.

"No," she insisted. Then, wondering if Bodie could hear what Maybelle had asked, she met his gaze and corrected her answer. "Yes."

His expression was wary, guarded, and she didn't like it.

"Look, Maybelle. I have to go. Thanks for being willing to go to Harvey's Farm with me, but I'm going to pass. Love you." She hung up the phone before Maybelle could say anything further, then addressed Bodie. "Not sure how much of that you could hear."

"Enough."

"Then you know I would love for you to go with me to get a Christmas tree."

He glanced behind him as if looking for a reason to say no. "I need to finish hooking up the plumbing to the tub. Plus, now that I have it here, I'm going put in the vanity."

She did want him to finish with the bathroom plumbing and the vanity. But at the moment, what she wanted most was for him to go with her to get a tree. The work at the house was important, but so was a tree, she reasoned. After all, how could she have an open house on Christmas Day without a tree?

"How long will that take? I can wait," she offered, then clasped her hands. "Or, better yet, I'll help you if you'll tell me what to do."

"Like you did with the painting?"

"Hey, I helped," she reminded, smiling, and grateful that his tense expression had eased.

"Helped make a mess," he reminded her.

"Yeah, yeah, but painting was a lot more fun with me helping. Admit it."

"Not going to happen." He took a step back in what she could only label as a retreat. "Take my truck and get what you need. I have a lot to do today."

"It's almost lunchtime, Bodie. We can get something

to eat, then go to Harvey's Farm. Or better yet, we can eat there."

Why hadn't she thought of that earlier? Bodie would love Harvey Farms. Or at least, she'd love showing it to him.

"You have to see it to believe it. Christmas trees for miles and miles. Plus, all kinds of Christmas goodies." She sighed at the memory of going with Aunt Jean year after year. Some years, her dad had gone with them. Some years, he hadn't been able to due to his pastoring work. The life of a minister wasn't a nine-to-five weekday one. Aunt Jean had always been there. Sarah had loved going to pick a tree with her each year.

"Go with me to get a Christmas tree and you can put the vanity in while I decorate the tree this evening," she suggested, wanting Bodie to go with her for so many reasons.

Rather than agree, he just eyed her skeptically. "You didn't get enough decorating this morning?"

"Nor last night," she confessed. If it were up to her, she'd have every inch of Hamilton House draped in garland and in the holiday spirit.

And Bodie Lewis in the holiday spirit, too.

"Thank you for helping me carry everything down, by the way. I never would have gotten so much done had you not been here."

He didn't quite meet her eyes, but said, "You're welcome."

She gave him a hopeful look. "So, you'll go with me to get a tree?"

"You don't need me to go. You have my truck key," he reminded. "Go find your tree. There will be someone to help you load it and I'll unload when you get back here. Problem solved."

He was right. She could do that. But...

"You might not get another chance to see Harvey Farms before you leave Pine Hill. It would be a shame to miss out on seeing something so magical."

"I've seen farms before, Sarah. Not a one of them was magical."

"That's because you weren't at a Christmas tree farm with me."

He shook his head, but a flicker in his eyes spurred her on.

"Mrs. Harvey makes a delicious soup and sandwich," she tempted. "Plus, in addition to trees, they have a gift shop that sells the most awesome homemade goodies ever. Oh, and you can buy fresh holly wreaths, too. We could get one for the front door."

One side of his mouth hiked up. "All that? Really?"

"Really," she agreed, not caring that he found her enthusiasm amusing. She wanted to show him Harvey Farms. "It's not quite as wonderful as the festival, but Harvey Farms is still like a dream come true."

"Your dream, maybe." He leaned back against the kitchen counter, crossed his muscular arms, and regarded her. "You know this isn't my kind of thing."

"Only because you've never been," she assured him, thinking how much fun she'd have showing him one of her favorite places, letting him see it through her eyes. Bodie didn't have a lot of Christmas spirit, but she suspected that came from lack of exposure.

Holiday happiness was contagious, and she wanted to infect him with a big dose of Christmas goodness.

"I'll be fine if I never go," he countered.

"Once you've tasted Mrs. Harvey's yummy soup you'll think otherwise. No one should go their whole lives without sampling some of her treats." Just recalling how wonderful the woman's past offerings had been had Sarah's mouth watering. "I'm sure Harry would love the opportunity to stretch his legs."

This point seemed to make more of an impact. He tilted his head and seemed to be actually considering it. "There is that," he admitted. "Though I could just take him for a walk around the block."

"Wouldn't he rather run through the woods? The trees are breathtaking. Like a forest of Christmas enchantment waiting to happen."

"A forest of Christmas enchantment waiting to happen?" Snorting with amusement, he shook his head. "You sure you don't work for a holiday advertising company?"

"Am I selling you on coming with me?"

"You're not going to leave without me, are you?"

Excitement filled her. "After you've worked so hard since you arrived, it would be my pleasure to take you to Harvey Farm today."

"Your pleasure to take me, eh?" A full grin broke out on his face. "In my truck?"

"Well, yes. Unless you want to strap the tree to the top of my car?" She batted her lashes. "Can't you see me driving us around with a tree hanging over both ends of my little car? No doubt that would be some type of traffic violation. Donnie would be waiting in his patrol car and would take great pleasure in giving me another ticket. I might lose my license."

He chuckled. "Then how can I say no?"

Her insides warmed. How could she have ever thought he never smiled? Sure, the smiles still didn't come as often as they should, but the man certainly could smile. And how! She'd also been right about how his smile transformed everything about him. She'd never admit it to the Butterflies, but she knew full well that Bodie was a very attractive man.

With a smile so brilliant it could top a Christmas tree and outshine any star.

"You can't. I'm irresistible," she teased and almost felt as if she really were with the way Bodie indulged her.

Too bad he planned to leave Pine Hill as soon as he finished at Hamilton House. If he were staying, it would be so easy to let herself fall for him.

But she wouldn't.

Nor did she want to think about his leaving. Not now.

For the moment, Bodie was going Christmas tree shopping with her and that was enough.

"An irresistible snowflake." He gave a resigned sigh. "Then I have no choice but to go."

"Yay!" Before she thought better of it, Sarah crossed the short distance between the kitchen island and the counter, wrapped her arms around Bodie and gave him a hug. "You won't regret this."

Although she did regret hugging him, because she'd swear he smelled better than Christmas morning itself.

CHAPTER SEVEN

ODIE HAD HEARD OF CHRISTMAS tree farms, but
Sarah was right that he'd never been to one.

Much less been to a Christmas tree farm with
someone like her.

That she found the place enchanting was evident in
the way she hadn't been able to sit still as they drove
up the long drive. Trees of various shapes, sizes, and
shades of green went on for as far as the eye could see
on both sides of the truck.

"Isn't it wonderful?" she asked as he parked in a
marked-off area.

She had no idea. But that there weren't more cars
was a plus. Being around a lot of people wasn't his
thing. Maybe they could get in, find a tree, and get
out.

"Wonderful."

"Just wait. You'll see."

Bodie's gaze cut to her. She was putting her hat,
scarf, and gloves on. Once she was properly bundled,
she turned and flashed a full wattage smile at him
that had his own lips twitching. How did she do that?

Rather than opening the truck door, she dug around in the mini-suitcase she called a purse and pulled out lip balm. Popping the lid off, she rubbed it over her lips.

"You want some? Can't have you chapping on my watch."

Eyeing her, Bodie shook his head. "No shiny lips for me. Thanks anyway."

She dropped the tube into her bag. "Ready?"

"As I'm going to be."

Laughing, she climbed out of the truck, Harry jumping out with her, and motioned for Bodie to get a move on. "Come on. Someone may be buying my tree."

"Wouldn't that make it their tree?" He grabbed Harry's leash and got out of the truck. He zipped up his jacket as he walked around to her side of the truck and hooked the leash to Harry's collar.

"Bite your tongue," she ordered, grabbing his hand and leading him and Harry toward a gated area where there were a variety of cut and live balled Christmas trees.

As with everything to do with Christmas and Sarah, there was nothing quick or easy about tree shopping with her.

They wandered around the farm as she inspected tree after tree. They all looked good to him. A tree was a tree was a tree, right?

Sarah had other ideas. None passed her inspection. She moved on from one tree to the next, taking them further and further away from the barn where most of the other visitors seemed to be enjoying the mini-shop/restaurant with a deli-style menu. There had only been a handful of tables with chairs, but they'd all been full when they'd peeped into the room to fill out a form and had been given a tag to put on the tree they wanted.

Sarah had been on a mission ever since. And it wasn't going well.

"None of these are going to work." Her forehead furrowed beneath the edge of her toboggan. "We're going to have to go out in the field and find the right tree."

Not surprised since she'd barely paused at any of the trees readily available, he asked, "Is there something I should be looking for to help you find the right Christmas tree?"

"We'll know it when we see it."

She meant she'd know it. They all looked the same to him. Still, she was right in that he was grateful to stretch his legs outdoors with Harry on a leash at his side.

"There," she breathed, pointing to his right. Her tone was full of awed wonder, as if she'd just spotted something spectacular.

Bodie looked, but just saw more trees.

She ran up to one, made her way around it, then clasped her gloved hands together as she turned to look at him. "Isn't it perfect?"

No, but Sarah was close.

The excitement on her pretty face was more enchanting than any tree could ever be.

Her long brown hair was tucked beneath her hat and the matching red scarf was wrapped around her neck and tucked beneath her thick white coat. Her eyes glowed as warmly as the hot cocoa she sometimes served him before he left for his hotel room each night.

Her nose had turned pink from the cold December air and so had her cheeks.

His gaze dropped to her mouth. Her lips were pink and shiny from the lip balm she'd put on before they'd gotten out of the truck. He'd told her the truth. Shiny lips weren't his thing.

Not on him. On Sarah? Shiny lips were downright kissable.

He looked up, met her gaze, and realized her attention was no longer on the tree, but on him, on how he was studying her.

The enchanting twinkle in her eyes from finding the tree was gone, replaced by something new, something foreign and exciting. Something alluring that beckoned him to move closer. He stepped nearer, his gaze dropping back to her shiny lips, before returning to her eyes.

Something tightened in his chest, making breathing difficult as he stared into her eyes, seeing things that could make a jaded man believe in Santa Claus and Christmas miracles.

Because Sarah made his chest flutter. Everything seemed possible—seemed *magical*—when she was near.

Her lips parted. To tell him he was crazy?

He *was* crazy. This was Sarah. Sweet, good Sarah.

Her eyes searched his, questioning, tempting.

He took a deep breath, the cold December air sticking in his throat.

"Bodie," she said, her voice a huskier tone than usual, as if maybe she was struggling to get her breath, too.

Just as he was on the verge of giving in to the urge

to touch his lips to Sarah's, Harry barked and jerked against the leash in Bodie's hand, pulling him back to reality and toward Sarah's tree.

Whatever magic was swirling in Sarah's eyes dissipated, and common sense returned.

What kind of Christmas spell had come over him to almost kiss Sarah? To convince him that she wanted him to kiss her?

"Harry, stop barking," he ordered, surprised the dog was pulling against the short length of the leash. But the dog kept barking, getting louder and more persistent.

Bodie frowned. "Quiet, Harry. You'll get us thrown out of a Christmas tree farm. I wouldn't mind, but Sarah might not forgive us."

Harry stopped barking, but he didn't seem happy about it. Standing at attention next to Bodie, he gave a low growl toward the tree.

"Maybe there's a squirrel in the tree," Sarah suggested, moving to check around the tree.

The penny dropped when he spotted a flash of brightly colored hair. Bodie shook his head. "More like a butterfly."

"A...oh," Sarah exclaimed as a bright green bundle peeked around from the other side. "Rosie!"

A red-faced Sarah jumped back, almost bumping into Bodie. He reached out to steady her, but she shook off his hand.

"Imagine bumping into you two here!" the older woman said as she tucked a stray blue hair back under her olive-colored hat.

Harry gave a low yelp, reminding everyone that

he'd known this person was there and that he'd tried to warn them.

Annoyed with himself that he'd been so caught up in Sarah that he'd not realized they were being watched by one of Sarah's spying friends, Bodie stooped to pet his dog, glad for the chance to clear his head of the Christmas spirit that had him acting a fool.

"What are you doing here?" Sarah asked.

"Same as you, I imagine. Looking for a tree," the woman, Rosie, said from deep wine-painted lips that stood out sharply in comparison to her neon green ski pants and pea-colored jacket.

"Mr. Lewis, too long no see." She held out her gloved hand. The green of her gloves matched the deep olive of her scarf and hat, but that was all that matched about her ensemble. She was like fifty shades of green.

He straightened and took the woman's green glove, meaning to give her hand a quick shake.

"Oh," Rosie exclaimed as she grasped his bare hand and didn't let go. "So big and strong."

As delicately as it was possible to wrench your hand free from a very green older lady, Bodie pulled his hand from her gloved one.

The woman batted her eyelashes, looking overly impressed. "Have you noticed how big and strong his hands are, Sarah?"

Sarah made a noise that went from sounding as if she were clearing her throat to an outright cough.

Bodie winced. An awkward situation was growing more and more awkward by the second. He'd had enough.

"Sarah must've been out here too long," he told Rosie, injecting a lot of concern into his voice and keeping a tight hold on Harry's leash as the dog still hadn't decided if Rosie was friend or foe. "I'm going to find someone to let them know we want this tree so we can have it loaded onto the truck, and I can get Sarah back home before she catches a cold."

"I saw that," Rosie accused Sarah the moment Bodie walked away. The older woman did an excited little green shimmy as she gave her an *I told you so* look.

Still a bit dazed from what had almost happened— from what she'd *wanted* to happen—Sarah fought to keep from going after Bodie to demand answers.

What had it meant, that almost-kiss they'd almost shared? Anything? Had he gotten caught up in the magic of this place, or did he truly feel something for her?

"Saw what?" she asked Rosie, trying to keep her voice calm and casual, even though she knew the odds were against her. Especially when she turned to see Maybelle and Claudia had joined them.

"Phew!" Claudia seemed a bit breathless beneath the green floral scarf she had tied around her head. "I didn't think we were ever going to find you."

Maybelle elbowed Claudia, then smiled at Sarah as if their being there was nothing out of the ordinary.

Both women also wore multiple shades of green—all of them either ugly all on their own, or never meant to be matched together. Usually the women were decked out in full style and never dull, but today must be Ugly Green Outerwear While Tree Hunting Day. Sort of like an ugly Christmas sweater party. If so, the trio were shoo-ins for a three-way-tied win.

Claudia's get-up was putrid green pants with old olive rainboots and an even older camouflage jacket. The scarf around her neck was a faded green knit number with lime polka dots that had seen better days. Maybelle wore tight lime green pants, green riding boots, a dressy green jacket that Sarah had seen her wear to church in the past, and a bright green scarf that she'd tied around her head. Apparently, she hadn't had any green gloves as she had on black cloth ones that she'd pinned a green ribbon to.

She loved her friends but would admit they made her eyes hurt.

"Don't go getting distracted by their nursing home camo, you know what I saw," Rosie warned, drawing Sarah's attention back to the grinning woman.

Sarah didn't know. Had Rosie seen…what, exactly? Nothing had actually happened, even though for a moment she'd thought Bodie was going to kiss her.

Yet she hadn't wanted him to kiss her. Not really. Had she?

Hadn't she learned anything from her ex leaving her?

Besides, a kiss probably didn't mean a thing to someone as worldly as Bodie. She shouldn't read anything into something that hadn't happened anyway. Bodie was no more destined to stick around in Pine Hill than Richard had been.

As much as she enjoyed Bodie being around, as much as she'd wanted to lean toward him moments before, she was grateful Rosie had shown up when she had. A kiss between her and Bodie would only further complicate things that already felt more than complicated enough.

"We lost sight of you," Claudia said, still sounding breathy as she ignored Maybelle's jab and Rosie's description of their outfits, "and had to split up to cover more ground. You and that man sure can move fast when you've a mind to."

Maybelle glared at her floral-scarfed friend.

"We were looking for a Christmas tree," Sarah defended. "This tree."

The perfect Christmas tree for Hamilton House's Grand Opening.

Eyeing the three women, she narrowed her gaze. "Why are you here?"

"What most people do when they go to a Christmas tree farm?" Maybelle told her with her usual dryness.

How the woman could produce sass in so much mismatched green was beyond Sarah. Had they really believed they'd blend with the trees?

"See, I told you that's why we were here," Rosie added, still looking at Sarah with a smug smile. "But then we spotted you and needed to come talk to you."

"I've talked to all three of you at different points this morning. Has something happened that you needed to talk to me right now?" She looked back and forth between them.

"Aren't we allowed to spot a dear friend and want to say hello?" Maybelle tsked.

"Yeah," Claudia agreed, rubbing her gloved hands over her camo jacket sleeves. "Didn't you want us to come over to say hi?"

Even knowing it was a deliberate guilt trip couldn't stop Sarah from automatically replying "Of course I wanted you to say hi."

"Yet you practically ran away from us," Claudia

accused, still rubbing her hands back and forth over her jacket sleeves as if she were trying to warm herself.

"I didn't run from you. It's not like you said my name or tried to get my attention."

"And we blended in so well with the environment that you couldn't see us coming?" Maybelle asked drily, gesturing to the clothes that almost looked as if they would glow in the dark.

"I was looking for a tree and didn't even know you were here," Sarah reminded them, eyeing the cartoon turtle embroidered onto the backs of Claudia's hands. Was she wearing one of her grandsons' gloves?

"Because you were distracted?" Rosie practically danced with excitement as she regarded Sarah.

Flustered, Sarah blinked at the trio. "Of course I'm distracted. I'm working on getting Hamilton House ready to open, and next weekend is the On-the-Square Christmas Festival." Plus, Bodie had almost kissed her. "There's just a little bit going on that might have me distracted, don't you think?"

"You're distracted, all right, but not from any of those things." Rosie giggled.

Sarah looked around to make sure Bodie hadn't returned and wasn't in hearing range. She couldn't see him or Harry at all beyond the trees.

They had ventured out further into the field than she'd realized. And, although there were other shoppers, none were easily visible as far out as they were.

No wonder her friends were out of breath if they'd been trying to find them.

Because no matter what excuses they made, she

knew that was exactly what they'd been doing—trying to find them. Trying to *spy* on them.

All that was missing was green paint smudged across their guilty, spying faces. But that did remind her—why were there only three of them? Was it possible the fourth was there too, just better hidden?

"Where's Ruby?" she demanded. "Perhaps hot on Bodie's trail?"

"What?" Claudia sounded offended as she raised her turtle gloves to her chest.

"Ruby is with Charlie this morning. They had other plans. As for us, we're watching out for you," Maybelle corrected, not looking one bit ashamed at having been called out. She even maintained her characteristic dignity in spite of her uncharacteristically mismatched outfit.

"Watching him for you," Rosie revised. "Easy on the ol' eyes, isn't he, Sarah?"

Sarah's cheeks probably matched her scarf, but she stood her ground. "I can't believe you three came here to spy on Bodie and me—in all of that ugly green."

Horrified at the thought of being a fashion miss, Rosie sucked in a loud, indignant breath. "We're camouflaged, not in ugly green."

"We needed to blend with the trees, so you wouldn't spot us," Claudia added, earning another scowl from Maybelle to which she mouthed, "What?"

"You and Bodie were so caught up in each other that you wouldn't have spotted me, either, if that blasted dog hadn't given me away when I came in to hear what was being said," Rosie pouted, not hiding her disappointment at having been caught.

Sarah closed her eyes, counted to ten forwards, then backwards. Lord, help her.

"I want you three out of here pronto," she ordered them. She hated to send them away like they were misbehaving children, but she did not want them playing spy or Cupid, or whatever other trouble they came up with. "Go home and never ever wear those clothes together again."

"What?" Claudia's brow rose, disappearing beneath her green toboggan. "Since when have you ever wanted to get rid of us?"

"I'd say that's obvious enough," Rosie pointed out. "Since she started wanting to be alone with Bodie Lewis. And who can blame the girl?"

"I'd say it was more like since you started spying on me and Bodie."

"Not on you," Maybelle corrected, waving off her concerns in a wave of ugly greens. "You're just an innocent bystander. It's Bodie we're keeping an eye on. Just in case."

"I volunteered to do the job without backup, but they insisted," Rosie informed her, seeming to think that if it had just been her then everything would have been fine, and Sarah wouldn't have minded.

Sarah gave Maybelle an imploring look. "You're the one who said he was squeaky clean. Just... just stop spying on him. Please."

"Oh, all right," the older woman gave in. "Girls, let's go get coffee and warm up. We'll look for our tree later and leave the lovebirds to themselves."

"We're not lovebirds," Sarah insisted as the older women walked away.

They weren't.

And, despite that almost-kiss, she and Brody weren't going to be, either.

CHAPTER EIGHT

WHILE THEIR TREE WAS BEING dug up, Sarah and Bodie had gone to Mrs. Harvey's café to get a late lunch.

"Okay, I'll admit it," Bodie said. "You were right."

"About?" Taking a sip of her hot cocoa, Sarah glanced at him from across the small wooden table where they sat.

"This." He gestured to the renovated barn with its country store and deli. The owners had even had a fireplace built complete with a large stone hearth, and a braided rug and rocking chairs in front of it.

The feel of the place spoke of times long gone; simpler times when life was good and dark shadows didn't haunt him.

"Mrs. Harvey's soup is the best I've had," he continued. Realizing how Sarah might take his comment, he added, "No offense to your own cooking, of course."

"Of course," she mimicked, a smile toying on her lips that he recognized from when they'd been painting and she'd dabbed him with paint. Sarah liked to tease him.

Bodie didn't mind. Sarah was...fun.

In a different time, a different world...no, he wouldn't go there, either. Just because he was inside a cozy country barn straight off a Christmas card didn't mean anything had changed. Not really.

She might have called the tree farm enchanted, but there were some things no amount of Christmas magic could fix. His messed-up head and body being two of them.

"You should consider serving Mrs. Harvey's soup to your customers at Hamilton House."

"Her peanut butter fudge isn't bad, either." Sarah took a bite to prove her point. "Mmmmm."

Watching her eat one of the candies she'd insisted they had to have, Bodie smiled. If a person was what he or she ate, it was no wonder Sarah was so sweet. The woman loved desserts.

"You sure you don't want a bite?" she offered, holding a piece out to him.

He nodded. "I'm sure."

"You shouldn't be." She tsked. "You just admitted that I was right about the soup. I think you should trust me on this and at least have a taste of peanut butter fudge."

Sarah might be sweet as sugar, but she was also as stubborn as a mule.

"One bite, then."

She rewarded him with a smile and a piece of fudge. "You won't regret this. It's delicious."

The fudge stuck to her fingers when Bodie attempted to take the bite from her fingers.

"Here," she offered, holding the bite up to his mouth, but Bodie managed to get most of the fudge in his grasp and popped the candy into his mouth.

The sweet peanut butter flavor practically melted in his mouth, but even though the fudge was good, Bodie thought Sarah had Mrs. Harvey beat. He preferred Sarah's oatmeal chocolate chip cookies any day.

He started to tell her so but noticed a flurry of green outside the window.

"Aren't those the moths?"

"Butterflies," Sarah corrected, frowning at the ladies in the window. "Nosy Butterflies."

Seeing that they'd been spotted, the three women waved, then came into the building. Harry lifted his head, eyed the trio, then laid his head back down on his front paws. His gaze never left them, though, as they made their way to where Bodie and Sarah sat.

"Brrrr, it's nippy out there."

"Nothing a little hot chocolate won't cure."

"Didn't you already have hot cocoa?" Sarah reminded, her gaze going back and forth between the women.

"On our way back up here, we found my tree and had to make arrangements for it. That sweet boy of Carrie's who works here offered to deliver it when he finishes his shift," Maybelle pointed out. "Now we're cold and need a round to warm us up."

"There's not an empty table," Rosie stated the obvious, giving Sarah and Bodie an expectant look since there were empty chairs at their table.

Wincing at how painfully obvious her friends were, Sarah met Bodie's gaze. Her eyes were full of pleading that he'd understand and not judge the women too harshly.

In all actuality, he found them entertaining, if a bit annoying. And he admired their dedication to Sarah. How many women out there had people who cared so much about them that they'd go out in such ridiculous get-ups? He'd venture to guess not many.

Sarah gave him an apologetic look, as if she expected him to be furious. *That* surprised him. Did she have any idea how often he spotted one of them around town? If he was going to get angry, surely she knew it would have already happened by now.

Leaning back in his chair to more fully eye them, he asked, "Maybe you'd like to sit at our table?"

All three women nodded their approval. As they began peeling off green layers, Bodie stood and helped them with their coats, putting the hideous combinations on the chair backs.

When they'd finished unloading their outerwear and had headed to the counter to order, Sarah sighed.

"I'm sorry."

"It's not a problem." He'd been interrogated by worse.

"See if you're still saying that by the time they're through with us. They don't understand the concept of subtle."

No. That much was obvious.

"What exactly is it they're doing?"

She shrugged. "Spying. Matchmaking. Who knows what all they're up to?"

The spying, Bodie was fully aware of. The blue-haired one had even pretended to be out running one morning, complete in a purple velour jogging suit. He'd managed to evade having to say more than a quick hello to her by keeping his head down and his headphones cranked up.

He understood why they'd want to know more about a man who was spending so much time at Sarah's home alone with her. The matchmaking, though... that one had him puzzled. Why would the women who obviously cared for Sarah try to match her with a stranger who wouldn't be in town long?

"Why are they matchmaking?"

"Because I'm twenty-five and single, and they believe it their duty to marry me off to the first willing man in Pine Hill." Realizing how he might take her words, Sarah's cheeks flushed as brightly red as Mrs. Harvey's apron.

Bodie tried to think of something to say that might ease her embarrassment, but what? Her friends were wasting their time if him settling down with Sarah was their hope. Bodie wasn't the sticking-around-in-one-place type, much less the marrying kind.

For that matter, he wasn't marriage material. Certainly not for Sarah, who deserved so much better.

"That's not what I meant," she attempted to clarify, her face growing more flushed. "I, you, I mean—"

"It's okay." He knew what she had meant and he would have said more but the blue-haired butterfly rejoined them.

Rosie leaned over to give Sarah a hug before sitting down in the chair next to Bodie. "Did you get that gorgeous tree you were looking at?"

Fortunately for Sarah, the Butterflies joining her and Bodie was the perfect distraction from her blunder. She and Bodie both knew he wasn't looking for a relationship. Neither was she. They'd only met a couple weeks ago.

Not to mention that Bodie planned to leave Pine Hill as soon as he finished her job. She held no false hopes that he might want to stay. Boring Richard hadn't wanted to stay. Why would someone as travel-seasoned as Bodie want to stick around?

"Mr. Lewis," Maybelle greeted as she returned to the table with her order, her blue eyes studying him as she sat down.

Bodie didn't look the slightest bit intimidated by Maybelle's stare. Leaned back in his chair, he held her gaze. "Maybelle."

"I see you got my name right this time," she said drily, as she arranged the items on her food tray.

"Yes, ma'am. I'm a quick learner."

He made his claim with a smile that made an approaching Claudia exclaim, "Look! He really is a quick learner."

"Or our Sarah is a good teacher," Maybelle countered, her tone still dry, as if she wasn't willing to give Bodie more credit than he deserved.

"Smiling never looked so good," Rosie said with an appreciative sigh.

The Butterflies had bought a half dozen cookies and a cup of coffee apiece.

Bodie's gaze shifted to Sarah questioningly.

Eyeing all three women innocently taking sips of

their coffee in sync, Sarah shook her head. "You don't want to know."

He also probably didn't want to know all the things he'd learn over the next several minutes.

Why Rosie and Claudia felt it necessary to tell him all about her was beyond Sarah. Once he'd flashed his smile a few more times, they had warmed up and were now recounting tales from her childhood she'd just as soon they kept to themselves.

Maybelle, on the other hand, sipped her coffee and watched him with suspicion.

"Then there was the time she decided she was going to take up a special collection for the Johnson family after their house burned down," Claudia told him, sounding very much like a proud family member. "Right in the middle of church services she walked up to the front and told the congregation about the little girl in her class whose house had burned. She insisted the family needed our help."

"She borrowed my handbag, dumped its entire contents on the pew, and passed it around for collection for the family," Rosie added, laughing at the memory.

"Never seen Rosie move as fast as she did that day, trying to keep prying eyes from taking note of her belongings," Claudia said, laughing at the memory. "Doubt those church pews had ever seen the likes of some of the items in her bag."

Sarah met Bodie's gaze and gave a little shrug. "Bethany Johnson was my best friend. I had to do something to help her even if it did get me grounded."

"You were grounded?" Bodie asked, looking amused at the story.

Grateful he wasn't bored, Sarah nodded. "It's not a good idea to interrupt the preacher during sermon, especially when he's your dad."

"Don't let her fool you. She has William wrapped around her finger and always has," Maybelle assured, her voice clearly trying to sound disapproving, though her gaze was indulgent when she glanced toward Sarah.

Sarah smiled. Her father loved her and had always provided for her every need. Yes, he'd often leaned on Aunt Jean and the women surrounding her, but raising a daughter alone couldn't have been easy for him. She'd never begrudge him accepting the help they offered as she cherished those times.

Just as she cherished the women embarrassing her with their tales.

When they started in with another story, she shook her head, but let them run with it. It wasn't as if she could stop them if she'd tried.

She'd heard their stories before, but while listening to them, she realized she didn't recall their having told them to Richard or any of her past boyfriends. She marveled that they'd opened up so quickly to Bodie. Without even trying, Bodie had them eating out of his hand.

Well, two of the three. Maybelle seemed intent upon withholding her approval.

When an attendant came in to say her tree was ready, a round of disappointment sounded.

"So soon?" Rosie pouted as Sarah and Bodie stood to leave the table.

Bodie pulled his coat off the back of his chair and began putting it on. "Got to help Sarah get this tree in the house and then get back to work. Nice running into you here."

As Sarah went to slip her arms into her jacket, Bodie came over to help her.

"Yeah, nice running into you here," Sarah repeated as she zipped her jacket. She met each of the Butterflies' innocent-appearing gazes. "Such a coincidence that we bumped into each other."

Maybelle picked up her coffee, brought it to her lips, said, "Isn't it, though?" then took a sip.

When Bodie's back was to them, Sarah made a gesture to show she was keeping her eyes on them, too.

All three women laughed.

Thanks to the help of a neighbor, Bodie got Sarah's "perfect" tree inside Hamilton House. No way could he and Sarah have gotten the tree out of his truck and inside without additional help. He'd mentioned as much to Sarah at Harvey Farms, but, smiling, she'd said they'd figure something out.

She'd given him the biggest grin when the neighbor had pulled in right across the street. When she'd asked for his help, "Robert" had about fallen all over himself doing her bidding and had produced a furniture dolly that had been a godsend.

"You sure this is where you want the tree?" Bodie asked while Robert and his furniture dolly were still there.

Big brown eyes full of question, Sarah looked at him. "You don't think it looks good here?"

What could Bodie say? It was a tree. It belonged outdoors.

"Looks great, Sarah," Robert said, looking at Sarah with googly eyes. She'd said they'd gone to school together. Had there once been more than friendship between them?

But that wasn't any of Bodie's business.

"My aunt always put her tree here because you can see the lights from outside thanks to the big window," Sarah continued, her gaze going back and forth between Robert and Bodie. "Where do you think we should put it?"

Bodie glanced around the room. Near the window was the only place the tree could go without doing major furniture shuffling.

"I think this spot does it."

The tree actually had him feeling a little anxious. What would it be like seeing the tree every day, a constant reminder of what had almost happened at the Christmas tree farm before her friend had interrupted?

What was he thinking? Nothing had happened at the Christmas tree farm. They had picked out a tree that a salesperson had helped load into his truck. They'd had soup and fudge at Mrs. Harvey's kitchen, followed by some chatting with her friends, and then they'd come back home. End of story.

Not that Hamilton House was home. Or that he thought of Pine Hill as home. He didn't.

What he did think was that he needed to get back to work.

While Sarah was seeing Robert out, Bodie made sure the tree was secure. He couldn't have it toppling over on her. Once he was certain it was steady, he straightened, annoyed at the pain that shot to his hip. Without thought—and quite stupidly, since Sarah could walk back in at any moment—he rubbed the area.

"Did you hurt yourself?"

Bodie turned towards the door and saw Harry and Sarah standing there. "Robert gone?"

"He is." Her eyes were full of concern. "You didn't answer my question. Did you hurt yourself carrying in the tree?"

Great. He couldn't have her worried that she'd caused him pain. He shook his head. "It's nothing more than an old injury."

"From your time in the service?"

Although he'd rather not go there, he wasn't going to lie to her, so he nodded.

"How old?"

This was what he got for giving in to the pain, for rubbing the area that was hurting. He should have known better.

"Is your injury why you're not in the military anymore?"

Her voice was so gentle, so full of empathy, that he couldn't stand it. He didn't deserve her empathy and he sure didn't want her pity.

"I'd rather not talk about it."

She sighed, but rather than push, she put her hands on her hips. "Okay, fine. We won't talk about your hip injury. Or your time in the military. Or anything else you don't want to talk about."

"Good."

Her expression said she didn't agree. Shifting her

gaze, she looked at the tree and her eyes took on some of their usual light.

"It really is a beautiful tree."

As it got her to change the subject, Bodie was happy to agree. "Best tree ever."

Surprised by his comment, she turned, smiled, then took on that eager-for-life, full-of-energy expression she usually had. The expression of a dreamer. "It's going to look even better when we get through decorating."

We? There was no "we" decorating her tree.

"I should get back to the bathrooms now. Those vanities aren't going to install themselves."

Frustration shone on her face. "You don't want to decorate the tree?"

"Not particularly."

"Okay. Back to the vanities." She sighed. "If that's what you want."

Hating that he'd yet again dimmed that dreamer light in her eyes, Bodie headed toward the bathroom.

Sarah had decorated a tree with Aunt Jean for many years. But because of the grand opening, she'd chosen a tree that was much larger and grander than any tree she could remember ever being at Hamilton House.

Then again, maybe her choice hadn't been because of the opening, but because of how happy she'd been that Bodie had gone with her to pick out the tree.

Despite the almost-kiss, their moment of awkward conversation, and the Butterflies' persistence, she really had had a great day with him.

Right up until she'd asked him about his leg, and he'd clammed up.

She'd noticed his leg bothering him before, a slight hesitation sometimes when he first stood, but she'd never mentioned it. She knew whatever had happened to him, whatever caused his pain, was why he was no longer in the military.

It wasn't that he didn't still want to be a soldier. It was that he couldn't be.

Why hadn't he told her what had happened? Maybe he had been on some top-secret mission he couldn't talk about. More likely, Bodie didn't like talking about anything personal.

Regardless, that something had wounded him so irreversibly triggered an ache deep in her chest. The thought that he had been hurt, possibly seriously... that he could've died, and she wouldn't have even known...had her taking a deep breath.

As she went outside to get the small stepladder out of the small storage shed, Harry at her side, she contemplated how much she actually knew about Bodie.

Or more accurately, how little she knew about him.

If she wanted to know more all she had to do was mention it to the Butterflies. They'd no doubt be happy to hand her a whole dossier on him, probably with color-coded tabs.

But Sarah didn't want the Butterflies to tell her more about Bodie. She wanted Bodie to tell her. She wanted him to want her to know who he was, what made him tick, his likes, his dislikes.

Ha. He was her repair guy. Not her boyfriend.

What made her think he would ever choose to tell her anything personal?

Just because she wanted to know didn't mean he wanted to share anything with her. If his reticence told her anything, it was that obviously he didn't want to open up at all. Not with her.

Making sure not to scrape the hardwood floors, she dragged the ladder into the living room and set it up near the tree. Grabbing some heavy-duty scissors, she climbed up the steps to cut away a few stray branches.

As she came down from the ladder, she regarded the tree and noticed one little branch near the top that was like a bad stray hair.

It had to go. Going back up the stepladder, she reached over to snip the little limb.

"What are you doing?"

Spinning at Bodie's voice, she almost lost balance on the ladder, only steadying herself at the last second.

Quick as a flash, he was near the ladder, ready to catch her if she fell.

"Be careful," he ordered.

"I was fine until you came in and startled me," she pointed out, a little annoyed.

"What if Harry had bumped against the ladder?"

Sarah glanced at where the dog lay on the floor watching her. "Harry looks comfy where he is."

"You don't know that he wouldn't hear a noise and bump against the ladder. You could've fallen."

"But I didn't." Which was a bit of a shame when she had a strong soldier waiting to catch her. Would

Santa put her on the naughty list if she pretended to slip and let herself drop into Bodie's waiting arms?

Now where had that thought come from? She did not want to drop into Bodie's arms. But she did appreciate his concern.

"This time," Bodie argued, putting his hand on the ladder to steady it should she do anything that might jar it. "I don't think you should be up on ladders."

"I'll have you know I've been using this ladder to decorate trees in this house all my life. I've got this." She gave him a challenging look. "Unless you've decided you want to help. In which case, I'll gladly hand over my stepladder to you."

"Is that why you're up on that ladder stretched out that way? Trying to get me in on decorating the tree?"

"Would I do that?" she asked innocently. Truly, she hadn't been. But it was so much fun to tease him that she couldn't resist.

He arched a brow. "You tell me."

"If you're volunteering," she said, "I could use help."

He looked up at her, waiting to see what it was she wanted him to do.

"Putting lights on a tree has never been my favorite part of decorating." Truer words had never been spoken. "I'm not sure if it's a patience thing or what, but I always get them tangled up around each other." She gave him her best *pretty please* smile. "If you'd help me get the lights onto the tree, I'd appreciate it."

Not looking thrilled at the prospect, he regarded her. "Put the lights on, huh?"

"Think you could handle the lights? If so, I could make us some cookies and milk."

"Your homemade oatmeal chocolate chip cookies?"

When she nodded, she could tell his interest was piqued. Or maybe it was just that he didn't want her up on the ladder again. Either way, he pretended to be considering.

"Guess I could. Of course, this does mean I'm still not getting your vanities installed."

Not caring a bit about whether he got the vanities installed that day or not, she grinned. "We have all evening. How long does it take to put lights on a tree?"

Bodie gave her a skeptical look. "If I truly believed it was only going to be putting lights on a tree, it would be one thing. But I have this feeling I'm going to be in here a while."

Sarah hoped so.

A little later, walking back into the living area with a tray of goodies, Sarah paused in the doorway to look at Bodie.

He might have only come back to help her decorate the tree out of guilt for shutting down her questions, or concern that she'd hurt herself on the ladder, but he was doing a great job. The lights were spaced evenly, just the way she preferred, and she hadn't even had to tell him.

Sarah really liked that about him.

She liked a lot of things about Bodie. Like the fact that he was humming along with the Christmas music she had playing. No doubt if she mentioned it, he'd immediately stop.

For whatever reason, Bodie didn't want to

like anything related to Christmas. Sarah didn't understand how that was even possible. How could she, when she loved everything about the holidays?

Maybe by the time he finished with Hamilton House, she'd have shown him what Christmas could, and should, be like.

CHAPTER NINE

BODIE WRAPPED LIGHT STRANDS AROUND Sarah's "perfect" tree, stopping every so often to make sure he had them evenly distributed, then moved on to the next layer.

How did she keep pulling him into all this Christmas stuff?

He had told her no, walked away, gone to the bathroom and cut the vanity free of its cardboard and Styrofoam casing. He'd heard her go outside, come back in, heard the Christmas music come on, heard her start singing while she trimmed the tree.

The more he'd heard, the more guilt had eaten at him. For however long he was in Pine Hill, he needed to help Sarah.

He'd abandoned the vanity and gone to help her, almost having a heart attack when he'd seen her on the ladder, looking like an angel tree topper who was about to topple.

At the moment, she was a cookie-bearing angel watching him from the doorway, thinking he was unaware she was there even though he'd been aware of every step she'd made since leaving the kitchen.

"You did check to make sure all the bulbs still work, right?" she asked, finally coming on into the room.

"You think I'm an amateur?"

"At decorating a tree?" She sat a tray down on a table. "I'd put money on it."

Turning from the tree, he eyed her. "How much money?"

"How much are you willing to lose?"

He chuckled. "Am I so bad at putting lights on a tree that you're confident I've never done this before?"

"Honestly? You're great at putting on the lights."

"You're just saying that because me putting the lights on means you don't have to."

"Guilty as charged," she admitted. "But I'm also serious. You're doing an amazing job."

Pleased at her praise, he asked, "What makes you think I'm any good at light hanging?"

"I was watching you check the spacing," she admitted. "The lights are going to be perfect. Turn them on if you don't believe me."

"I'll finish putting the lights on, then we'll see."

Sarah lingered over the cookies and milk. Overall, it had been such a good day. She wanted to pause time where it was and not risk ruining it with opening the box of ornaments.

Opening those ornaments shouldn't be a bad thing. Decorating the tree was her idea. Yet she couldn't bring herself to walk over to the box.

As excited as she was about the tree, all along she'd been dreading this part. Seeing the ornaments her aunt had made, that they'd made together over the years, and knowing that Aunt Jean wasn't there this time and never would be again... It wasn't going to be easy.

She told Bodie a joke she'd heard while out delivering meals. He laughed, finished his milk and cookies, and stood. Although he'd been sleeping on the rug in front of the fireplace, Harry lifted his head to keep an eye on Bodie.

"There's more if you want another."

He patted his flat stomach. "I'm good."

Yes, he was. A good distraction from what she knew was about to happen.

"I need to get back to work."

Dismay filled her at the idea of being in the room alone, decorating the tree alone when she had so many cherished memories of doing so with her aunt. She wanted Bodie to stay. Yes, he'd already helped her with the lights when she knew he didn't want to but surely staying a little longer wouldn't be too much to ask?

"You've already done so much to help me today, and I know I'm being silly, but, I... I'd really appreciate it if you'd decorate the tree with me."

He looked torn, as if everything in him was saying that he should get out while he could, but something held him in place. "It's been a long time since I've helped decorate a tree, Sarah. Hanging the lights is my extent of my tree-decorating abilities."

He was turning to go, would soon be back in the bathroom working on getting everything ready for her future guests. It's where he should be. Where she needed him to be. He was her repair guy, nothing more.

"Please don't go."

He met her gaze and studied her for long moments, then seemed to see beneath the surface, that this had nothing to do with trying to get him into the Christmas spirit and everything to do with her and what was going inside her head. Inside her heart.

Despite his tough exterior, she knew Bodie wouldn't leave her when she'd asked him to stay. Strange to think how fully she trusted him to be good to her when she and Richard had dated for over a year and she knew he wouldn't have hesitated to leave.

"You're the boss," Bodie said, as if that explained why he was still standing in her living room. "If you want me to decorate a tree, I'll decorate a tree."

She wanted to hug him.

"Thank you." She clung to her cocoa mug and pretended to take another sip. Pretended because the cup was empty.

"Can I carry that to the kitchen for you?"

She started to say no but a trip to the kitchen would delay what she wanted delayed.

"That would be great." She put her mug on the tray and she and Harry followed him to the kitchen. After he sat it down on the kitchen counter, she rinsed out their mugs and saucers, then placed them inside the dishwasher.

When she turned, Bodie was leaned against the countertop, watching her. Harry stood next to him, waiting to see what they'd do next or perhaps just hoping they had a few leftover cookies they planned to share with him.

"We don't have to decorate the tree tonight."

Oh yeah, he was on to her. His insight had her feeling guilty that she was dilly-dallying, that she was putting any type of damper on Christmas. She was supposed to be giving him Christmas joy.

"Then it would just be waiting."

"I'm sure there are other things waiting on your attention that you've been putting off."

"Plenty."

"Then do those and come back to the tree when you're ready. For that matter, you could help me install the vanities."

Sarah closed her eyes. "I feel ridiculous."

"Because?"

"Because I am so excited about that tree and yet I am procrastinating on decorating it."

"Maybe you need to buy new decorations," he suggested, the simple phrase clearly broadcasting that he'd accurately read what was bothering her.

She could. Except money was an issue. As would be looking at a tree in Aunt Jean's house that held ornaments other than the ones Sarah cherished. She shook her head.

"I love those ornaments. Forgive me. I'm just being silly."

"She must have been a wonderful person."

"She was." The tears she'd been holding back filled her eyes. "I've tried to keep myself busy enough that I haven't thought about just how different all my Christmases are going to be without her."

She hadn't wanted to do this, but talking to Bodie was so easy.

"Aunt Jean was the closest I had to a mother—

while also being so much more. It makes me sad that I'll never see her smile again or have her teach me something new." She pointed toward a quilt rack in one corner of the room. "She made that. It's one of my favorites. There's a trunk full of them in my bedroom. She made and did so many things, helped so many people, and was just such a talented person. She donated dozens of quilts over the years. Baby quilts, charity quilts, Quilts of Valor for soldiers—those were her favorite to make. Probably because Roy died in the service." Sarah sighed. "I tried to soak up everything I could, to do good things like she did, but there was so much more for me to learn from her."

If ever Bodie was going to tell Sarah about his quilt, now was the perfect opportunity. He could explain about her quilt. Her note. Her impact on his life. That, like her aunt, she helped so many people, too.

She'd helped him. Maybe she'd be glad to hear that. Maybe it would help.

But he hadn't planned to tell her about the quilt he treasured even more after getting to know the woman who'd made it. What would be the point?

"I imagine she was very proud of you."

How could her aunt not have been proud? Sarah was the best person he knew. Good, wholesome, unjaded by the cruelties of the world. He wanted to protect that. To protect her from the things he'd seen and done. To wipe away the sadness in her eyes.

Sarah nodded. "She was proud, but always pushed me to do my best. She believed in serving others and lived her life doing so."

"Nothing wrong with that life philosophy if you're able to do it."

"As a young widow, she took care of her in-laws and then, much later, she took care of me."

"She never had children of her own?"

"No. They'd planned to start a family after Roy came back from the war."

"But he never came back," Bodie finished for her.

She gave him a trembly smile. "Did you fight in any wars, Bodie?"

Not ones where the enemy fought out in the open. His enemy had always been hidden, avoiding open battlefields and attacking from the shadows, hiding among the innocent and wreaking destruction on their lives.

Taking the lives of his brothers in arms.

His stomach knotted. His vision blurred. His fingers dug into his palms as his hands clenched.

Bodie closed his eyes.

"I'm sorry. I didn't mean to pry."

Fighting the shadows, he opened his eyes, met her still-watery gaze.

"Well, I guess I did mean to pry," she corrected. "I'm curious about you, about your time in the service."

"I didn't fight in a war like your uncle Roy."

"But you did fight?"

Tapping his fingers against the kitchen island, he shrugged. "Every soldier is in a battle against terrorism."

She nodded as if she understood, but he doubted she did. He doubted anyone did unless they'd lived it.

"You were a good soldier."

He'd thought so, but then he'd awakened to

screams, awakened to die inside even though his body had somehow managed to survive. A good soldier would have protected his unit.

His gaze shifted to hers. "What makes you say that?"

"Because I know you."

"You've known me a couple of weeks," he said. "You know very little about me, much less whether I was a good soldier."

"Knowing a person is about so much more than just time." She put the dishtowel on the counter and closed the few steps between them. Reaching out, she touched his chest with her pointer finger. "I know what's in here. It tells me that you live by a high code of ethics."

Her finger burned through his shirt, warming the flesh as if she touched him with a branding iron.

"It comes out in everything you do." She stared at where her finger touched him. "Although you have this big bad aura that warns not to mess with you, you've got a big heart."

"Don't fool yourself into thinking that I haven't done bad things," he warned, not liking her assessment. She was making him out to be a hero when he was anything but. He wasn't good. "I've done things that would make you not like me very much."

He'd done things that made him not like himself very much... but he'd still done them because they'd been necessary to get the job done. He'd still be doing the government's bidding had he not gotten injured.

Flattening her fingers against his heart, she studied him. Bodie's heart pounded against his ribcage, against her hand.

"I believe you've always acted for what you felt was the greater good."

She was making him out to be heroic. He wasn't, and he didn't want her thinking he was.

"Greater good is oftentimes a matter of perspective."

"I trust you."

"You shouldn't." After all, in a way, he was deceiving her by being there without telling her the reason why. He'd come to thank her and instead had gone to work for her.

"I don't believe you'd ever hurt me," she continued, staring up at him with her big brown eyes filled with exactly what she claimed—trust.

"Not intentionally." He wouldn't. He'd do everything in his power to leave her as bright-eyed as he'd found her.

"But unintentionally you might?"

"It's possible." Feeling more and more uncomfortable with their conversation, he straightened his shoulders, pulling himself back just enough that Sarah's finger fell away. "Let's decorate the tree."

She wrinkled her nose. "Do we have to?"

"After all the work to get that tree? You better believe we have to decorate it."

Taking a deep breath, Sarah nodded, but within minutes, when faced with the packed boxes, she looked doubtful again.

He didn't fully understand her hesitation. She lived in her aunt's house, amongst her aunt's things. What was so special about the ornaments that unpacking them played such havoc on Sarah?

Walking over, he put his hand over hers. "You've got this."

A small sound escaped her lips, she inhaled, then nodded. "You're right. I do."

Half the tree was decorated and already it was looking amazing. Sarah inspected the ornaments Bodie held, trying to decide if she was going to use them. Her dread had significantly eased at Bodie's constant jokes and teasing.

"Hey, Sarah?" Bodie lifted the lid off a box of glass ornaments that had belonged to Aunt Jean's in-laws.

Knowing another joke was on its way, Sarah shifted her gaze to Bodie.

"What do you call an obnoxious reindeer?" he asked, giving her an expectant look.

"I don't know, Bodie. What do you call an obnoxious reindeer?"

"RUDE-olph."

Giggling a little, she rolled her eyes. He was intentionally keeping her focused on him, and she appreciated his effort. She appreciated most everything about Bodie.

"How is it that you know so many Christmas jokes when you profess not to like Christmas?"

"It wasn't by choice," he assured. "Lou has a new one written on a dry-erase board each morning."

"And you committed them all to memory? Saving them up for moments like these?"

"I read them all," he clarified. "Hard not to since the sign is right next to the cash register. As far as memorizing them, I never had any intention of repeating them."

She lifted one of the antique glass ornaments from

its box, running her finger over its smooth lines, before hanging it on the tree. "So why are you?"

The corner of his mouth twitched. "You're smiling, aren't you?"

"Kinda hard not to with your corny Christmas jokes."

"Not mine. Lou's."

She pulled another ornament from the box, deciding she was going to hang the glass ball in honor of the Hamiltons. "Tell me another."

"What does a sheep who doesn't like Christmas say?"

Putting the ornament on the tree, she turned, met Bodie's gaze and waited for the punch line.

"Baaaaaaa humbug."

"Good thing you're not a sheep or you'd be baaing all the time." Sarah snickered at the thought, then went back to the box see what was next.

"Oh, here's another ornament I made," she cooed, lifting the angel out of the box and holding it out for Bodie to see.

"Nice," he enthused with a teasing tone. "How old were you?"

She arched her brow. "You implying it looks like I was young?"

He laughed. "Just curious."

"Third grade."

His forehead furrowed. "How do you remember that?"

"Because I put the red hair on the angel because my schoolteacher had red hair. I thought she was beautiful, like an angel. I remember telling everyone that when I grew up, I was going to be her."

"I'm glad you didn't."

"Grow up to be her?"

He nodded.

"Schoolteacher is a noble profession."

"Agreed, not what I meant."

She waited for him to elaborate and wasn't surprised when she had to prompt him. "What did you mean?"

"That, although I'm sure your third-grade teacher was great, she wasn't you."

"And being me is a good thing?"

"Look at how many people you help, how many lives you touch," he pointed out. "Being you is more than good, Sarah. The world needs more people like you."

Heat flooded through her at his compliment. "That's a nice thing to say, Bodie."

He shrugged as if what he'd said was no big deal. "It's the truth."

"You're not just saying that to keep me from getting all weepy over these ornaments again, are you?"

The corner of his mouth lifted. "Would I do that?"

She laughed. "I wouldn't blame you. Thank you for your patience and your jokes. I'm sorry about earlier."

"It's fine. Everyone has off times."

Something in the way he said the words had Sarah glancing toward him, wondering what lay deep within him, what caused his "off times." "Do you?"

"Have off times?" He hesitated, then shrugged again. "Of course."

Not necessarily surprised that he'd shrugged off her question rather than give her an in-depth answer, Sarah inwardly sighed. She wanted to peel back his layers and expose what made him tick. No, not true. She wanted him to peel back those layers and choose to let her see. She suspected whatever had injured his leg was at the root of Bodie's off times. How could it not be?

"Well, if you ever need someone to help you through your off times, or to just distract you with corny Christmas jokes, I'm your girl, because you're definitely seeing me through mine."

His facial expression went tight for the briefest moment, but then just when she thought his eyes were going to take on that stoic, bleak look they'd had when she'd first met him, he surprised her by grinning. "Do you actually know any corny Christmas jokes?"

Despite knowing the absolute joy moving through her at his grin wasn't good for her long-term well-being, she couldn't stop the ecstatic feeling at the way that Bodie was teasing her, was enjoying himself, was determined she enjoy herself.

"Do I know any Christmas jokes? Seriously?" She put her hands on her hips and gave him her most dazzling smile. "I am the *queen* of Christmas jokes."

He arched his brow in challenge. "Let's hear them."

"Hey, Bodie?"

"Not a knock-knock joke, I hope."

She looked upward. "Quit ruining my joke and play along."

His lips twitched.

"Why was Santa's little helper depressed?" she asked.

He waited.

"Because he had low elf esteem." Trying to keep

from bursting out in laughter, she thrust up her arms in victory.

He snorted. "And you called my jokes corny."

"But you laughed," she pointed out with a little sway of her head.

"That I did," he agreed, a wry grin on his face.

Fifteen minutes later, the tree was done.

"Hit the lights."

"How about I just turn them on?"

"You knew what I meant," she mock-accused, enjoying how he kept teasing her. She knew why he was doing it, that he wanted to keep her smiling. He was doing a great job, so great she really did feel ridiculous that she'd hesitated on decorating the tree.

Grinning, Bodie pushed the on switch for the lights.

Sarah's breath caught. "Wow. That is the most beautiful Christmas tree ever."

"I bet you say that about every tree."

"Only when it's true." She clasped her hands together, turned to him and smiled. "Oh, Bodie, thank you for helping me. With the stress and with the tree."

His smile was real, reached his beautiful blue eyes, and put the tree to absolute shame.

"You'd have done the same for me."

She had done the same for Bodie. Not that Sarah knew it.

She'd made and donated a quilt that had, for whatever reason, resonated deep within him, shrouding him in selfless goodness that had shut out the darkness and wrapped him within its healing powers.

What would Sarah say, think, if she knew he had her quilt?

Part of him didn't think she'd mind, that she'd love the fact that her quilt meant so much to him.

Another part wondered if she'd consider him a crazy stalker with nothing better to do than track down a quilter and take on her home repairs.

Yeah, that didn't make him sound crazy. Much.

Uncomfortable with his thoughts, he glanced around at the empty ornament boxes.

"I'm going to carry these to the attic."

"I'll help."

There were only a few, but more than he could get in one trip, so arguing was futile.

Regardless, gathering up the empty boxes changed the subject and that was his main objective. His and Sarah's conversation had too many personal undertones.

The single trip up the stairs didn't bother his hip.

Once they got the boxes stored, he turned and found Sarah eyeing the cluttered corner of the attic. It appeared to be the odds and ends storage area, full of bits of furniture, trunks, boxes, and who knew what else beneath the stacks, drop cloths, and layers of dust.

"What's all that stuff?"

"Who knows?" she answered. "Once the estate was settled to where I could get started on the repairs, my priority was downstairs in hopes of getting things ready for the open house. I haven't gone through things up here, beyond throwing out whatever got damaged when the roof leaked. Once I get the suites up and going, I'll need to process all of this in hopes that some of the furniture will be useable."

"What happened to your aunt's furniture?"

"Everything from the downstairs suites is either stored upstairs, in my dad's garage, or piled up in corners. The mostly empty upstairs rooms are from where she sold things over the years."

"If any of the items she sold were like some of the antiques downstairs, then it's a shame she had to let them go."

"There were some beautiful pieces. But she needed the money." He could hear the pain she felt that her aunt had had to sell her furniture, that Sarah hadn't been able to help her. "Best I can tell, over the past five years, she was supplementing her income by selling things out of the house."

"Why didn't she open the B & B herself to bring in some income?"

Sarah shrugged. "Good question, and not one I have an answer to. Certainly, she and I talked about opening one often enough."

Sarah glanced over at the pile of stuff again.

"I have to admit, part of the reason I've put off going through this stuff is because of the heartache of going through more of Aunt Jean's things, rather than not having the time." At his look, she added, "Don't get me wrong. I've been busy. My aunt kept things just done enough that no one suspected she was having money issues. Once she passed and I really looked around, I could see a lot of little things that should have been repaired or replaced years before. The house, the yard... so many things had been neglected."

"I'm sure she did what she could."

Sarah nodded. "Right up until she got sick just after Thanksgiving, she was a fireball of energy. But, truthfully, most of her time was spent helping me. From the time I could walk and talk, I could always count on Aunt Jean and the Butterflies to make any project I dreamed up happen."

Bodie tried to imagine Sarah's childhood, the love that was directed at her from so many people, and he couldn't. She was easy to...well, for her friends and family, she was easy to love.

Take him, for example.

He wasn't in love with Sarah, but even as jaded as he was, he cared about her well-being. Sarah exuded goodness, so it was no wonder others wanted to help her, to be a part of that goodness in some way.

A temporary way to feel good about himself.

Suddenly claustrophobic in the attic, he took a step toward the door. He was ready to get back to work. Real work. The work he'd agreed to do. Not all this Christmas stuff she kept pulling him into.

"You were lucky to have had your Aunt Jean."

"I was." She nodded, then gestured to the cluttered section of the attic. "Maybe you can help me go through that stuff, too. It's probably junk or she'd have sold it before she sold her furniture. But at some point, I do need to sort it."

He doubted he'd be there that long. Despite the detours, like taking most of the day to help Sarah with her Christmas tree, he was making good progress on finishing up her remodel and repairs. He'd complete his work, then head to Texas.

Sarah smiled at him and that fluttery feeling swept

across his chest again, threatening to steal his breath and his peace of mind.

The sooner he finished with Hamilton House and got out of Pine Hill, the better.

CHAPTER TEN

"YAY, IT'S THE SECOND-BEST DAY of the year!"

Knowing where this was going, Bodie glanced up from where he worked in the second suite's bathroom but didn't say a word.

Sarah looked as if she were about to burst with happiness. "Are you going to ask me why it's the second-best day of the year?"

"Nope."

"Bodie!"

He couldn't help but grin. She looked more like a little girl dancing around with excitement than a grown woman.

"Not that I don't know, but tell me. Why is today the second-best day of the year?"

She rewarded him with a smile. "Because it's On-the-Square Christmas Festival day."

"Where you have ornament hunts, present picks, and a parade?" he teased, thinking he never should have looked up and seen the gleam in her eyes. Looking into Sarah's eyes tended to have him doing things he knew he shouldn't do.

"You *have* been paying attention," she praised in a playful voice. "It's also where we sell our snowflakes. Since you helped cut the pieces for some of them, you should be extra excited because you, Bodie Lewis, helped make today happen."

He gave her a dubious look.

Unfazed, she asked, "You are coming by our booth, right?"

Ugh. He knew where this was going. Knew he needed to steer clear.

"I hadn't planned to go to the festival. I figured I'd stay here and finish up," he admitted. He was almost done with her original requests. There were still a few items to complete, but he'd systematically crossed off Sarah's list of tasks one by one.

A look of horror fell over her face. "How can you not go? I understand that you didn't really get to celebrate Christmas while you were in the military, but guess what, Bodie?" Her chin lifted as she stared him down. "You aren't in the military anymore, so you should celebrate Christmas and you should definitely go to the Pine Hill On-The-Square Christmas Festival because who knows if you'll ever get the opportunity again?"

He knew.

He wouldn't.

Once he finished her house, it was unlikely he'd ever set foot in Pine Hill again. A sobering thought, but a realistic one.

Sarah would go on spreading snowflakes and Christmas cheer and he'd go back to his life. Not the life he'd wanted or envisioned, but not a life that seemed as dark and dreary as he'd once thought it would be, either. Still, it would be a life that had no point of intersection with hers.

"Say you'll go," Sarah pleaded with her words and her eyes. She could give Harry a run for his money on the full imploring puppy eyes.

"You need my help with something?"

She laughed. "That isn't why I want you to go, but I can always use another helping hand if you're volunteering."

Curious as to her reasons, he asked, "Why do I need to go, then?"

"Because you'll have fun."

Fun. How long had it been since Bodie had done something just because it was fun? How long since he'd even thought about the word "fun" prior to meeting Sarah?

Thinking back, he'd admit these past couple of weeks with Sarah had been the most fun he'd had in years. He truly enjoyed spending time with her and taking in how she looked at the world through her Christmas-colored goggles and belief in ultimate goodness.

Not that Bodie hadn't enjoyed his time in the military or his off time with his buddies when they'd gone skiing or backpacking. He had. But time with Sarah was a different kind of fun. Lighter, fluffier, more child-like and innocent.

"And because I'd really like you to be there," Sarah continued, upping the ante. "I want you to go to the Christmas festival. Please go."

Her words got to him. Sarah wanted him at the festival. How could he say no?

"If you need my help, I'll go," he agreed. He'd pretty

much do anything to help her. Wasn't that his ultimate purpose for being there? That he enjoyed spending time with her was just an added bonus.

"If that's the only way you'll agree, then yes, I need your help." Her smile was brilliant. "Never let it be said that I turned away a volunteer."

"Never. What do you need me to do?"

"Want to help with the ornament hunt?"

"'Want' is a strong word, but why not? What's the worst that can happen?"

"Great, but first we need to deliver the snowflakes and other ornaments to the booth. It's early, but they'll be setting everything up."

"And you're not there?"

"Not yet, but I should be, so let's get a move on."

Sarah's smile was so bright at the idea of them going together that he found himself glad he'd given in to her pleas.

Then again, he enjoyed being with Sarah, and if that meant helping with an ornament hunt and attending a booth at a Christmas festival, he would.

It was noon by the time Sarah and Bodie got the boxes of homemade ornaments unloaded. Several volunteers were already there and had set up their booths on the courthouse lawn. The large, commercial-style tent that contained the festival included several tables and boards and backdrops that divided up areas. One section was the homemade ornaments booth, another the Pick a Present game, and another baked goods and hot cocoa.

The Sunday morning ladies' class from church

sponsored the baked goods and the money went to a cause of their choice each year. The proceeds from the game and ornament sales were solely to help fund Sarah's special projects.

"Slide that last box up under the edge of the table with the others," she advised Bodie, stepping back so he could see where she meant.

As she stepped back, she bumped into Harry.

"Sorry, boy," she told him, patting him on the head. "You need to move over there," she told the dog, pointing to the side of the table. "That way you won't get stepped on while we're getting this set up."

Putting the box on top of another, Bodie straightened. "There you go bossing—I mean, directing—again. Me, Harry, whoever is within hearing range."

Standing from where she'd been petting Harry, she put her hands on her hips. "Yeah, well, if I didn't know better, I'd think you liked being bossed—I mean, taking direction, Bodie."

"The Army taught me well."

"Let's see if they taught you about arranging ornaments on this display," she quipped, handing him a snowflake from the box she'd just opened.

Other volunteers had set up pegboard backdrops painted to look like Christmas trees to separate the ornament booth from the others. Hooks were scattered on the boards. On each hook, she and Bodie hung ornaments, essentially decorating the pegboard trees.

"Not much arranging involved when all we're doing is hanging them on pre-placed hooks," Bodie mused.

"We're not done yet," she warned, gesturing to the group headed toward them with a live Christmas tree in tow. Harry got to his feet to inspect as the noisy group neared. Two teen boys carried the tree. A few other volunteers carried cardboard boxes. All were singing Christmas carols. Maybelle, Rosie, and Claudia, dressed in matching red coats and Santa hats, led the way and the songs.

"The hornets are here," he drawled, eyeing the approaching three women and their entourage. "How come I get the feeling things are about to get crazy?"

"Butterflies. Not hornets." Sarah slapped his arm but couldn't quite smother her laughter. "Surely you aren't afraid of them?"

"Those butterflies of yours aren't the gentle, fluttery kind. They're more like wasps with colorful wings."

Sarah laughed. "They'd love that you said so."

"Just in case, don't tell them. They might hurt me," he said with a grin.

"Yeah, yeah. I saw how you had them eating out of your hand at Harvey Farms," she reminded, handing him another ornament.

"Ho, ho, ho," Claudia said, spreading more Christmas cheer as they neared the booth.

"Afternoon, hun." Maybelle stepped up to Sarah, leaned in and kissed her cheek. "Looks like you have everything in the Christmas way, here."

Maybelle's gaze went to Bodie as she said the last.

"Not everything," Sarah admitted. "But we're working on it."

One of the teens who'd been patiently standing beside the live, balled tree, pulled out his cell phone. Maybelle was having none of it.

"Boys, set that tree up at the end of this table and go back to get the other one for the opposite side," she ordered, motioning for the young man to put his phone away. "You have the lights, Sarah?"

She nodded. "Thanks to Bodie. He helped carry everything and is going to help with the ornament hunt."

Rosie reached out and squeezed Bodie's upper arm. "Good thing you're here to save the day after Sarah's help cancelled on her."

Bodie shot Sarah a *see, I told you* look. Wasps with colorful wings. With the way her friends had been behaving, the description semi-fit. She'd often thought of them as bees over the years. Hard workers, full of energy, and always buzzing around.

"Rosie, behave," Maybelle ordered, clucking her tongue at the other woman. "Claudia, you have the tree skirts?"

"Like you'd let me forget."

"I just don't want to have to walk back to our cars this quickly after arriving."

"Admit it. You're getting old," Claudia accused.

Maybelle's brows touched the tips of her dyed hair. "Old? Me? Over my dead body."

"Something like that," Claudia said under her breath, winking at Sarah.

"What did you say?"

"Nothing," Claudia denied, taking the Christmas tree skirts the Butterflies had hand-quilted years ago from a bag and shaking them out. "Nothing at all."

"That's what I thought."

Sarah covered her mouth to stifle a smile.

Despite Claudia's digs, Maybelle started whipping out orders again, telling the boys to adjust where they'd put the tree and having Claudia wrap the skirt around the ball base. "Mr. Lewis, grab the box of lights and do the honor of putting them on the tree."

"Me?"

"You have a problem with that?" Maybelle's narrowed gaze said he'd best not.

"No, ma'am. Just that having never put lights on a tree before, I'm getting ample experience while in Pine Hill."

"Well, it was high time you learned, son." Maybelle's drawn-on brows rose as she gave Sarah a look that told her she'd realized that Bodie had just admitted he'd helped decorate Sarah's tree.

Sarah just smiled, refusing to say anything that might give the Butterflies something more to latch onto.

"Sarah, you get the extra ornaments organized so as soon as we sell one, we can easily replace it with a fresh one."

Sarah and Bodie exchanged a look and Sarah fought laughing as Bodie held his hand to where only she could see his face and he mouthed the word, "Wasp."

Maybelle's gaze fell to Harry. The dog sat at perfect attention, quietly taking in the commotion. His head cocked as his gaze met Maybelle's, as if he was waiting for her to give him orders, as well.

"You best be on good behavior," she warned the dog. "Stay out of the way and no barking at the customers."

Seeming to understand, Harry settled back into his corner, laying his head on his legs, and watching Maybelle as if he wasn't sure about her.

Fifteen minutes later, the trees were positioned to Maybelle's specification. The boys had gone to run errands for one of the women working the game portion of the tent, and Maybelle, Claudia, and Rosie were checking out the baked goods and discussing who'd made what this year with the other volunteers.

"Okay, you're right. The wasps scare me," Bodie said under his breath.

Sarah laughed. "There goes my big, brave, tough soldier image of you. Taken down by a group of elderly church ladies."

"Pretty sure Maybelle was a general in a previous life. I can't figure the sweet grandma-looking one out, Claudia. She comes in with a sharp tongue here and there just to keep you on your toes. Ruby seems to spend more time in marital bliss than flittering around with the rest of the swarm." He finished wrapping the lights on the tree and plugged the end into the generator. "The other, Rosie, is a friendly sort. Always smiling. A few times now, she's invited me to stop by so she could bake cinnamon bread for me."

Sarah's eyes widened. "Did you go?"

He shook his head. "Every instinct said for me to just say no."

Sarah feigned disbelief. "Rosie offered some of her grandmother's cinnamon bread and you said no?"

He stared at her as if he didn't see what the big deal was. Sarah didn't believe that Rosie's grandmother's cinnamon bread would have wooed Bodie, but she was amused that Rosie had offered.

"Too bad for you," she told him. "Rosie's grandmother's cinnamon bread is legendary. It's a secret family recipe and she rarely offers to make it."

"I'll keep that in mind if I'm invited over again."

A smile played at Sarah's lips. "You do that."

Bodie stepped back to survey the trees he and Sarah had decorated with the various ornaments for sale, along with the festooned pegboards.

"Not bad, if I do say so myself."

"They're beautiful," Sarah agreed, looking wistfully at the trees. "Someone should buy the entire trees with everything on them so they could have these in their home exactly as they are right now."

"That would be something," Bodie agreed, turning an ornament to a better angle.

Sarah reached for the ornament at the same time, their hands brushing against each other's. Her gaze cut to Bodie's.

She had taken off her gloves some time back, to avoid the ornament hooks snagging on the material. Despite the chilly December air, her fingers hadn't felt cold, but she imagined they did next to Bodie's warm ones. She didn't pull her hand away from his, just looked up at him, thinking how glad she was he was there, how much she looked forward to what the afternoon and evening would bring.

If Bodie were gone by Christmas, then this year, the On-The-Square Christmas Festival would likely be her most favorite day of the year rather than second-best.

Good thing she'd have her Grand Opening to keep her busy, with no time for dwelling on how much she would have enjoyed spending the day with Bodie, wrapping him in Christmas joy.

His blue gaze held hers, and then he smiled. Sarah felt as if she were a Christmas tree someone had just flipped the light switch on. She lit up so brightly that she was sure she shone for miles.

Her breath caught, getting trapped in her chest and making her feel a little lightheaded as her eyes searched his. For what, she wasn't sure—she just knew that she looked into their blue depths for something more than what was on the surface.

"Thank you for coming today, Bodie."

His fingers moving slightly against hers, he shrugged. "So far it hasn't been too bad."

"Not too bad," she agreed, staring up at him and marveling at how she could feel so close to someone she'd only known a few weeks. "Good news is that the best is yet to come."

"That best being the ornament hunt?"

"The ornament hunt, the parade, the tree-lighting ceremony, the booth sales, the games, the sleigh ride." She let out a happy sigh. "I'm glad you came with me. Very glad."

"Me, too," he surprised her by saying and by moving his hand over hers and giving a gentle squeeze.

Sarah's gaze dropped to where his hand held hers, then lifted back to his eyes, seeing that something more she'd been searching for earlier.

That something that said he felt the connection between them just as she did.

That maybe she wasn't the only one struggling to pull the cold December air into her lungs.

"Sarah, I—"

"Wow. You two have been busy," Rosie exclaimed, coming back to the booth and breaking up whatever magic had been stirring in the air. "The trees are the prettiest I've ever seen."

Immediately, Bodie's hand dropped and he stepped away from Sarah and the tree.

"I was just telling Bodie the same thing," Sarah said as she rearranged the ornament where their hands had been and fought disappointment at how quickly Bodie's gaze had become shrouded, at how lonely her hand felt without his near.

At how much she wanted to know what he'd been about to say, to do.

Internally, she groaned at Rosie's timing.

But maybe it had been for the best. For a second, she'd gotten caught up in the moment. She had actually been wishing she and Bodie could become something more than what they were. That he'd choose to stay in Pine Hill, to date her and see what developed between them. But that was ridiculous. Of course Bodie didn't want to stick around. There was nothing in Pine Hill to draw someone so worldly.

She already knew *she* wasn't reason enough for someone to stay.

Catching on that she must have interrupted something, Rosie looked back and forth between them. Sarah prayed her friend would use discretion with what she said.

Rosie just smiled and talked about the tree and how all the other booths were coming together.

Maybelle and Claudia came up, both of them carrying a cup in each hand.

"We brought hot chocolate to keep you warm during the ornament hunt."

"Thank you," Sarah said, taking the steaming cup although she couldn't say she felt cold, thanks to the outdoor heater running beneath the booth checkout table. Anyone visiting their booth that evening would get a reprieve from the outdoor chill.

Or maybe it was the memory of Bodie holding her hand that warmed her insides.

"Harvey Farms is doing sleigh rides again this year," Ruby informed them unnecessarily as she joined them. "Charlie's over with them now lining up a ride for us later in case they sell out again." She sighed. "Cuddling up next to him in the sleigh is my favorite memory from last year."

Sarah loved the addition of sleigh rides to the On-The-Square Christmas Festival. For the past few years, she'd wanted to go, had always thought a sleigh ride as something super romantic and straight from a fairy tale. Richard had thought the sleigh rides a silly waste of money and had refused to go even when Sarah had offered to pay. She should have known right then and there that he wasn't the man for her.

How had she ever thought he was?

Thinking back, maybe she had known all along that she and Richard weren't really meant to be. She just hadn't wanted to acknowledge that Richard hadn't been right for her.

Why? For fear of being alone?

No, she wasn't afraid to be alone. Maybe it was more that she'd been so anxious to have what her parents had had before her mother died, what Ruby and Charlie had enjoyed for fifty-plus years.

But maybe that life wasn't for her. Maybe she was meant to live alone, as Aunt Jean and Maybelle had done.

She glanced toward Bodie, wondering what he thought of sleigh rides. He was leaving. Soon. Yet the idea of a going on a sleigh ride with him, with him looking at her the way he'd been doing moments before, appealed far more than it should.

Sliding an empty box that had held ornaments under a table, Bodie didn't seem to be thinking about sleigh rides or their moment at all.

When he straightened, he slid his hands into his jean pockets. "Anything else you need me to do before we head to the ornament hunt?"

Yes. I need you to tell me what you were going to say to me before Rosie showed up. I need to know if I imagined that you wanted to kiss me.

Even if Rosie wasn't standing there, Sarah wouldn't have said the words out loud, but oh, how she wished she knew the answers.

To cover her wayward thoughts, she glanced at her watch. "It is about time we head toward the church."

The ornament hunt was held a block over from the square at the church's playground.

From inside the community room, Sarah, Bodie, and a couple of other volunteers gathered bags of prize-stuffed plastic ornaments and headed to the playground to "hide" them.

Bodie had attached Harry's leash to a fence post and the dog barked when he spotted them.

"I hate that he's tied up," Sarah mused as they began hiding ornaments around the playground.

"Better that than him finding the ornaments and demolishing them before your kids have a chance to hunt them."

"He might think he was in the greatest game of Christmas Fetch ever." Sarah smiled at the image of Harry happily hunting the ornaments.

Bodie chuckled. "Possibly. Either way, Harry and all these ball-shaped ornaments wouldn't be a good combination."

She didn't think Harry would make any trouble, but it probably was better to leave him on his leash and tied to the fence.

Sarah "hid" an ornament on each swing seat. Bodie paused from where he was tucking one into a patch of higher grass at one of the swing frame's legs.

"You're sure it's okay that we're just putting most of them in plain sight? Isn't the objective to hunt for the ornaments?"

"We want this to be easy and fun for all ages."

He didn't look convinced. "Won't the older kids grab up all the ornaments in the open rather than leaving them for the younger kids?"

Placing ornaments on the slide's steps, Sarah shook her head. "We start by letting the two-year-olds in first. Then, thirty seconds later, the three-year-olds. Thirty seconds after that, the four-year-olds go in and so forth up to the ten-year-old cut-off age. It's a little chaotic, I guess, but it gives the younger kids the opportunity to find the easy ones first."

"Sounds like a plan."

"It worked well last year and will hopefully do so again this year." Sarah tucked an ornament up beneath the end of the slide. "Mainly, our goal is for the kids to have a great time."

"How many kids will hunt?"

"Last year, we had around seventy. We're hoping to break a hundred this year."

Sarah glanced around at the playground, looking for barren areas to put the rest of their ornaments.

Red, gold, green, and silver plastic ornaments were visible wherever one looked. She smiled. The kids were going to have so much fun.

Bodie mused, "There's ornaments everywhere."

"Two thousand or so."

He whistled. "That's a lot of candy-stuffed plastic."

"Not all of them have candy. I told you some have gift cards to local business and a few other small prizes."

"Which leaves a lot filled with candy," he reiterated, grinning. "It wasn't a local dentist who sponsored this event, was it?"

A hundred and four children had arrived to hunt ornaments. Sarah was over the moon. Bodie had stepped back, moving to where he had Harry tied, so he wouldn't be in the way and could hang out with the dog.

And observe Sarah.

Watching her with the other church volunteers, the kids, and the people from her community was seeing her in her element. He hoped after she opened the bed and breakfast that she would be able to continue her work with the church. Her deep love for it shined through in all she did.

Not to mention what a blessing she was to those she came into contact with. And those she didn't come into actual physical contact with.

Such as himself, before he sought her out.

She glanced up from where she stood near the gate, talking with the families of the children who would soon be rushing into the playground with their large red stocking-shaped plastic sacks, and caught him watching her. Her gaze searched his, questioning him.

Bodie winked, surprising himself.

Her eyes widened. Then, smiling, she winked back, looking quite pleased as she turned toward a journalist from the local paper who was taking photos of the anxiously waiting kids.

At Sarah's wink, Bodie's chest did that fluttery thing that made him feel a little light-headed. He dug his fingernails into his palms.

Harry glanced up, whimpering as if he knew something weird had happened.

"Yeah, I know, boy." He bent, petted the dog. "I know."

The fluttery feeling in his chest wasn't some missed medical ailment.

It was his reaction to Sarah. He'd never known anyone like her.

Holding up a battery-operated microphone, she got the attention of the crowd, and with the help of several volunteers, got the kids into age categories. Making sure each child had their ornament-collecting bag, Sarah opened the gate and let the two-year-old kids begin hunting.

Or more aptly, the two-year-old kids' parents, as they encouraged and helped each toddler collect ornaments and drop them into their stocking.

Keeping an eye on her watch, Sarah let group after group into the playground. She laughed at something one of the parents said before turning her smile to an older man who'd come to talk to her.

"Pretty, isn't she?"

Having heard her approach, Bodie continued to watch Sarah rather than turn to Maybelle.

"You don't have to say anything for me to know your answer to my question," the older woman pointed out, leaning against the fence and watching a smiling Sarah encourage the children.

"What is it you'd have me say?" Bodie asked.

"That you aren't going to hurt my girl."

Bodie shifted his gaze to Maybelle and fought wincing beneath her all-knowing blue eyes. "Why would I hurt Sarah?"

Maybelle was taking no quarter. "You tell me."

"I'm her handyman. She's my boss. Nothing more." His mind flashed to when he'd held her hand earlier. Did all handymen get fluttery feelings in their chest when they held their boss's hand? Did all handymen look into their boss's eyes and get swept away by what shone in Sarah's pretty brown eyes?

Maybelle snorted. "You trying to convince me or yourself?"

"There's no need for me to convince myself. It's true." It was. He felt protective of Sarah. She'd done something nice for him and he wanted to do something nice for her. He'd attached so much emotion to his quilt that it was only natural he'd feel a connection to its maker. That was all that fluttery feeling was, all that his holding her hand had been.

Maybelle harrumphed. "If you believe that, then you're not nearly as smart as I've given you credit for."

Bodie ignored her jab, glanced around. "Where are the rest of your cronies? I thought you traveled as a pack."

To his surprise, Maybelle's painted lips curved

upward. "Not always. The rest of the girls are working at the booth and I'm meeting Sarah's father here to clean up after the hunt."

Bodie crammed his hands into his jean pockets. "You need an extra set of hands?"

Obviously pleased with his offer, Maybelle chuckled. "Don't let it be said that I ever turned down a willing volunteer."

That her words were echoes of Sarah's caused Bodie's lips to twitch.

Sarah might not have had her birth mother to shape her into the woman she was today, but the Butterflies and her aunt had sure stepped up to the plate, influencing so much about her.

Except for maybe Rosie, as he didn't see Sarah dying her hair in punk rock blue and chasing men around anytime soon.

Then he noticed an older gentleman spinning Sarah in a mini-dance to the Christmas music. She kissed his cheek, then burst out laughing. The corner of Bodie's mouth hiked up. Maybe Rosie had influenced her more than he'd thought.

"You sure you won't stay in Pine Hill?" Maybelle asked.

Bodie's gaze cut to her. "Positive. I'm only here to help Sarah. As soon as I finish at Hamilton House, I'm gone."

"Interesting wording for your reason for being in Pine Hill."

Yes, he supposed to Maybelle, it was.

Rather than question him further, she leaned against the fence and watched the ornament hunt in silence except for a quietly spoken, "A shame you aren't staying, though."

Sarah laughed so hard she had to pause to catch her breath at the almost eighty-year-old Clyde's impromptu lesson of the Christmas boogie while his great-grandchildren hunted ornaments. Then she straightened, adjusted her scarf and hat, and glanced toward Bodie.

He wore a serious expression. No wonder, with Maybelle perched against the fence next to him and Harry. There was no telling what she'd said.

When Sarah's gaze met his, she smiled and waved. Despite whatever had caused his solemn expression, he gave a half-grin and nodded his acknowledgement.

Sarah's heart spluttered the way it always did at a Bodie smile.

"He's cute." Carrie came over to where Sarah was and flicked her gaze toward Bodie. "I thought it the day he came to the community room, asking if you were there, but he seems even more so now. I think it's how his smile crinkles his eyes."

Feeling self-conscious, Sarah nodded. Not that "cute" seemed like the right word to describe Bodie. Cute implied something cuddly, and Bodie wasn't that. But she agreed—Bodie's smiles were noteworthy. Her hand burned within her glove with memory of his touch and she wondered if it were possible for Bodie to cuddle.

"How's the remodel going at Hamilton House?"

"Almost finished with the downstairs. We're on schedule to open on Christmas Day." Oh, how she loved saying that. "Bodie is doing a fantastic job. If you know anyone who needs some work done, let him know."

Not that she was lining up work in hopes he'd stay in Pine Hill. Just...

"That's great." Carrie's gaze went to the ornament hunt. "I think all the ornaments have been found, if you want to call time."

Kids and families were still searching, but a few of the kids had already sat down on the cold ground and were opening their ornaments to ooh and aah over the contents. One of the two-year-olds had chocolate running down her chin and was giving her mother a toothy grin.

Sarah didn't see anyone finding new ornaments; nor did she spot any that hadn't been discovered. Using the microphone, she thanked everyone for participating, reminded them that photos with Santa were available at the photography business on the square and told them not to forget the parade at six.

With the children and their families clearing out, Sarah and the other volunteers walked around the playground, checking hiding places, and not finding any additional hidden ornaments.

Maybelle joined her. "Looks like you had more kids this year."

"We did," she agreed, excited by the event's success. "Over a hundred. Did you see those happy little faces?"

Pride shone on Maybelle's face. "You did good."

Ecstatic that she'd made Maybelle proud, Sarah leaned over and kissed her cheek. "Thank you, Maybelle. That you think so makes my day."

"Nothing you don't deserve." Pulling her coat tighter around her, Maybelle gestured to Sarah's hands. "Now, give me that bag. I'll clean up any stray bits of trash so you can get over there to that fellow waiting on you."

Sarah glanced at where Bodie had untied Harry's leash from the fence and was squatted down next to him. One of the families who'd hunted ornaments was talking to him, their kids petting Harry. Harry rolled over onto his back, obviously eating up the attention, and the kids gave him more rubs.

Bodie laughed at something and Sarah's heart hiccupped.

"You like him."

"Harry?" Sarah shrugged, purposely misunderstanding Maybelle. She bent to pick up the plastic top to one of the ornaments and dropped it into the sack she hadn't handed over to Maybelle. "What's not to like?"

"Not the dog. The man." Maybelle sighed. "You really don't know much about him."

"I know enough."

"Then you're admitting he's more than your handyman?"

Watching Bodie with the children, with Harry, a mixture of pleasure and sadness filled her. She shook her head. "He's not."

"No?"

Sarah stooped to pick up a stray candy wrapper, then turned to her friend. "No."

Maybelle laughed. "Girl, you are as transparent as glass."

"Doesn't matter," she admitted, not looking toward

Maybelle. The woman already saw too much. She didn't need to see Sarah wishing things were different.

Things weren't different.

"He'll be leaving soon, and I won't ever see him again." Ouch. That hurt to say out loud. But it was true and she needed to not forget.

As if she could.

"There is that," Maybelle agreed, studying her far too closely. "Just so long as you're sure."

Sarah was sure. But that wasn't going to stop her from enjoying the rest of the day or her time with Bodie.

He was still in Pine Hill, was still her handyman and friend, and that was enough.

It had to be.

CHAPTER ELEVEN

ALTHOUGH MAYBELLE HAD OFFERED TO take over the clean-up, Sarah stayed until the church playground and the community room was restored to normal operating order. Bodie had stuck around and helped break down the registration table and carry it inside the church, Harry at his side.

"Walk me back to our booth?" Sarah asked. "After that, you can grab something to eat. I recommend Lou's booth or the Rescue Squad's. You can check out the other venues, and maybe by then, it'll be close to time for the tree lighting."

"What are you going to do?"

"Take a shift at the booth," she reminded him. "If there's plenty of help, I'll check out the other vendors at the end of my scheduled time. If not, I'll help for as long as I'm needed and the ornaments hold out."

"Harry and I will walk you there."

He didn't promise more than that, but Sarah hoped he would stay for the parade. There was something magical about the floats different organizations put together, the high school band playing Christmas tunes, the fire trucks and rescue vehicles, seeing Santa's float as he waved at the kids. Surely, if Bodie saw the parade, he'd want to experience more of this wonderful event and would stay for the tree lighting later, too.

"I heard the ornament hunt was a huge success," Claudia praised when Sarah and Bodie arrived back at the church's booth. "I've seen quite a few kiddos running around with stockings full of goodies and smiles on their sweet faces."

"It went even better than last year." Sarah paused in front of the table serving as the checkout area. Warm air from the heater hit her pants legs, rising up her body, and she relished the warmth. It wasn't crazy cold outside, but the heat still felt good after being out of the much warmer tent. Sarah wasn't ready to loosen her hat or jacket, but she did peel off her scarf and gloves so she'd be able to handle the ornaments more easily. "How are we doing here?"

Claudia gave a thumbs-up. "Already sold lots. We've already dug out some of the reserves to restock and the sale has barely started."

"Yay!"

Bodie stood to the opposite side of the booth, one hand tucked inside his jeans pocket and the other holding Harry's leash. Harry looked bored at the calmness of the booth after the chaos of the ornament hunt. Bodie looked unsure as to his next move.

Was he planning to leave? Or just lingering for a few minutes before taking her suggestion to get something to eat?

Smiling, she couldn't resist deepening her voice and asking, "You here for an ornament, sir?"

He snorted. "To put on my nonexistent tree?"

"You could hang it from your truck mirror."

His brow lifted. "You want me to decorate my truck with Christmas ornaments? I know you love Christmas, but that's taking things too far."

"Have you seen some of the vehicles around town? They're decked out with lights and wreaths. I don't think one little ornament is going to de-masculinize your truck."

"I've seen some of them. That's why I'm leery. I give you an inch and you're going to have my truck wrapped in garlands, lights, and a giant red bow before you're through."

At his description, Sarah laughed.

"You have a point, but we do have some lovely snowflakes." She did a game show hostess move, using her hands to point to the ornaments on the tree and on the peg board behind her. "It would be a shame not to have one as a keepsake of your time in Pine Hill."

"I need a keepsake?"

"Of course." No way could he look at a snowflake bought here and not think of her. Selfish, perhaps, but she didn't want Bodie to drive away and never think of her and Pine Hill again.

The thought of him forgetting...hurt.

His mouth twisted a little, then he surprised her by asking, "Any particular ornament I need?"

Surprised he was actually considering it, she glanced behind her, then over at the tree. She took in each ornament, contemplating it, then moving on. When her gaze fell on the snowflake they'd been adjusting when he'd held her hand earlier, she walked over and took it off the tree.

Recognizing the ornament, his surprised gaze met hers. "That one?"

He knew why she'd picked the snowflake, why it was special. Perhaps she should be embarrassed she'd made such a telling choice, but now that she'd chosen it, no other would do.

"Absolutely this ornament. Check out the fancy white sequins and the glistening faux pearl beads and how the lights reflect off them." She did another showy saleswoman hand gesture, trying to make light of how much she wanted him to have it. "This snowflake is a work of art."

He chuckled. "For the low price of?"

She told him, reminded him it was a fundraiser for a good cause, and waited to see what he'd do.

He met her gaze, and something softened in his blue eyes. "Be hard to pass up a once-in-a-lifetime deal like that."

"Exactly." Wanting to fall into his gorgeous eyes and soak in whatever was shining there, she smiled. "Shall I wrap your snowflake in tissue paper?"

"On one condition."

Her hand halfway to the tissue paper, she paused. "What's that?"

"It doesn't hang in my truck."

Sarah laughed. "Deal, but where are you going to hang it?"

"On your tree." He shrugged. "If that's okay."

Her cheeks heated to the point where she loosened the top button of her jacket. "Yes, of course."

"Consider it an early Christmas present."

Sarah's knees wobbled. "From someone who doesn't believe in Christmas?"

"I never said I didn't believe in Christmas," he corrected. "Just that it's only another day in my world."

"Not this year," she pointed out, wrapping the ornament in the piece of white tissue paper, then placing it inside a small paper bag.

He snorted. "Christmas couldn't be just another day to a complete Scrooge with you around, Sarah."

Pleased he thought so, she handed him the bag. "Thank you for your purchase, sir. We appreciate your business and hope you'll be back next year."

The words came out automatically, as something she would have said to any customer. With Bodie, she found them to be desperately true. She did hope he'd be back next year.

They both knew he wouldn't be.

"Did you sell Bodie an ornament?" Claudia asked, coming over from where she'd been helping another customer to see what Sarah was doing.

"She did, and if she can sell an ornament to the likes of me, your booth will sell out tonight."

"Oh, I hope so!" Claudia said, clasping her gloved hands in glee. "That would be wonderful. The money helps fund so many wonderful projects throughout the year."

Bodie nodded, then put the paper sack inside his jacket's pocket.

"You off to Lou's booth?" she asked, wondering if how much she wanted him to stay showed on her face.

"You can't go," Ruby told him as she joined them in the booth. "You haven't gotten to say hi to my Charlie yet. He's dropping by in a few minutes. Being around that man of mine is a privilege not to be missed."

Claudia rolled her eyes. Sarah stifled a smile. Bodie looked hesitant.

"The tree lighting is at seven. You could stay until then," Sarah suggested.

"I planned to go back to the house and put the hardware on the bathroom vanities."

"That's one of the finishing touches, isn't it? You're that close to having the bathrooms completed?" Claudia asked, sounding impressed.

Sarah nodded. "He's done a great job making sure we're ready by Christmas."

"Sarah!" Ruby scolded, clicking her tongue. "I know you want to get Hamilton House open, but give the man a break and let him enjoy the festival."

Sarah opened her mouth, set to defend herself, but, eyes twinkling, Bodie spoke first.

"Yeah, Sarah, don't be such a Scrooge. Let me enjoy the Christmas festival."

Shocked at his public teasing, her jaw dropped a little.

"You stay here and enjoy the festival, Bodie. Sarah will get over you taking one night off to enjoy the second-best night of the year," Ruby assured him, giving Bodie's arm a motherly pat. "Just you wait until the sun sets and all the booths and businesses have their Christmas lights going. And then, when they light the tree," Ruby sounded almost as enthusiastic as Sarah as she spoke of the event, "it's pure magic."

"Can't say as I've ever experienced magic."

"Stick around and you will before the night's over," Ruby promised, patting Sarah's hand this time. "Now, I'm taking my place over on the other side of the tent to sell baked goods and hot cocoa. You enjoy the festival."

When Ruby left to work the other booth, Claudia greeted a customer she knew as she showed her an ornament.

With Bodie standing a few feet from her, Sarah waited for him to say what he was doing one way or the other. Stay, she mentally whispered. Maybe she would be able to leave the booth, find him prior to the tree lighting, and they could experience it together.

How wonderful would it be to share that with Bodie?

"Is Ruby's best night of the year the same as yours? Christmas?"

Her eyes searching his, Sarah shook her head.

His brows lifted and he teased, "What day could possibly be better than Christmas?"

"I know, right?" Sarah asked with a smile. "To me? None," she assured. "To Ruby, it's her and Charlie's anniversary."

"That makes sense." Bodie looked impressed. "Where are the other Bees?"

"Butterflies," Sarah corrected, glancing toward Claudia to see if she was eavesdropping. As one of the woman's daughters was now visiting the booth, Claudia was too busy oohing and aahing over her grandson to have noticed anything else.

"Rosie is over at Lou's food booth, plying him with her grandmother's cinnamon bread," Sarah told Bodie. "Apparently, Alberta Jennings invited him to go on a sleigh ride later tonight."

"I bet that didn't sit well," Bodie mused.

"You'd win that bet. Although she's refused to settle

down since her last husband died, Lou is special to Rosie."

"Nice enough fellow," Bodie agreed.

Sarah knew Bodie stopped by the diner early most mornings. Even if he hadn't told her, the Butterflies kept her posted about his comings and goings around town.

She thought they'd quit following him eventually, but they refused to quit dropping his name every chance they got.

"Maybelle should be this way in a bit," Claudia added, letting Sarah know the woman had been following the conversation after all. "She's having coffee with your father and that sweet couple from over on Bell Street while entertaining herself by watching Rosie hem and haw over Lou."

Sarah could see it unfolding exactly that way. Her father would be discussing the weather or his upcoming Sunday sermon with the couple. Pretending to listen, Maybelle would be calmly sipping her coffee while enjoying the show—because if Alberta was making moves on Lou, Rosie would be fit to be tied.

Another customer arrived and Sarah waited on the woman, smiling and selling her five ornaments. While she wrapped them in tissue paper, she chatted with the woman and watched Bodie squat to pet Harry from her peripheral vision.

"Sarah, I hate to leave you alone, but would you be okay for a few minutes if I go to watch my granddaughter in the Little Miss Pine Hill Christmas pageant? I totally forgot about it when I signed up for this time frame."

"I'll help in the booth while you're gone."

Both Sarah and Claudia looked at Bodie in surprise. The customer Sarah was waiting on did, too.

"Thank you," Claudia told him, looking pleased. "I'll be back as quickly as I can." She paused. "Actually, if those judges have eyes and a brain, I may be a while as I won't be back here as long as my sweet girl is still in the running."

"We'll be fine," Sarah assured her, bagging up the five ornaments and handing them to her customer. Another two had stepped up and were looking at ornaments.

While they were looking, Sarah motioned for Bodie and Harry to come around the table. Apparently remembering his spot from earlier, Harry went back to lie beneath the table, but kept his head up to take in what they were doing.

"I'll walk you through checking out this dear lady," she told Bodie, but as Bodie stepped up to help another couple who wanted to purchase several of the ornaments from the pegboard, she realized instruction wasn't necessary.

Bodie paid attention to details. He'd watched her and Claudia wait on a few customers and no doubt could write a textbook on the dos and don'ts of ornament selling by this point.

For the next hour and a half, they sold ornaments nonstop as more and more people arrived at the festival.

"She won!" Claudia beamed as she returned to the booth, her cheeks rosy and her eyes full of pride. "Annabelle is Little Miss Pine Hill Christmas."

"That's awesome," Sarah said, giving Claudia

a high-five as the woman joined them behind the checkout table.

"Congrats," Bodie added.

"It was only fitting. All the girls were wonderful, but my Annabelle outshined them," Claudia assured in her most proud grandmother tone. Bodie and Sarah exchanged a look, smiling.

"She takes after her grandma that way," Sarah said, earning a happy grin from Claudia.

A half-dozen new customers arrived, entering the booth to check out the ornaments displayed on the pegboards and to congratulate Claudia on her granddaughter's success.

"Phew, you can tell it's getting close to time for the parade," Claudia observed as she smiled at a woman purchasing a snowflake.

"Most definitely," Sarah agreed, eyeing the building crowd prior to greeting a precious girl who had been in her Sunday school class the previous summer and who held three ornaments. "Hi, Chevell, did you find everything you needed?"

The girl nodded, then said quite loudly, "I'm buying these for my teacher." Then, she leaned forward and whispered, "Really, they're for my mom, but I don't want her to know."

Chevell's mom looked amused and indulgent, holding her young son and watching over Chevell while she shopped.

While Sarah wrapped the ornaments, Bodie collected the girl's money and gave her change.

"Thanks for your business, Chevell." Sarah winked at her. "I hope your *teacher* loves her gift."

The little cutie grinned, then winked back before

rejoining her mother. Chevell held up her paper bag to her mother, then turned and waved goodbye at Sarah and Bodie.

Sarah sighed with happiness. "That, Bodie Lewis, is what Christmas is all about."

"Buying presents?"

"No," she corrected with a scolding look that prompted a laugh from him. "The excitement Chevell felt at getting her mom a special gift. The joy she experienced at the thought of giving her mom those snowflakes is what Christmas is about, what it should be about."

He didn't comment, just grinned, then turned to wait on another customer.

They were still working the booth when Sarah heard the whine of the fire truck sirens, signaling the start of the parade.

The parade would make its way down Main Street, turn onto the square, go around the courthouse, then head toward the church. Once past the church, the participants would park their floats in the church parking lot and disband to walk back to the square to enjoy the festivities.

Sarah wanted to shoo Bodie out of the booth so he could watch the parade. But the booth was busy, and, surprisingly, he seemed to be enjoying himself while talking to their customers, especially the ones who spotted Harry and made a fuss over the dog.

"Not sold out yet?"

Sarah grinned at the balding, uniformed man in his early sixties strolling up to their booth. "Not unless you're here to buy us out, Sheriff Roscoe."

He gave a hearty laugh. "Now, Sarah, you know I'd

be in all kinds of trouble if I bought out one booth and didn't buy out the others. Showing such favoritism would be the end of my career."

The sheriff and his department had made several hefty donations to support Sarah's projects and his deputies had been known to volunteer on several occasions to lend a helping hand. She adored them all. Except for perhaps that ticket-writing Donnie.

"There is that," she agreed with the sheriff.

He gestured to Bodie. "Who's this?"

As if the Butterfly-aiding-and-abetting law enforcer didn't know. But fine, she'd play along.

"Bodie Lewis. He's helping at Hamilton House." She glanced at Bodie, who had finished waiting on his customer and was now watching them.

"Heard about you," the sheriff acknowledged Bodie, sticking his hand out to shake. "Hear you've got an impressive military background. Appreciate your service, young man."

His face looking a little taut, Bodie shook the sheriff's hand. "As I appreciate yours."

Although Bodie had likely meant his law enforcement career, the sheriff puffed his chest out with pride. "I served in the Army myself, back in the good ol' days when..."

He continued talking military with Bodie, but Sarah lost track of the conversation as she waited on a repeat customer who wanted two dozen snowflakes.

"I use them to decorate Christmas packages, rather than hanging them on my tree," the woman enthused. "I got so many compliments on the ones I bought last year that I'm doubling my order this year."

Although she really wanted to listen to the sheriff

and Bodie's conversation, Sarah beamed at the woman and set about helping her pick snowflakes.

Bodie had no idea how good Sheriff Roscoe was at police work, but he liked the blustery, talkative lawman who'd done two tours of duty in the army.

What he didn't like was the man's questions about why Bodie had chosen not to re-enlist. There were some things Bodie didn't want to talk about— especially the demise of his career.

"Probably same reason as you." Probably not. "Was the right time for me to get out."

There wouldn't have been a right time for him to get out had he not gotten hurt. He'd planned to be a lifelong military man.

"You looking to stay around here?"

Bodie shook his head. "I'll be moving on as soon as I finish at Hamilton House."

"Too bad. I'm looking for someone to replace one of my officers." Sheriff Roscoe shook his head in disappointment. "Donnie took a desk job with the state. He's better suited for that, anyway."

"Donnie left the sheriff's department?" Sarah exclaimed, pausing in her snowflake wrapping to gawk at the sheriff.

"Don't worry, Sarah. Your speeding ticket still stands."

Sarah gave him a beatific smile and went back to wrapping while she said, "If Donnie's no longer with the department, shouldn't that old ticket be torn up?"

Sheriff Roscoe laughed. "That's not how the law works. You go too fast, you get a ticket and you pay the price. Next time, make sure there isn't a next time."

Sarah gave an exaggerated sigh.

"It was worth a try." She smiled at her customer. The woman chuckled.

"Now," the sheriff turned back to Bodie. "As I was saying before Lead Foot there interrupted," he jerked his thumb in Sarah's direction, "I'm looking for a good man to take Donnie's place on my team."

"Are you trying to hire Bodie?" Sarah was obviously not through with the conversation.

"I've got to replace Donnie to make sure someone's around to write little speed demons' tickets."

"Oh." Claudia joined in from where she was helping a customer. "You should hire Bodie. He could write Sarah tickets when she drives too fast."

"I do not typically drive too fast. If I didn't know better, I'd think there was a conspiracy to make sure I keep my car going at a snail's pace," Sarah accused, winking at her customer as she put her tissue-wrapped snowflakes into a bag. "Oh, the joys of living in a small town."

"Isn't it grand?" her customer asked.

"That it is. Wouldn't live anywhere else," Sarah agreed, handing the woman the paper bag. "Thank you so much for shopping with us. We hope everyone loves their snowflakes again this year and that we'll see you next year, minus the discussion on my driving habits."

While Sarah collected the woman's money, Bodie regarded the sheriff.

"Think about it, son," the sheriff suggested. "Be hard to find a finer place to live than Pine Hill."

"I appreciate the offer, but I really am just passing through. I have a job lined up I'll be starting in January."

With Lukas at iSecure. He'd be back to making the world a safer place and helping his friend have more time with his wife and baby once Kelly delivered.

Though his work wouldn't really make the world a safer place, he corrected his thoughts. More like he'd be making the person or persons he was hired to protect safer.

"I've read your background." The sheriff's cheeks turned a little pink as he seemed to recall why he'd performed a background check. "You're more than qualified," the sheriff continued. "Have more training than most of the men in my department. You change your mind and decide to stick around, give me a call. I'll arrange an official interview."

The sheriff handed him a business card, and they shook hands again.

Out of respect for the sheriff, Bodie put the card into his jacket pocket. He'd toss it later as he had no intention of calling the sheriff or of staying in Pine Hill. His life was elsewhere.

His gaze cut to Sarah and she motioned to where her father and Maybelle headed toward them. "Looks like our shift relief is on the way."

Bodie glanced at his watch, surprised at how much time had passed while they'd been selling ornaments. Sarah greeted Maybelle and her father, kissing them each on the cheek.

"If you two hurry, you can catch the last half of the parade," her father suggested.

"Oh, let's." She turned to Bodie and grabbed his hand.

He glanced toward Harry.

"The dog can stay with us if you want," Maybelle offered, giving Harry a squinty-eyed look. "He won't misbehave on my watch."

Bodie doubted anyone misbehaved on Maybelle's watch, but he shook his head. "Harry will go with us."

At hearing his name, Harry's head lifted and Bodie motioned for the dog to join him. Harry was immediately at his side, raring to go, and Bodie clipped the leash to his collar.

Straightening, he turned to a visibly excited Sarah and couldn't resist grinning. "Let's watch this Christmas parade you keep talking about."

CHAPTER TWELVE

SARAH STOLE A LOOK AT Bodie, hoping to see complete enchantment on his face at the parade floats passing by.

Not exactly enchantment, but he didn't look bored. Keeping a tight rein on Harry, who was distracted due to all the people and noise, he was hunkered down next to the dog.

"Hey, Sarah!" Carrie's son, Jeff, called as the local high school football float passed by. A handful of candy rained down several feet in front of them onto the paved street.

"He's obviously not the quarterback," Bodie mused.

Picking up the candy from the pavement, Sarah laughed. "You're right. He's not our quarterback, but he is one fantastic receiver and a great member of our church youth group. An awesome kid."

Sarah handed the candy she'd picked up to a couple of nearby kids, then she rejoined Bodie.

"Looks like he has a little crush on the special projects director."

"What?" Sarah frowned, shaking her head. "No.

I'm sure he doesn't.—What about you? Did you have a teenage crush?"

He shrugged. "Not really. My teenaged fantasies all revolved around becoming a soldier."

"Seriously? No special girl from your past who still holds your heart?"

Now why had she asked that? It wasn't as if it mattered to her whether he did or didn't have someone special waiting for his return someday.

"I rarely dated, and it was nothing serious when I did. It wouldn't have been right to try for something more when I knew I'd be leaving with no return planned." He stroked his hand over Harry's neck. "So, no, there isn't anyone special from my past."

She barely heard the last part as the high school band moved their way, playing an upbeat Christmas tune and making conversation temporarily impossible. Which was just as well, as she might have said something silly, such as that she was glad he didn't have someone special waiting on him.

How selfish of her to feel that way. She should want Bodie to have someone, to feel love and happiness.

Yet, hearing him say that there wasn't someone special, that there never had been, pleased her in ways it shouldn't. In ways that a friend shouldn't feel about a friend.

Ignoring her tumultuous thoughts, she swayed and sang along with the upbeat band. Later, in the quiet of the night, she'd think over the day, over how much fun she'd had with Bodie, and maybe then she could label the giddiness in her belly when he smiled.

After the group passed, when they could hear each

other talk again, Sarah asked, "How about band? Do you play an instrument?"

Bodie straightened from where he'd been squatted with Harry and glanced toward her. "What is this? Twenty questions?"

"Just curious about you."

"I was a boring kid in high school, Sarah. No sports, no band, no clubs, very few girlfriends. Just school, ROTC, and working for my stepfather. That kept me plenty busy." Before she could ask another question, he turned the tables. "How about you?"

"Me? I did a few school clubs, no sports or ROTC, and spent all my spare time away from school with my father, with Aunt Jean and the Butterflies, at church, or some combination thereof."

He adjusted Harry's leash handle. "You left out the boyfriend part."

Her cheeks heated. Not from the thought of anyone from the past, but at the way Bodie looked at her, the way he seemed edgy as he waited for her answer. As if her answer mattered. As if *she* mattered.

"I had a few boyfriends during high school," she admitted. "Mostly guys I met through our church youth group. Nothing serious."

"How about since high school?"

Yeah, she didn't like this table-turned thing. She longed for a relationship like her parents had had, a relationship like Charlie and Ruby still had—but her own relationships had never even come close.

"There were a couple of guys I dated for a short time during junior college, none serious until I met Richard."

"That's the last guy?" The corner of Bodie's jaw gave

a visible twitch, as if he'd fought clenching his teeth and his muscles had protested.

She nodded. "I shouldn't say we were serious, because he never was. Leaving Pine Hill was always his goal, not a life with me."

Just as leaving was Bodie's goal.

"He never even asked me to go with him, which was just as well since I wouldn't have left." *Not for Richard.* Now where had that thought come from? She wouldn't leave Pine Hill for anyone. Her life was here—the people she loved, the places she loved. She couldn't imagine ever willingly walking away from her beloved hometown. "Anyway, Aunt Jean died, Richard left, I inherited Hamilton House, and I've been too busy to think about dating since."

His brows rose. "And yet you claim the Butterflies want you married off to the first willing man."

Sarah's cheeks heated at the memory of having told him that. A group of baton twirlers walked past them as the parade progressed.

"Not giving in to them isn't always easy, but that particular issue hasn't really been a problem all that often. I never meet anyone who catches my eye, and I've been busy this past year."

She had been busy. No one had caught her eye.

Except for the man standing next to her.

The twirlers moved on and several floats with scouts and various kids' groups passed.

"Look, there's the sheriff's department float." She pointed toward the upcoming float, then waved at Sheriff Roscoe and the deputies as they passed. "I was afraid we'd missed it."

"What's this Sheriff Roscoe was saying about you getting a ticket?"

Sarah narrowed her gaze and gave the meanest look she could muster. "Don't go there."

He laughed.

"Okay, I won't." He hesitated, then added, "Speedy."

Sarah rolled her eyes.

Bodie's gaze went back to the parade. "How about we find Lou's booth and grab a bite to eat before the parade ends and there's a rush?"

She didn't really want to miss the rest of the parade, but she was starving, and the booths would get busier and busier as the parade participants returned to the square, so Sarah nodded. Maybe they could get their food and find somewhere to eat where they could still watch the parade.

If not, then maybe Bodie would check out the other booths with her, play a few games, and sample some of the homemade goodies being sold.

"Harry seems to like Lou," Sarah said in between bites of her chili. The dog had finished the plain burger Bodie had bought him and was lapping water from the bowl Bodie had gotten out of his truck earlier in the day.

Lou had made a big to-do over the dog, making sure Bodie got extras for him. Apparently, Lou had even begun to let Harry inside his place when Bodie came by for breakfast.

"Lou seems to like Harry, too. He offered to buy him from me one morning last week."

"What?" Sarah gasped, her gaze going to the black

and white dog. "Surely he knew you wouldn't sell Harry?"

Though his mouth was full of chili, Bodie shook his head and reached down to pet the dog.

"How long have you had Harry?"

"Not nearly as long as you'd think."

That piqued Sarah's curiosity and she stared at him, waiting for him to elaborate. As usual, she had to prompt him.

"Where did you get Harry?"

"He was my best friend's dog."

There was a story there, but Sarah knew she'd have to pry it from Bodie. "How did Harry end up your dog?"

"I stole him."

Sarah's jaw dropped. "What?"

"Gotcha." Bodie laughed. He popped the last bite of his chili into his mouth, put his plastic spoon back into the empty bowl, then wiped his hands over his jeans.

Pleased he'd teased her, Sarah put her hands on her hips. "You may as well keep talking, because you know I'm not letting you stop with that smug little 'gotcha.'"

He grinned, glanced toward the dog who was lapping at his water. "Lukas gave him to me."

The named clicked.

"The Lukas you listed as a reference?"

"Yes."

"Your references were your stepfather and your best friend?"

He nodded. "Can't think of any reference that would mean more than one coming from those two men. They're the most honest, trustworthy men I know."

When he worded it that way, Sarah couldn't really question his choices further. But she did have questions.

"Why did your best friend give you his dog?" She couldn't imagine anyone willingly giving up such a great pet.

Bodie hesitated a moment, then said, "Lukas has a baby on the way, and I guess he thought Harry would be better off with me." He finished his water. "Done?"

Not by a long shot, but it was obvious he didn't want to discuss anything personal any longer, so she nodded and gathered up her trash. He offered to take it with his, but she followed him to the bin.

They watched the end of the parade, then made their way around the booths, Sarah saying hi to her friends and neighbors, Bodie mostly watching in silence and only speaking when spoken to.

More and more people glanced at their watches, then stopped what they were doing to head toward the far side of the courthouse yard.

"It's almost time for the tree lighting." Yeah, that had been her voice hitting several octaves higher than normal, but she was excited.

Turning toward Bodie, Sarah caught him looking at her and suddenly felt self-conscious. Did he find her excitement childish?

If so, too bad. She loved Christmas and wasn't ashamed of that fact.

Lifting her chin, she asked, "What?"

A half-grin on his face, he shrugged. "Just you."

Yeah, like she was going to leave it at that. He should know better.

"What about me?" she pushed as they walked toward where the tree lighting would take place.

"You and your excitement for all this."

"'All this' is a big deal to me and to Pine Hill. Although I love the On-the-Square Christmas Festival for so many reasons, the tourist dollars the event pulls in are vital to local businesses on the square. Not to mention the organizations that set up booths on the courthouse lawn, such as my special projects and the ladies' class at church. Plus, events like these will bring in guests for Hamilton House, which is a huge added bonus." Sarah gave a little shrug. "Mostly, though, I love that these events draw us together as a community."

He nodded as if he understood, but Sarah wasn't sure he did. He'd told her he was from Houston. Maybe big cities didn't have the sense of community she enjoyed in Pine Hill.

Or maybe it wasn't big cities lacking a sense of community, but Bodie himself who lacked it.

If that was the case, then certainly, that would make it easier for him to never stay in one place for too long. A sense of community meant strings, attachments to a place or to a group, meant being a part of something that was bigger than oneself.

A sense of community was important. At least, to Sarah it was.

She supposed to Bodie, his sense of community came from being in the military, his brotherhood there—although she couldn't say for sure, since he never talked about it.

"Come on," she encouraged as the crowd of people grew thicker the closer they got to the tree. "Let's get as close as we can to watch the tree lighting. If it's like years past, my dad will be leading a prayer prior to the lighting and I don't want to miss it."

Watching the tree lighting wasn't nearly as interesting as watching Sarah's face as Pine Hill's mayor spoke, read a short Bible passage, then called on Sarah's father to come up to say a prayer for their community and to bless their holiday season.

"I don't know why, but I always get nervous when he speaks in public like this," Sarah whispered to Bodie, reaching out to take his hand as her father took the microphone and she bowed her head.

When the prayer ended, Sarah didn't let go, just whispered, "Amen," and kept her eyes on the unlit tree as the ceremony proceeded.

Her gloved hand inside his was warm, her grip firm, as if she had no intention of letting him let go.

On the count of three, the tree lights came on, lighting up the twenty-plus-foot-high live Fraser fir tree like a Christmas beacon on the courthouse yard.

"Wow," Sarah breathed, turning to look at him with excitement in her eyes. "It's not as magical as our tree at Hamilton House, but isn't she gorgeous?"

Our tree. She should have said *her* tree. But he didn't correct her, not wanting to take anything away from her happiness.

"She?"

Looking very serious, Sarah nodded. "Oh, yeah. This tree is female."

"You know that how?"

"She was planted when I was ten years old. Since then we've had a few talks over the years."

"You talk to trees?"

"Only ones that get decked out in Christmas lights."

Bodie laughed, then glanced around. People were milling around, sharing their appreciation of the tree's beauty, taking photos of the tree and of others standing in front of the tree. Some had headed back off to various booths or to shop the open businesses.

"Let's!"

Bodie looked at Sarah, not sure what she meant.

Pulling out her phone, she gestured to the tree. "Take a selfie with me?"

Why anyone, let alone Sarah, would want a picture with him was beyond Bodie, but if that's what Sarah wanted, that's what he'd do.

Turning so their backs were to the tree, Sarah held up her phone, then frowned at the image. "You're too far away. Move closer."

Bodie moved closer, not surprised when Sarah wrapped an arm around his waist and smiled up at where she held her phone as high as she could reach with her other arm.

"Smile and say 'cheese,'" she ordered, moving her thumb to snap the picture. "Ack, this is harder than people make it look. I need one of those stick things."

"Here, my arms are longer," Bodie offered, taking her phone. He hugged her close and then, making sure he had the tree behind them, he took their picture.

"Thank you," she said, taking the phone from him

and checking the image. "Look, you got Harry's face in it, too, but just barely. Okay, now a funny one."

"A what?"

"Come on. Make a funny face." Sarah leaned in close to him, held her phone out in front of them, stuck her tongue out at the corner of her mouth, looked upward and clicked the phone again.

Glancing down at the photo on her phone, she laughed. "That's your funny face?"

He glanced at the photo. He was looking at her rather than at the phone camera. "Looks funny to me."

"O-kay." She laughed again, then moved away from him and aimed her phone in his direction. "Let me take one of you and Harry."

"Why?" Bodie frowned. He wasn't much for pictures. Never had been. Which was just as well, as he'd never wanted his image to end up on social media. When one worked in the shadows, one didn't post pictures.

Not that he was working in the shadows anymore. Not yet, anyway.

"Because after seeing how hilarious you were in our funny picture, I have to have one of you and Harry. Try smiling this time."

Bodie shrugged, got down next to Harry, then smiled for Sarah. It wasn't as if smiling was difficult when she was around.

Obviously satisfied with her picture, she rewarded him with one of her smiles, pocketed the phone, then took his hand. "Let's go have some fun scoping out our competition."

Bodie laughed. "Ah, so it's not all fun and games at the Christmas Festival."

Sarah smiled at him. "Did I say 'scoping out our competition'? Oops, I meant, 'supporting the other booths.' Those 's' words trip me up sometimes." She hesitated. "You are okay with staying a while longer?"

He should have left hours ago. But he hadn't. What could staying longer hurt?

"Let's go scope out—I mean, support other booths."

"But only if we're not needed at our booth," she reminded, grinning at him.

"Our booth first, then support other booths."

Her smile lit up her entire face. "You're going to be glad you stayed."

Possibly.

He suspected the day would linger in his mind much longer than the images on Sarah's phone.

Their booth was having a post-tree-lighting rush. Bodie and Sarah jumped in to help as Maybelle, Rosie, and Claudia were busy waiting on customers. As she often was, Ruby was off somewhere with Charlie.

When the rush passed, Sarah and Bodie offered to stay, but the Butterflies refused.

"There's another round of volunteers signed up who should be here any moment," Rosie assured.

"Plus, we're almost sold out." Claudia gestured to the pegboards, which were starting to look bare. "We've depleted our reserves, so this is it."

"Go," Maybelle insisted. "I signed on to stay until close. Your dad and some other volunteers are going to help with shutdown. Working in the booth makes me feel useful since these legs of mine are too old to walk around much more tonight."

"You heard her, folks. She admitted she's old," Rosie called out with glee. "Anybody get that recorded? I'd be up for watching an instant replay."

Just as Sarah and Bodie were leaving, a distressed Ruby rushed into the tent.

"This is terrible." The dyed redhead looked as if she were about to burst into tears. "My Charlie had a tumble and is feeling sore. Nothing serious, but rather than stay, he wants to go home."

"Oh, Ruby!" Sarah wrapped her arms around her distraught friend and gave her a hug. "You're sure he's okay? Is there anything we can do to help?"

"Do you need us to drive you home?" Maybelle asked, moving close as well.

"No, no," Ruby insisted, sounding stressed. She dug around in her coat pocket, then pulled out a slip of paper. "That's not why I'm here. Our grandson is visiting from out of town. He and his girlfriend are helping Charlie to his car, driving him home, and making sure Charlie gets inside and settled."

"Does your grandson need help getting him inside your house?" Bodie asked, wanting to help Sarah's friends any way he could. Plus, he genuinely liked the older man.

Sarah shot Bodie a look of gratitude, but Ruby shook her head. "Charlie insisted he was fine and didn't need help. He's probably right, but he gave me such a fright when he went down. Thank goodness he didn't break anything or need stitches."

Assured he wasn't needed, Bodie stepped back, looking around to make sure none of their current customers needed assistance.

"Still," Ruby continued. "Although I'm not sure

about the girlfriend, I'm glad our grandson is staying with us, just in case."

The women surrounded Ruby with their support.

"I know you're worried about Charlie. It's a good thing Rick is here to help you."

"Sounds as if he's going to be just fine, but you keep a close eye on him."

"If you need anything, anything at all, you call."

Ruby nodded, then took a deep breath, and visibly pulled herself together.

"I need to get going. I'm supposed to be following in our car, but these," she waved the paper she'd pulled from her pocket, "sold out almost immediately, and I couldn't bear for our reservation to go to waste."

Bodie wasn't sure what the paper was, but the other women seemed to understand. Their eyes grew wide, then they nodded in agreement.

Rosie patted the woman's hand. "That's so sweet of you, but I talked to Mrs. Harvey and she saved one for me. I'm meeting Lou at our designated time and he's going with me." She waggled her drawn-on brows. "Thanks anyway."

Ruby's gaze went to the others.

Maybelle shook her head. "I'm working the ornament sales until we sell out or close down."

Claudia also shook her head. "I promised my daughter she could drop the grands by my place later. They're going to stay the night and go to church with me in the morning. I'm heading home as soon as I finish here."

All eyes turned to Sarah and Bodie.

"Oh, Ruby, I couldn't."

"Why not?" the Butterflies all asked simultaneously.

"Well, I...We..." Sarah's face was flushed as she turned to him. "What do you think? Would you want to go?" Her eyes were full of longing. "I mean, I've always wanted to go on one of Mr. Harvey's sleigh rides, but that doesn't mean you want to. Or that you have to. I mean, I understand if you don't want to."

Sarah was rambling and Bodie felt obliged to rescue her.

"If you want to, I'm fine with whatever," he agreed.

At his words, all the Butterflies lit up like lightning bugs. That might have had him backtracking, except Sarah's eyes glowed with pleasure and she moved from Ruby to wrap her arms around him in a hug.

"Oh, thank you. Thank you. Thank you. You don't know how much this means to me."

Harry made a little whimper sound from where he slept beneath one of the tables. Bodie knew how the dog felt and fought whimpering himself. A carriage ride with Sarah. Maybe he should do Sarah a favor by grabbing the dog and running while he still could.

Not that he'd ever been one to run, but with the way his mind kept going back to the way their hands had brushed against each other earlier, how their almost kiss at Harvey's Farm replayed through his mind, how just being near her made him feel better inside, their going on a sleigh ride together knowing he'd soon be leaving felt like stepping into crossfire.

CHAPTER THIRTEEN

BODIE FOUGHT TAKING A STEP back from the sheer force of their smiles that even Sarah's hug couldn't shield him from.

He had just agreed to go on a sleigh ride. With Sarah. No. Big. Deal.

Right. That's why all the women in the booth were looking at him as if he'd morphed into a Prince Charming who was about to sweep Sarah off her feet on a romantic carriage ride.

"It would be a shame for Ruby's reservation to go to waste," he tried, hoping to clarify why he'd agreed.

The Butterflies weren't buying it. Nothing he could say would convince them he'd agreed for any reason other than that Sarah wanted to go.

"A shame, indeed," Rosie agreed, snatching the reservation slip from Ruby and handing it to Sarah. "Look at the time!" she exclaimed. "You and Bodie have the last ride of the night."

"Ooooh," Claudia praised. "That's for a full twenty minutes."

"The best ride of the night," Ruby beamed. "My Charlie would settle for nothing less."

Glancing down at the paper, Sarah nodded. "Thank you, Ruby. Now, go check on Charlie and don't forget to let us know how he is."

There was a flurry of kisses and hugs, then Ruby was off.

Claudia and Maybelle's attention returned to customers who were now ready to check out. Rosie stared at Bodie and Sarah expectantly.

"Maybe you'd like to visit the other booths now?" Bodie asked, knowing he'd like to do that. Or pretty much anything that got them out from under the watchful eyes of the Butterflies.

"Thanks for that," Sarah told Bodie as soon as they were out of earshot of the church booth. Maybelle and the others had really laid it on thick.

And perhaps in Sarah's desire to go on the sleigh ride, so had she.

Letting Harry's leash out so the dog had a few feet of leeway, Bodie glanced at her. "For rescuing you from the Butterflies?"

"That, too, but I meant for agreeing to go on the sleigh ride."

Guilt hit her. He really had been put on the spot. No wonder he'd agreed. He'd probably feared the Butterflies would serve him for Christmas dinner had he refused.

"We don't have to go," she said. "Not if you don't want to. The others never have to know."

Not that they wouldn't. The Butterflies had eyes

and ears everywhere. No doubt word would get back to them if Sarah and Bodie never showed for Ruby's sleigh ride.

Still, she'd deal with them when the time arose if that was what Bodie needed from her.

Bodie gave a tug on Harry's leash, and stopped walking. "Do you want to go on the sleigh ride, Sarah?"

She bit the inside of her lip, then nodded. "I do. A lot. I mean, I've really wanted to go, well, my whole life. Who doesn't want to go on a Christmas sleigh ride? But last year..." How did she explain the fiasco of her relationship with Richard? "Well, it didn't work out. So, yes, I would like to, but that doesn't mean you and I have to go. There's always next year."

Watching her closely, he took a deep breath. "Like I said at the booth, if you want to go, we'll go. It's not a big deal. Let's not make it into one."

He sounded so matter-of-fact about it she could almost believe him.

Almost.

"I..." she hesitated, not sure what to say, then smiled. He was right. It wasn't a big deal. She needed to quit acting as if it were. They were just two friends going on a free sleigh ride they'd been given. She needed to remember that. "Thank you, Bodie. From the bottom of my heart, thank you."

At her words, Sarah swallowed back the knot forming in her throat.

Not from the bottom of her heart. Her heart was not involved in this. She was just feeling gratitude for the wonderful friend he was.

This year, she was going on a sleigh ride. With Bodie.

"Step right up, folks," a teenaged boy called as they passed his booth. "You need to play to win because winning is what it's all about."

Surprising Sarah, Bodie walked over to see what the boy's game involved.

"Buy a ticket for a chance to win the lady a stuffed Christmas toy."

The booth was a throwing game. The contestant threw a red ping-pong-sized glowing ball into a small opening on a painted reindeer face. The opening appeared barely large enough for the ball to fit through.

"You want a stuffed Christmas toy?"

Not that she doubted Bodie's abilities, but the hole was *tiny*. Sarah gave Bodie a skeptical look. "You think you can win?"

He glanced back at the game board, then nodded.

Cutting her gaze to the teenager, she asked, "How many chances does he get?"

"Each ticket buys three chances to win."

"Three chances? How many does he have to get to win?"

"Just one." The boy walked over and put the ball through the opening, showing that it did fit—with no margin of error. "Ready to try your hand?"

Pulling out some cash from his front pocket, Bodie paid the boy who then handed him three glowing balls.

Bodie cupped the balls in his hands, examining each one for about a millisecond before choosing one and handing the other two to Sarah. "You want to go first?"

She looked at him in question. "What?"

"Go ahead." He gestured for her to throw.

"No sports, remember?" she reminded, knowing her throws would be a waste of his money.

"Me, either, remember? It's for fun, right?"

"Right." She eyed the board, aimed the best she could, then underhand tossed the ball toward the deer's missing nose. The glowing ball bounced off the board and onto the ground.

"Whoops," the teen said. "Try again."

Sarah looked to Bodie to see if he minded her wasting a second one of his chances. He nodded for her to go ahead. She aimed and this time tried throwing overhanded. The ball bounced off the board again and was further away from the opening than the first time.

She laughed and turned to Bodie. "Okay, that was all kinds of ugly. Let's see what you've got."

Taking off his jacket and handing it to Sarah, along with Harry's leash, Bodie eyed the opening with such a serious expression he seemed to be mentally calculating thrust velocity and wind dynamics as he took aim, flicked his wrist just so, and threw the ball toward the deer's face.

The ball went straight into the nose opening.

"You got it!" Sarah exclaimed, bouncing with excitement and giving him a congratulatory hug. Harry awarded him with a single bark, too.

"Hey, dude. You win," the teen said, impressed.

"I thought you said you didn't play sports," Sarah teased as she handed his coat back.

Bodie grinned. "By choice—not from a lack of skill."

Sarah imagined there wasn't much Bodie couldn't do if he set his mind to it.

"Pick your prize," the boy told Sarah.

While Bodie put on his coat, she glanced over the stuffed Christmas toys and picked a silly-looking elf because it made her think of the joke she'd told when they'd unpacked Aunt Jean's ornaments.

The joke made her think of Bodie's laughter. Which made her feel warm inside. She looked down at the big-eared elf in its green hat and outfit and smiled. She couldn't have made a more perfect choice.

As they walked away, Bodie eyed the toy. "Now I know why Santa's elf had low elf esteem."

A bit breathless that his mind was on the same wavelength, Sarah hugged the elf. For a few moments, they walked along in silence, but finally, Sarah couldn't hold it in any longer.

"I'm wondering why you didn't play sports. That's some throw you have."

He shrugged. "I was interested in being a soldier, not in sports. That doesn't mean I never played with friends or in pick-up games. Just that I never had interest in devoting myself to a sport."

"What other hidden talents do you have?"

Looking at her out of the corner of his eye, he shook his head. "None I'm telling you about."

The reminder of how very different his life had been from hers hit full force. He'd seen and done things around the world unlike anything she'd ever see or do.

She was content with that. Some, like Claudia, dreamed of traveling the world. Sarah believed everything she wanted, needed, was right in Pine Hill.

Would Bodie ever consider settling down in one place? Her chest constricted a little that their dreams weren't more in sync.

They popped into art and crafts tents, sampled homemade fudge that almost compared to Mrs. Harvey's, listened to music performed on a stage that had been set up at the far corner of the square, then, when it was time, they made their way to a side street where Mr. Harvey was picking up and dropping off guests for their sleigh ride through the city park.

"Look, they're dressed like Mr. and Mrs. Claus," Sarah exclaimed, loving the added touch.

"Just so long as those horses aren't flying reindeer in disguise," Bodie mused.

"Where's your sense of adventure?" Sarah challenged. "Flying reindeer have got nothing on Bodie Lewis."

He grinned. "So you say."

The couple before them told Mr. Harvey thanks and goodbye while Sarah gave Mrs. Harvey the reservation slip.

Then they greeted Mr. Harvey, who helped Sarah into the sleigh and waited for Harry to jump up, then Bodie, before he climbed into the front and told them a few rules for their safety.

"Now, y'all just forget I'm here, sit back, and enjoy," Mr. Harvey concluded before signaling for his Clydesdales to take off on the path they'd already trodden numerous times that night.

The night air was crisp, but with her coat, hat, scarf, and gloves Sarah hadn't been overly cold up to then. The moving sleigh created just enough wind to put a chill straight through her and she spread the carriage's thick, fuzzy blankets over her and Bodie.

In all her sleigh fantasies, she hadn't been cold in a single one. Nor did she remember being cold on the one she'd taken with her father all those years ago. Then again, it had been in the middle of the day with her father.

Harry seemed intrigued by the sleigh ride, standing at attention and moving from Bodie's side of the sleigh to hers. Fortunately, he didn't bark, as Mr. Harvey had warned that if Harry barked, it might spook his horses.

"This is Harry's first sleigh ride?"

"As far as I know."

"Yours?"

He nodded.

She shivered and pulled the heavy blanket up further around her.

"Cold?"

She nodded. "A bit."

"Here." He pulled her closer and adjusted the blanket to tuck it in more securely around them.

With her being so close to Bodie, Harry jumped up onto the seat in the spot she'd vacated, pulling his leash across her. First, he looked out of the sleigh, then settled down next to her, his head lying across her blanketed lap.

"Sorry," Bodie apologized.

"No problem. Harry adds extra warmth."

Obviously thinking her comment meant she was still cold, Bodie wrapped his arm around her, hugged her close, and made sure the blanket covered her.

Ah. This was more like her fantasy sleigh ride.

A beautiful starry night through the park with a gorgeous man holding her close. Even Harry lying against her was near perfect.

Sighing with contentment, she lay her head against

Bodie's strong shoulder, snuggled into his warmth and closed her eyes.

That's when she felt it. The tiniest of nature's kisses that wasn't a kiss at all.

She opened her eyes and looked around them with disbelief. The night sky illuminated by the occasional light pole was sprinkled with white specks.

"It's snowing!"

Bodie laughed. "Guess you can't have a sleigh ride without snow."

"Guess not." She stuck her tongue out and caught a flake, then laughed. "I can't believe it's snowing."

Bodie couldn't believe it was snowing, either.

He couldn't believe a lot of things.

Had someone had told him six months ago when he'd been lying in a hospital bed in Germany, alive but wishing he wasn't, that in December, he'd be in a horse-drawn carriage driven by a man who looked a lot like Santa, with a beautiful, smiling woman cuddled up in his arms and a dog he owned sleeping beside her, well, he'd have thought them delusional.

If someone shook him right now and he awakened to find this was all just a dream, that wouldn't surprise him at all. Maybe he'd never awakened from the hospital bed and this alternate world only existed in his head.

"It's like a dream come true," Sarah said, cuddling up against him as her words echoed his thoughts.

Only this, riding in a sleigh with her and Harry, wasn't his dream. Never had been.

His dream was being a soldier. Of fighting against bad guys for freedom and justice for all.

Unbidden, he was hit with flashes of the day his Humvee had exploded around him and his unit as an IED went off. The jolt of remembered terror and pain hit him like a body blow, threatening to rob the moment of everything good.

He closed his eyes, squeezing them tight against the ebb of darkness that he expected to engulf him.

"Bodie?" Sarah reached up, touched his face. "Are you okay?"

Through her glove he could feel her warmth, could feel her concern, could feel a lifeline to reality. This reality. A reality where he was in a quaint little town in a horse-drawn carriage with a woman as sweet as the fudge they'd eaten earlier.

Bodie opened his eyes.

Glancing down at her, she came into focus and the darkness left as quickly as it had snatched at him.

"I'm fine," he said, grateful he was telling her the truth and hating that his murky thoughts had invaded this precious moment. He wouldn't let them.

Apparently, neither would she, because her gloved hand palmed his cheek in what could only be called a caress as she smiled up at him. "I'm glad."

"So am I."

With that she snuggled back into the crook of his arms and he held her close as the sleigh pulled them along the small river that ran through the park. The moonlight dabbled light off the water. The falling snow sprinkled the ground.

Bodie reminded himself again that this wasn't his dream, but it was hers, and he was so glad he could give it to her. In exchange, he'd allow himself for the moment to relish the warmth and goodness Sarah so freely gave.

The ride only lasted twenty or so minutes. Bodie had cared nothing about going on the sleigh ride, but by the time Mr. Harvey delivered them back to the drop-off point, he admitted he wasn't ready for the ride to end.

Riding in the sleigh with Sarah snuggled against him and snow falling around them had been surreal, like being trapped inside a magic snow globe where everything was perfect. Where he was a different person and not some jaded, broken man who'd only just begun to put his shattered life back together.

When Mr. Harvey stopped the sleigh, Bodie thought their adventure complete, but apparently Mrs. Harvey had other ideas as she joined them, camera in hand.

Rather than getting off the sleigh, Mr. Harvey told them to smile for the fancy camera his wife held.

"What is it with you people and pictures?" Bodie mumbled.

"Yeah, yeah," Sarah teased. "Why don't you make that funny face for me again?"

As she'd probably intended, Bodie smiled.

"Now," Mrs. Harvey instructed. "If you look up, you'll see that dear sweet husband of mine stopped in just the perfect spot for the next picture. As it just showed up there earlier tonight, we've decided 'twas a Christmas miracle and meant to be."

Bodie and Sarah looked up and spotted the mistletoe at the same time. When they looked back at each other, Sarah's eyes had widened.

"Now, now," Mrs. Harvey tsked, motioning for them to cooperate. "Don't be shy."

Shy had nothing to do with it.

"I think she wants you to kiss me," Sarah said slowly, her eyes growing even larger.

Bodie's eyes might be huge, too. His hesitation certainly was.

"Doesn't matter what she wants. We don't have to kiss just because there's planted mistletoe hanging from a lamp post."

Uncertainty and what could only be labeled as disappointment shone on Sarah's face.

Bodie's stomach knotted. Did she want him to kiss her?

Memories of standing by their Christmas tree at Harvey Farm, of holding her hand earlier, swamped him, stirring his insides into a muddled mess.

He'd wanted to kiss her on both occasions. He wanted to kiss her now.

That didn't mean he should.

"Quit making a big deal out of this and just kiss me," Sarah ordered, sounding thoroughly fed up with the whole thing.

Bodie hesitated. When he still didn't move, Sarah gave him a huffy glare. "Look, we may as well do this. The Harveys aren't going to let us out of the sleigh until we do."

"You're sure?"

She rolled her eyes. "Oh, good grief, just kiss me and get this over with."

Not sure he wanted to kiss Sarah under these circumstances but realizing the longer he hesitated the more awkward this would become, especially for

Sarah, Bodie leaned in and touched his lips to hers, then backed away. The kiss, if you could call it that, lasted a millisecond.

"That was too fast," Mrs. Harvey complained, her white brows drawn together in a frown. "I didn't get a picture."

Sarah gave him a look that said not to argue, but to just do what the woman wanted. "Guess you have to kiss me again."

Bodie sighed. "Guess I do."

"Slower this time, so she can get the picture and we can go help with clean-up."

Bodie leaned in, touched his mouth to Sarah's again. This time, he lingered long enough to fully register how soft her lips were.

He kissed Sarah.

And she kissed him back.

He really was lying in a hospital bed somewhere dreaming, because no way was this real.

No way could Sarah be kissing him the way she was.

As if the kiss wasn't staged but was something magical, something she wanted and was enjoying.

"Oh! That's perfect," Mrs. Harvey interrupted the moment. "I got it. All the photos will be available for pickup at our place on Monday morning."

Slowly, Bodie and Sarah parted. Sarah looked at him with the same wonder and awe as she'd looked up at the snow.

As if he enchanted her and filled her with happiness. As if she trusted him completely.

His promise to Maybelle rang through his mind, causing him to swallow the lump in his throat. He shouldn't have kissed Sarah, shouldn't have let them get into a situation where the kiss could even have happened.

He didn't want to hurt Sarah. Couldn't let himself hurt her.

He needed to protect her. Even if that meant protecting her from himself.

CHAPTER FOURTEEN

WATCHING BODIE AND A HANDFUL of others work to break down the tent, Sarah stood in the lightly falling snow, holding Harry's leash and her stuffed elf.

Maybelle joined her. "How was the sleigh ride?"

"Good," she said, keeping her eyes trained on Bodie.

They'd sold out of ornaments. Maybelle, her father, and the other volunteers were just packing everything up when Sarah and Bodie returned. They'd had plenty of volunteers. Bodie had asked Sarah to stay back with Harry while he went to help. She hadn't argued. She'd needed a few moments to contemplate her and Bodie's kiss.

He hadn't wanted to kiss her. Why had he been so reluctant to play along with a quick, staged kiss beneath the mistletoe?

While Bodie helped the men take down the tent, was he thinking about their kiss, too? Wondering what it meant?

"Good," Sarah repeated without meaning to.

Sarah didn't have to look at Maybelle to know her brow had lifted. She could feel that arch.

"That's all I get? A one-word answer twice over?"

Rubbing her gloved hand over her elf to smooth down its floppy ears, Sarah fought grimacing. What would Bodie say if he could even hear them—if she told Maybelle the truth, that the sleigh ride ended with a kiss that had her head spinning?

She'd never again see mistletoe without thinking of Bodie. How could she? Bodie's second kiss had been sweet and tender... just what a kiss following a magical sleigh ride should be.

But that didn't mean she should or even wanted to tell Maybelle about it. She didn't know what their kiss meant.

Who was she kidding? Nothing. The kiss meant nothing. No big deal, remember? Wasn't she the one who had told Bodie that? So why was she twisting herself into knots over a mistletoe kiss when she knew better?

Bodie was leaving. She needed to just forget that kiss had even happened.

"It was cold." Sarah kept her voice rather blah and didn't meet Maybelle's eyes for fear the woman would see right through her. Instead, she wished she could read what was going on inside Bodie's head as he worked alongside her father and people she'd known all her life.

"That doesn't sound like fun." Maybelle's gaze bore into her. "Rosie mentioned the Harveys had some nice additions this year."

Maybelle's nonchalant tone did nothing to hide that she was fishing for details.

In Sarah's fluster over her and Bodie's kiss, she'd forgotten all about Rosie and Lou. Now there was a subject that might deter her friend from further prying.

"How did their sleigh ride go? Has Rosie finally admitted she has feelings for Lou? I mean, she did make him her grandmother's cinnamon bread."

"Apparently that stuff works. He admitted he's crazy about her."

Maybelle's sassy tone suckered Sarah in and she couldn't resist looking at the woman.

Maybelle's pale blue eyes lit with delight when they connected with Sarah's. No doubt she knew she had Sarah under her power, and she'd soon confess everything.

But her friend had a bombshell of her own to drop first.

"Lou asked Rosie to marry him at the end of their sleigh ride."

Surprise and excitement filled Sarah. "Seriously? That's wonderful."

Not looking surprised or excited, Maybelle nodded. "Lord only knows why that man wants to marry her."

"Did she say yes?"

Maybelle snorted. "What do you think?"

Sarah's heart sank. "She said no?"

"Of course she said no. We're talking about Rosie."

"Poor Lou." It was common knowledge he'd had a thing for Rosie for years. "He must be devastated."

Maybelle's gaze dropped to where she was hugging the elf. Sarah resisted the urge to hide the stuffed toy beneath her coat.

"Rosie told him when he proposed properly with a big, blingy diamond and down on one knee, she might reconsider. Until then he can sit next to her in church and she'll let him hold her hand."

Picturing Rosie telling Lou just that, Sarah smiled. "Lou may have to get Alberta involved again to get Rosie in a more agreeable state of mind."

A sly smile dug wrinkles into the corners of Maybelle's eyes.

Realization dawning, Sarah's eyes widened. "Alberta didn't invite Lou to go on a sleigh ride with her, did she?"

Maybelle looked offended. "She most certainly did."

Sarah wasn't buying it. She knew her friend too well and recognized that smile.

"Because you put her up to it?" she guessed.

Maybelle's smile said it all.

"Rosie is going to kill you if she finds out."

"Finds out what?" Maybelle asked, not seeming concerned. "I haven't admitted to a thing."

She didn't need to. Sarah smelled a Butterfly. A matchmaking one.

"What did you think about the mistletoe?" Maybelle asked, adjusting her scarf. "I thought it was a nice touch to the end of a romantic sleigh ride."

Sarah's mouth dropped. "You did that, too?"

"I'm good, Sarah." She said it as a statement of simple fact. "But it's been years since I could climb up a lamppost to hang mistletoe. I doubt there were any ladders lying around waiting for an old woman to use."

"True," Sarah admitted. "Yet you knew exactly where the mistletoe was."

The older woman's blue gaze sparkled. "Pay attention, girl. I said I couldn't climb a lamppost. Not that my eyes and ears don't work."

"Rosie told you about the mistletoe? That's how you knew?" Sarah clarified, shifting her elf and Harry's leash. The dog was lying near her feet with his head on his paws, watching the tent being packed away and every so often looking up at Maybelle with suspicion. Smart dog.

"Rosie told me."

"You're saying you had nothing to do with the 'Christmas miracle,' as Mrs. Harvey called it, of the mistletoe appearing earlier tonight?"

"Lou kissed Rosie beneath that so-called Christmas miracle." Maybelle sounded right proud. "You think she wasn't telling everyone with ears about how he was so overcome by their kiss that he proposed?"

It's exactly what Rosie would do. Maybe Maybelle had been innocent.

"Lou and Rosie weren't the only ones beneath that mistletoe."

Sarah's face heated.

"Oh, look, I think they're done," she rushed out, taking a step toward where the crew had finished packing up the tent. Just in time to keep from tripping, she remembered she had Harry's leash and waited for the dog to jump to his feet and join her in heading toward Bodie.

"That's okay, Sarah," Maybelle called from behind her, her voice full of merriment. "I always did say a picture was worth a thousand words."

Bodie wasn't at Hamilton House when Sarah got home from her post-church lunch with her father the following afternoon. As much as she hated to admit it, her mind had been on Bodie rather than her father's sermon.

When he hadn't shown at her place prior to church services, she'd consoled herself that she'd see him later that afternoon.

Coming home to an empty space where he usually parked his truck had disappointed her.

Surely, he'd be by in a few? Not that there was much left to be done on the specific jobs she'd hired him to do.

He'd stayed well under her budget, which meant she could afford some of the projects she'd planned to put off. If he was willing, she'd ask him to start on renovating the upstairs or at least as much as he could get done prior to his leaving for his job in the new year.

The advertisements she'd purchased were set to start running this week, but she'd been actively promoting on social media for months and had visitors lined up for the new year. Soon, Hamilton House would be filled with guests, she hoped and prayed.

She sighed. If only Hamilton House opening didn't mean Bodie would be gone.

If only he wasn't leaving, then she could allow herself to think on their kiss, could allow herself to think about him, and dream of what might be.

She didn't want him to leave, but he would. And soon.

Trying to change the course of her thoughts, she went to her bedroom. After programming her phone to play Christmas music, she flipped on her sewing machine and pulled out the fabric she was making into quilt blocks.

If anything could give her peace, it was sewing. She'd always found taking pieces of material and transforming them into something beautiful, something useful, to be cathartic. An added benefit was that it was something that made her feel closer to Aunt Jean. As she ran the material through the machine, she could hear her aunt's voice telling her to make sure she kept the seams at a quarter inch.

Oh, how she wished Aunt Jean was there, so she could've met Bodie.

After completing several pieces, Sarah stood, set up her ironing board, and turned on the iron so it could heat while she placed a sewn section of fabric on her ironing board.

Although pressed for time with the B & B, she planned to complete another Quilt of Valor in the upcoming year, and at least one annually for all her years to follow. Doing so was yet another legacy to her aunt. And to her mother.

Sarah smiled at thoughts of the quilt she always gravitated toward at her father's house. The quilt her mother had made him while he'd been away in the service, that she had given him upon his return.

Had Aunt Jean fantasized that each Quilt of Valor she so lovingly made was for Roy? Had those fantasies fueled her constant need to make and then donate the beautiful patriotic quilts?

Taking the iron, Sarah pressed the seams down so the material would lie flat.

She was a lot like her aunt. Hadn't she dreamed of a love of her own during all the hours she'd put into the special quilt she'd made following her aunt's death?

She'd poured so much love, so much emotion into every stitch as she'd grieved her aunt. Somewhere, there was a soldier who would return to his love, her quilt in tow, and they'd have happiness.

She'd pour just as much emotion into this new quilt, would send it off to wrap another soldier in love and good wishes.

Lord willing, she'd continue to do so as her aunt had.

Just as she finished pressing the newly sewn pieces, she heard a vehicle pull into her driveway. Her heart kicked into overdrive. That was Bodie's truck.

Grateful her bedroom had a window on the driveway side of the house, she walked to it and saw Bodie getting out of his truck, Harry jumping out right behind him. Joy spread through her.

She shouldn't feel such happiness at his arrival, but she did. He'd been at Hamilton House so much that his not being there when she got home had felt wrong.

After unplugging the iron, she practically ran to the foyer. Not waiting for him to knock, she opened the front door.

He stood on the porch, hand poised to knock.

"Hey there," she breathed, smiling at him. Realizing he wasn't smiling back, Sarah's smile fizzled.

Looking at Bodie like this was a flashback to seeing him for the first time when he'd shown up at the community center. Just like then, his expression was tight, withdrawn, almost tormented. What had happened?

"Is everything okay?" she asked, reaching out to touch his jacket sleeve.

Rather than reassure her, he looked back into her yard, his gaze stopping on where Harry sniffed at a bush at the yard edge. "You busy?"

Not sure what she'd expected, her hand fell to her side. "Not doing anything that can't wait."

It wasn't as if she was on a timeline to finish the quilt. But even if she'd been busy, she'd have dropped everything to talk with him when he seemed so upset. Something was wrong.

Still gazing out at Harry, he stuffed his hands into his jacket pockets. "I had it in my head what I wanted to say to you, but now that I'm here, words are failing me."

That sounded ominous. She knew he was essentially finished with the work she'd hired him to do, having only a few small things left undone. Had he come to say goodbye?

"You want to come in? Have you eaten? I could heat something up for you."

His gaze came back to hers and he shook his head.

Did that mean he didn't want to come in? Hadn't eaten? Or that she couldn't heat something up for him?

Talk to me, Bodie. Tell me what's wrong, what's changed from last night when we were so happy in that sleigh?

Unless he regretted their ride, their kiss.

And was leaving.

"You want to go for a drive?" he surprised her by asking.

"Uhm, yeah. A drive would be great. Let me get my coat and keys. I'll be ready in a few. Feel free to come in and grab something out of the fridge if you're hungry."

Where had all the things he'd planned to say gone? Bodie wondered. He'd had everything all planned out in his head long before he'd pulled into Sarah's driveway.

He'd had most of the night to think on it, because he sure hadn't been sleeping. Thankfully, it hadn't been nightmares that had robbed him of rest. Instead, Sarah had been heavy on his mind.

He'd kissed Sarah. He shouldn't have kissed her.

He was leaving. Sarah had looked at him as if she wanted him to stay.

He couldn't stay.

He needed to put his life back together, to make a new life for himself, to feel whole again. iSecure was giving him that opportunity, and Bodie was grabbing it with both hands.

Wasn't that what he'd told himself as he'd been aimlessly driving around all morning?

When Harry came bounding up the steps, Bodie let them both inside the house. As was their routine, Harry paused, waiting on the rug as Bodie wiped his feet, then took a towel off the coat rack to check Harry's feet so the dog wouldn't leave muddy paw prints everywhere.

Thankfully, Harry didn't seem to mind the extra attention and had taken to stopping on the rug automatically after the first few times Bodie had ordered him to do so. When finished, Bodie hung the towel back up on the rack and followed the dog into the living room. His gaze immediately went to Sarah's tree.

It was the middle of the day, but she had the lights plugged in and twinkling and there were already presents wrapped beneath it. Her comment the night before was correct. Their tree was more beautiful than the town's tree.

Their tree.

His fingers had wrapped around the ornament in his pocket moments before on the porch and now it called to him. Taking it out of his pocket, he unwrapped the snowflake from its protective tissue paper, then looked for a spot on the tree. Finding an area where he could put it, he hung the ornament, then stepped back to make sure it looked right.

"What do you think, Harry?"

At his name, the dog lifted his head from where he lay in front of Sarah's fireplace. He cocked his head, but lost interest when Bodie didn't say anything further because Sarah entered the room.

"I think it looks great."

He thought she looked great. She'd put on her coat, her hat, scarf, and gloves. Her cheeks glowed pink and her eyes were bright.

"Thanks," he told her. "Ready?"

She spread her arms, drawing attention to her winter get-up. "Do I look ready?"

One side of his mouth lifted as he met her gaze. "Ready for what is the question."

"For whatever today's adventure is," she assured him. "I've got my keys in my pocket." She jingled them as she stepped into the foyer, then motioned for him to join her. "Let's go."

Bodie followed her, opened the door and let Harry and Sarah go out, then made sure the handle was locked before pulling it closed behind him.

Harry followed him to the truck and hopped up onto the seat. Bodie brushed off the seat. "I should have let him in on my side." There was just enough of a sprinkling of snow still on the ground that Harry's feet had left wet marks on the seat. "Sorry."

"Not a problem." She wiped the seat dry with her gloves, then climbed into the truck.

Bodie closed her door, went around and got into the truck. Once he had the engine started, he turned to her. "Which direction do you want to drive?"

"Anywhere is fine. Surprise me."

He backed up the truck and pulled out of her driveway.

After several minutes passed with no conversation, Sarah reached out and grabbed his hand. "Are you going to tell me what's bothering you? I know something is."

Bodie's gaze dropped to where her gloved fingers wrapped around his bare fingers, firmly holding onto him.

Would she still want to hold his hand when they'd finished their talk?

"I shouldn't have kissed you last night."

Sarah's hand tensed, but she didn't let go as her gaze bore into him. "That's what this is about? That stupid mistletoe kiss?"

She was right. The kiss had been stupid on so many levels.

"That and a lot more I need to tell you."

She sighed. "Then tell me."

Wondering at why this was so much harder than anything he'd done before, he sucked in a lungful of air, then went for broke. "I came to Pine Hill to find you."

"I know. To answer my help wanted ad."

Staring out at the road, he gripped the steering wheel tight with his free hand. "I didn't know anything about your help wanted ad until everyone assumed that was why I was there."

Sarah was quiet a few seconds, then asked, "Then why?"

"I have your quilt."

Sarah wasn't sure she'd heard Bodie correctly. "Pardon?"

With one hand, he gripped the steering wheel as if it were a lifeline. With his other hand, he flexed his fingers beneath hers, but Sarah didn't let go.

"The quilt you donated to the Quilts of Valor Foundation," he clarified, keeping his gaze toward the road. "I have it. It's in the duffel bag behind your seat."

"How...I... Wow." Bodie was the soldier who'd received her quilt? All the hours she'd put into that quilt, thinking of who it would go to, not once could she have imagined someone like Bodie.

"I came to Pine Hill to say thank you."

Trying to let what he was saying sink in, Sarah stared at his tense profile. "And you went to work for me instead?"

Still not looking her way, he shrugged. "You needed my help and I owed you."

"You didn't owe me anything." Sarah's stomach lurched as ugly realization hit. "That's what all this has been? Repayment for my having donated a quilt? That's why you're at Hamilton House? Why you've worked so hard?"

He'd helped her out of a sense of obligation. Had that been what everything between them had been about? Even his kiss?

Of course he'd felt obligated.

They'd been sitting beneath mistletoe with her ordering him to kiss her. The whole time he'd been in town, he'd done everything she'd asked of him. She'd thought it was because he cared about her— as a friend, at the very least. But now... He'd played along with the kiss. How could he have not, without embarrassing her in front of the Harveys?

She was embarrassed now.

He met her gaze for a second before returning his focus to the road. "The pattern of stars, the hand-quilting, the time you put into that quilt, the words you wrote in the attached note about life in Pine Hill and thanking me, an unknown soldier, for making that life possible..." His voice held awe. "I don't think you understand how much your quilt meant to me."

Bodie had her quilt. The one she'd started prior to Aunt Jean getting sick, the one she'd quilted by hand while sitting at the hospital with her aunt hour after hour. The quilt she'd let dry her tears of sorrow when her aunt had passed.

She'd almost kept that quilt. Instead, she'd reminded herself of why she'd made it, reminded herself that there was someone out there who needed it more than she did. So, instead of keeping it, she'd written a note of all notes, expressing her gratitude for her life and all her blessings, her gratitude for those who made her life in Pine Hill possible.

Bodie had been that someone, that soldier.

"I know how much it meant to me to give it," she began, heat flushing her face. Her heart pounded, rattling her ribcage.

"Then you understand why it was just as important to me to give something back to you."

All this time, he'd been working with such dedication at Hamilton House because he was reciprocating kindness for her quilt. All his attention to detail, taking his time to do things the right way, being nice to her, helping her with anything she asked, it had all been because of the quilt.

Her insides shredded into little bits as a mix of emotions hit her.

Please don't cry, Sarah. Please don't cry. Grasp onto how angry his having deceived you this way makes you feel, but don't cry.

"I didn't need your charity."

"But I did need yours."

Stunned at his soft confession, Sarah's attempt at holding onto anger became more difficult and she stared at him. "I don't understand."

Still watching the road, Bodie winced. "Maybe going for a drive for this conversation wasn't a good idea."

"We can turn back," she suggested, determined that they would have this conversation without any more delays.

Seeming to recognize where they were, he drove

a little farther, turned into the city park, and pulled into a parking place. They were the only ones there.

Sarah refused to let thoughts of the night before, when they'd also been at the park, into her mind. She needed to keep clear-headed.

"Unfortunately," Bodie said as he put the truck into park, "I can't turn back time."

"Not what I meant. But is that what you want? To turn back time?"

He tapped his fingers against the steering wheel but didn't answer, just seemed to be considering his next words.

"What would you do different if you could turn back time?" she pressed, knowing that whatever was going on in his head was important, that as deceived as she felt, this conversation needed to take place. She couldn't let him retreat without having told her everything.

"I'd have thanked you for my quilt and left Pine Hill immediately."

Ouch. His answer stung. Because he'd rather not have gotten to know her?

"Actually, that's not true," he revised, raking his fingers through his short hair. "Hamilton House wouldn't have been ready by Christmas if I hadn't stayed."

"If you believe that, you don't know me as well as I would have thought. I'd have found a way," she assured him. Even if it meant she had to watch online how-to videos and suffer through trial and error or beg the men and women at church to come help her, she'd have finished by Christmas Day to have her open house.

"My being here made it easier."

"True." His being there had made the suites perfect—better than she'd envisioned them. His being there had been wonderful and had filled the void in Hamilton House she'd felt since Aunt Jean had died. But that made his revelation sting even more. It had felt wonderful to her. It had felt like obligation to him, and that spoiled everything.

Lifting her chin, she stared him straight in the eyes. "I appreciate you helping me, Bodie, but your coming here wasn't necessary."

"It was."

Refusing to soften at the look in his blue eyes, she kept her head high. "I didn't give that quilt to make someone feel obligated to me."

"Thankful isn't the same as obligated," he pointed out.

"Is that why you kissed me last night? Thankfulness?" Her voice held a nasty edge she didn't like and could barely even recognize as her own. What was wrong with her? She didn't talk this way. Didn't feel this way.

Which was what exactly? Defensive? Bitter? Hurt? She had no right to feel any of those things. Yes, he should have told her the truth about the quilt. But he'd come to thank her. He'd stayed to be kind. Did she really have any right to resent that?

"I kissed you because you told me to."

Sarah winced. She'd ordered him to kiss her, really.

"But the truth is," he continued. "I wanted to kiss you, Sarah. Just not because Mrs. Harvey said to or because there was mistletoe, but because I like you."

Warmth filled her and she disliked herself for it. *No,*

no, no. She shouldn't feel this way, couldn't let herself feel this way or read anything into his confession.

"I like you, too." She sure shouldn't have made a confession of her own.

"But you shouldn't."

Yep. At least they agreed on something.

Growing restless with the non-moving truck, or perhaps a bit agitated at the high emotions in the cab, Harry climbed between Bodie and the steering wheel to press his nose against the window, then whimpered.

"You need out, boy?"

The dog whimpered again.

Opening the door, Bodie let Harry jump out.

"Stay close," he ordered as the dog took off to inspect a nearby tree. Keeping an eye on the dog, he continued, his voice low, as if he really didn't want her to hear what he said next. "I was in a bad place when I was given your quilt. Physically, mentally, emotionally."

The pain in his voice cut into her like the sharpest sword.

"What happened to you, Bodie?"

Chapter Fifteen

BODIE RAN HIS PALMS OVER the steering wheel, knowing he had to talk to Sarah about what had happened. Reliving the events that led him to Pine Hill wasn't going to be easy, but she deserved the truth.

"I almost died."

Sarah face paled at his words. They were harsh. They were also true.

"I should have." Parts of him had—or so he'd thought at the time. Lately, since meeting Sarah, glimmers of those parts he'd thought were forever gone had revived, sparking to life.

"No," she denied, placing her hand on his arm. "You shouldn't have."

"You don't understand," he started again, forcing his next words from his mouth because he had to confess the truth. "We'd left a small village where we'd been staked out for a few days. All of us knew something didn't feel right and we were relieved when we got the orders to get out. None of us wanted to be there. We'd not gone a mile out of town when the IED went off."

"Bodie," Sarah gasped, her hand squeezing his arm in a gesture meant to comfort.

Back then, nothing had comforted the raw pain inside him. Nothing until he'd been awarded a beautiful work of art she'd made, held her quilt, read her note, and known he needed to recover so he could thank her in person.

"I don't remember much after that. Just a blinding pain, seeing things no person should see, and then nothing." He twisted in the seat to face her, to let her see his shame. "No one else survived, Sarah. Just me."

Her face paled even further. "I'm so sorry, Bodie."

"I have flashes of being found, of being put in a helicopter, then not much else until I woke in a hospital in Germany two weeks later." He swallowed and continued, hating to tell her of his gruesome past, trying to gloss over details, but needing her to understand. "I was there for several more weeks. Next, they sent me to a stateside army hospital where I stayed for a month or so, then a rehab facility for another couple of months, before being discharged to stay at a friend's place. I was there until the day we met."

"Your friend Lukas?"

Bodie nodded. "It was while I was in the Army hospital that I was presented with your quilt. One of my nurses was involved with the Quilts of Valor Foundation and thought I needed it." He took a deep breath. "She was right."

Sarah placed her hand on her chest. "I'm glad she gave it to you."

"Me, too. After the presentation, I read your note

and it sparked the first flicker of light I'd felt inside me since the accident." He looked at her, hoping she understood what he was saying. "I didn't deserve to survive, Sarah, not when the others didn't. Although my body had been healing, my mind hadn't even started. I was their commanding officer and I failed to keep them safe."

Something he'd never completely forgive himself for. How could he?

"I wanted to have died with them. Until I held your quilt and read your note." He'd read that note so many times that he'd worn the paper ragged, could quote her words about a blessed life that she owed to men and women like him, about how much she appreciated the sacrifice he made, prayed for him, and hoped he found the peace she knew. That night had been his first without waking, covered in sweat, to the sounds of screams in his head.

Beneath her quilt, the nightmares slowed. He'd wanted to get better to find her, to thank her in person for making the world brighter, making his world brighter.

"That's why I had to come to Pine Hill, to find you. I needed to tell you thank you for doing what the doctors hadn't been able to do."

Sarah's head spun from everything Bodie was saying.

Her heart ached from his words, from the thought of his beautiful body having been hurt, from his mind having been tortured by gruesome memories and survivor's guilt.

"You weren't what I expected to find," he admitted,

laughing a little. "That's why I assumed Carrie was pointing to Maybelle that day. She fit with my image of who'd made my quilt."

That explained a lot.

"But it was you," he said. "I'm glad it was you."

"Why didn't you tell me this before now?"

"I was going to show you my gratitude by helping with Hamilton House, then I'd leave without ever telling you I had your quilt."

She let that sink in. "So why tell me now? What's changed?"

"Me."

She waited for him to say more, but then, as usual, had to prompt him.

"How did you change, Bodie?"

"More like what—or rather, who—changed me." His gaze went to where Harry was playing with a stick he'd found. "Just like with your quilt, you changed me."

Sarah sucked in a breath.

"You are so full of goodness that being near you makes me feel hope again. How can I not believe in goodness when all I have to do is be near you to feel it?"

Gratitude. He was full of gratitude toward her. She was glad, but...

"I...thank you."

"I took the job with Lukas at iSecure because it's the closest I thought I could be to getting my life back. Now I see it for what it is. An opportunity to work my way back to doing what I love, a chance to serve and protect again. I get to be whole again." Excitement underlined his words, emphasizing their truth. "I'm not telling you all this because I expect anything from you. I don't. I just needed to tell you everything."

"But that still doesn't explain why you chose to tell me now. You could have kept it a secret—I'd never have known."

Maybe that would have been better. She didn't want his gratitude. She wanted... she closed her eyes. What she wanted didn't matter, not when she heard the truth in Bodie's voice, the excitement at the prospect of his future...far away from her.

"There's more I need to say."

She swallowed, wondering what could possibly be more than what he'd already revealed.

"I'm falling for you."

Startled at his confession, her lips parted, but no words came out.

"I'm not sure any man could spend time with you and not fall for you, Sarah."

"Oh, there have been plenty who haven't." She couldn't believe Bodie was saying he had. Yes, she'd seen the look he sometimes got, had felt the changes in him, but she hadn't dared believe he was falling for her.

"Then they never really saw the woman I see. They couldn't have."

Stunned, Sarah stared at him. Was it possible Bodie was the hero she'd dreamed of while sewing the quilt? Her knight in shining armor who'd never leave her? Or was he just feeling misguided gratitude? And did any of this change his plans? Was he still leaving?

"That's a sweet thing to say," she began, her mind full as she tried to comprehend what was happening.

"I'm not a sweet man, Sarah. What I'm saying is the truth."

"You're the sweetest man I've ever known, Bodie."

A redbird flew low where Harry played, grabbing the dog's attention, and he took off after it, barking and chasing it towards the woods.

Frowning, Bodie opened the truck door, and half stepped out. "Harry!"

Slowing, the dog looked their way.

"Come here."

Harry hesitated, gave one last look of longing in the direction the bird had flown, then bounded toward them full speed, not slowing until he reached Bodie.

"Good dog." Bodie squatted and gave the dog a good rubbing down and more words of praise.

Shivering from the cold air filling the truck through the open door, Sarah watched them, while processing everything he'd said.

Bodie had come to find her and now he was falling for her.

With the way her heart fluttered when he was near, when he'd kissed her the night before, it would be so easy to fall for him, too.

But as wonderful as the thought of falling in love with Bodie was, she knew that didn't change the fact he was leaving.

Leaving was in his blood.

Pine Hill was in hers.

Sadness filled her at what might have been if either of them were different people, had different dreams. Part of her wanted to beg him to stay, to give them a chance to see what could be.

But doing that, only to have him eventually leave... she just couldn't.

Richard leaving had stung, had left a void in her life, and he'd never been sweet to her or made her belly feel like a shaken snow globe.

Bodie leaving was already going to hurt much worse than that sting.

If she were to let herself to fall for him, and then she lost him, she might never recover. Hadn't her Aunt Jean only loved one man her whole life? Her father only one woman? She couldn't allow her heart to belong to a man destined to leave.

Biting into her lower lip, she fortified her resolve that she and Bodie could only be friends. She'd known it from the beginning. The night before had messed with her head, but they could move past that. She'd chalk it up to a romantic sleigh ride and a magical mistletoe kiss on her part and misguided gratitude on his.

He'd leave and occasionally they'd think of each other with remembered fondness. Nothing more.

Harry jumped back into the truck cab and Sarah welcomed his wet kiss against her cheek, laughing as he continued to lick her, putting her hands up to protect her mouth from his affection.

"Settle down, Harry."

"He's fine," she assured him, giving the dog a scratch as he settled onto the seat next to her. "I'm going to miss him after you leave."

After he left. Sarah's words rang through Bodie's head. He was leaving, had never thought he wasn't. Yet, hearing her say the words left him feeling heavy, as if gravity tugged hard on him, trapping him against the seat.

Sarah's gaze met his. A mixture of resolve and perhaps a glimmer of something more shone there. "I'm going to miss you after you leave, too."

He'd been happy in Pine Hill. But he'd been biding his time until he could get back to a life of high stakes and travel. He'd loved that life. Missed that life.

Working for iSecure wouldn't be the same as his time in the Army. He didn't fool himself that it would. But once he put his time in as a glorified babysitter to the rich and famous, Lukas would move him into more challenging jobs. Jobs Bodie welcomed and that his friend needed to avoid now that he was about to become a father.

"Is your new job dangerous work?"

Had she read his mind?

"People or places who aren't at risk don't need to hire a high-end security firm."

"Which means I asked a silly question." She gave him a smile that almost seemed to tremble as she said, "I'll worry about you."

Yet another reason why he shouldn't have spent so much time with Sarah. She had such a big heart that he knew she really would worry.

"I'm not worth it."

"How can you say that?" she demanded, her face flushing. "You are, Bodie."

Unable to stop himself, he touched her cheek, traced his thumb across her smooth skin. "You only think that because you don't know the things I've done."

"Those things don't matter."

She was wrong.

"What matters are the things you do in the future."

What he'd do in the future was leave.

She didn't say the words, but they echoed throughout the truck cab. He drove her home, neither of them saying much.

"Come in?" she invited when he pulled into Hamilton House's driveway.

Bodie hesitated, then nodded. There were only a few things that needed to be done for him to finish with the suites completely.

"I didn't mean for you to come in to work," she told him when he headed toward the hallway leading to the suites. "We could watch a movie or play a game or something."

"Or I could knock out the rest of the work tonight."

"In a hurry to finish?"

Stopping, he didn't turn to look at her, just stood still, taking a deep breath. "Despite what you may think, I will miss you, Sarah."

She didn't say anything, didn't ask him to stay, and for that he was grateful.

Staying wasn't an option.

For so many reasons. Not the least of which was that Sarah deserved so much better than a messed-up man such as himself.

"I'll be in the suites."

A couple of hours later, Bodie glanced around the suite, happy with what he saw. The walls were painted, the trim work and crown molding repaired and painted, the hardwood floors gleamed. The antique tiles of the fireplace were cleaned, newly grouted, and the freshly stained oak looked fantastic.

Walking into the bathroom, he glanced around, checking each item to make sure everything still worked perfectly. Lights, electrical outlets, sink, shower, tub, toilet. All that was lacking were Sarah's finishing touches.

The suites were ready for furniture and then they'd be ready for guests. He still had a few things he wanted to accomplish, and he'd be her muscle on anything she wanted done the next couple of days.

Then, he'd leave.

"You missed your calling."

Turning to her, Bodie studied her make-up-free face, her slightly puffy eyes and pink nose and realized that while he'd been admiring his work, she'd been crying. Over him.

Guilt hit him. When he'd told her he was falling for her, he hadn't meant to hurt her. He'd...he'd just needed to tell her the truth. About the quilt, about him, about how she made him feel.

Like he could step into the sunshine and live.

"You sound like my stepfather," he told her, watching her closely, trying to read where her thoughts were. "This is what he wants me to do, only in Texas."

"Texas is a little far for me to use you as my handyman."

"A little."

"While you've been busy in here, I've been working in the kitchen. Hungry?"

They ate sitting at the kitchen island. As always, Sarah had outdone herself.

"Your guests are in for a treat."

Though she was much quieter than her usual chatty self, she still smiled. "I hope so. Getting great reviews from these first few guests will be key to my success."

"Hamilton House will be a success." Of that, he had no doubt. Sarah was a woman who could accomplish anything she set her mind to and do it with a smile on her face.

"Because?"

Thinking how much he was going to miss talking to her, he grinned. "You won't allow anything else."

"I hope you're right, because there are so many things beyond my control." She stood to clear their dishes while Bodie wiped off the island.

"You'll be fine."

She closed the dishwasher, faced him. "So, what's next? We'll get Aunt Jean's furniture from my dad's and get the suites set up tomorrow evening?"

He nodded. "Anything else you want me to take care of?"

"The upstairs rooms need pretty much the same work as you did for the suites downstairs."

He knew what she was leading up to. Part of him wanted to say he'd help her with the upstairs rooms, personally ensure that Hamilton House was ready for her to fill every space the way she dreamed.

But he'd done what he'd come to do. More than he'd come to do.

Staying longer only delayed the inevitable.

Still, he couldn't bring himself to say no, just studied her a moment more, then sighed. "Show me what you want done, Sarah, and we'll see."

"Yes, Maybelle," Sarah said into the phone as she poured a glass of juice early the following morning. "I'll be at church within the hour and will handle the extra meal deliveries today since Ruby and Charlie won't be there."

Charlie was going to be fine, but Ruby insisted he take it easy for a few days. Sarah didn't blame her.

She chatted with Maybelle for a few minutes longer. Mostly, she listened to Maybelle inform her what a huge success everyone said their booth had been.

She glanced at her watch. "Oh, sorry, Maybelle. It's later than I'd thought. I've got to run. Love you and see you in a few."

She hung up the phone, then rushed to finish getting ready. When she was, it surprised her that Bodie wasn't there. He must have gotten hung up at Lou's. Or maybe he was making arrangements for help to move the furniture back into the suites.

No problem. He knew where the spare key was hidden to let himself in.

Only when she stepped outside onto the porch, she froze, almost falling to her knees.

Not because of the cold December air or a chilly gust of wind.

There, draped over the porch railing, was Bodie's quilt.

The quilt she'd made while dreaming of him before she'd ever even known him.

She walked over to the railing and, hands shaking, she touched the soft cotton material she hadn't seen since donating it to the Quilts of Valor Foundation.

The material that had once dried her grieving tears, that had wrapped around Bodie's broken body and soothed his wounded warrior's soul. Her quilt, this quilt, had given him comfort, had been a light in his world full of darkness.

But not anymore. He'd let it go. Let *her* go.

Eyes watering, the red, white, and blue blurred and she gave in to the sorrow sweeping through her as she accepted what stared her in the face.

What she'd known all along and why she hadn't asked him to stay.

Bodie had done what he'd always been going to do. He'd left.

"What do you mean he's gone?" Maybelle asked as they filled disposable trays with today's lunch offering in the church kitchen.

"Did he tell you he was leaving?" Claudia pushed, dipping a large serving of green beans into a cup then putting a plastic lid over it.

Sarah resisted the temptation to brush back a stray hair from her ponytail with her gloved hands, then shrugged. She'd teared up this morning on her porch as she'd carried the quilt inside, placing it in the rocking chair across from their Christmas tree. But she'd refused to let herself cry. Instead, she'd draped the quilt across the chair, given it one last look, then headed to church.

As much as she didn't want to talk about Bodie with the Butterflies, there was no point in delaying the inevitable. Actually, she was surprised that they hadn't called to tell her he was gone long before she'd found the quilt.

"He didn't have to tell me in words."

"Then how do you know?" Rosie insisted.

"He didn't show at Hamilton House this morning," she admitted, not wanting to mention the quilt. Silly as it was, the quilt felt private, something intimate between the two of them. "I called his hotel. He checked out during the night."

That he'd left in the middle of the night without saying goodbye stung.

"He's gone." She couldn't put it much more simply than that.

"He didn't say a word? He just left?" Maybelle's brows arched high.

"That sums it up." She understood Maybelle's surprise. Sarah had never imagined him leaving without her having a chance to tell him thank you.

Or to pay him for the last week of work he'd done.

She hadn't thought him a coward, the type to steal off in the night instead of saying goodbye. But what did it matter? They'd had no future together. Why draw out the goodbyes? Maybe it was just as well he'd left as he had.

Had he thought she'd try to convince him to stay?

"Did something happen? You didn't fight, did you?"

Sarah shook her head. Their talk in the truck qualified as something that had happened, but the things they'd said were private and she wanted to keep them to herself.

"Your sleigh ride must not have gone nearly as well as mine," Rosie mused, looking concerned as she closed a tray lid and placed it inside a bag.

"Well, there sure wasn't a proposal."

Sarah had said her comment as a joke, but the way the three Butterflies stopped what they were doing to stare at her, mouths agape, said they hadn't taken her that way.

"Did you want there to be a proposal?" Maybelle asked, her brows deeply veed.

"Of course not. Bodie and I are—were," she corrected, "just friends."

"Personally, I think he's a friend you should take off after, so you can travel and see the world with him," Claudia suggested.

"That's your dream, Claudia. Not mine. I'm happy in Pine Hill."

Maybelle said, "You really need to talk to that husband of yours about taking you on vacation."

"He says for our fiftieth wedding anniversary, he'll take me anywhere I want," Claudia assured. "So, I'm biding my time to tell him I want to visit Europe. Only a few more years to go."

"Harrumph," Maybelle snorted. "What's he going to do if you book something sooner? If you want to travel, then, woman, travel."

Claudia's eyes grew huge, then she shook her head. "This is about Sarah, not me. I'll travel someday."

Maybelle, Rosie, and Sarah sighed simultaneously. If Sarah had the extra money, she'd book Claudia on a trip herself.

They resumed their assembly line preparation of food trays to be delivered to shut-ins.

Sarah held her breath, hoping the women would not resume the conversation about Bodie. She should have known better.

"Is Bodie coming back?" Claudia asked.

Sarah shook her head. "He was only here to get Hamilton House ready by Christmas. He did that. There's no reason for him to return."

He'd done everything she'd asked of him and more. Maybe someday she'd tell the Butterflies about Bodie's quilt. That he'd been the soldier her quilt had gone to, that he'd come to find her, to thank her, and had ended up staying to help her.

He had.

He'd done a fantastic job on Hamilton House. She'd get Carrie's son and some other young men from the congregation to move the items out of her dad's garage back to the downstairs suites. Then she would decorate the rooms and would move forward as if nothing out of the ordinary had happened.

As if Bodie had been just another repairman.

CHAPTER SIXTEEN

"**M**AN, I APPRECIATE THIS MORE than you know."
Bodie took Lukas's outstretched hand and they exchanged a bro hug. He hadn't expected Lukas to be waiting at the hospital entrance for him. He'd called to tell his friend that he'd just pulled into the hospital parking garage and had gotten Kelly's room number so he could meet his friend there.

"No problem."

"You're sure? I know you'd taken on that undercover job in Kentucky, but I needed someone I trust to take my place on this one."

Bodie followed Lukas's lead down the hospital hallway to an elevator bank. "I finished what I was hired to do in Kentucky, so your timing was perfect."

"Not my timing. This baby's." Lukas combed his fingers through his hair. "Didn't she know she had another month before she was due—and that I had a really important job that was supposed to be my last out-of-country trip until after she arrived? Doctor said she's doing great, though, and is a strong little thing."

"Takes after her mother, then?"

Stepping into the elevator, Lukas grinned. "I caught that, but yeah, you're right. Looks just like Kelly."

"Physically, you're good?"

Bodie shot his friend a look of challenge. "You want to try me and find out?"

Lukas laughed. "After the night I've had? I don't think so. You might take me, and I'd never hear the end of it."

"I'd take you after your best night."

"Maybe in your dreams."

Bodie snorted, but let it drop. "You going to watch after my dog while I'm out of the country?"

"My dog, and you'd better hope he doesn't decide he's missed home. What'll you do if he chooses to stay when you get back?"

"I'm not worried, but if Harry wanted to stay with you, I wouldn't force him to leave."

His friend, and boss, stared at him. "There's something different about you."

Bodie glanced toward Lukas and shrugged. "Same old me."

"Actually, that's it. You are more like the old you. Much more so than when you left here."

In some ways, Bodie felt more like his old self. In others, he felt nothing like the man he'd been in the past. His time in Pine Hill had changed him.

"What happened in Kentucky?"

Bodie shook his head. "Not much. Just worked in a small town no different from hundreds of others."

Lukas looked like he was about to ask more, but they reached their floor and the elevator door slid open.

As they stepped out of the elevator, Bodie glanced at his watch. "My flight's in four hours?"

"Yeah. Sorry to do that to you, but swapping my flight for yours was the best I could do to get you where I needed you to be in time." His friend gave a wry look. "As much as I hated to pull you into the company sooner than we'd agreed, I'd have hated leaving for two weeks right now even more."

Bodie shrugged. "You were the one saying I needed more time to heal before I started work. Not me."

"I wanted you to go home, see your family, kiss a girl. You know, have a life for a bit and get your head on straight before stepping into the company."

"I have a life." He wouldn't respond to the comment about getting his head on straight. There was no denying there had been a time when his head had been messed up. In some ways, it might always be because he couldn't un-see things he'd seen.

Nor would he respond to the comment on the kissing a girl.

Because he couldn't un-see Sarah, either. He'd never forget her.

Lukas stopped in front of a hospital room but didn't open the door. "What gives?"

Bodie glanced toward his friend questioningly.

"You zoned out on me. Sorry, man. I didn't mean to bring up bad memories."

That's when it hit him that he'd thought of what had happened and he'd been okay. The darkness hadn't clawed at him. Sure, the memory still gutted him, but he could remember it without despair threatening to take over.

Which made him feel stronger than he'd felt in a long time.

His body was healing. His mind was healing. He was on the brink of starting a new career, one that would eventually put him back in the action and allow him to help his best friend.

He met Lukas's concerned gaze. "I'm good."

Lukas studied him a moment, then nodded. "For the first time in months, I believe you are. I don't know what happened in Kentucky, but something must have."

Sarah's sweet face flashed through Bodie's mind. Her smile. Her laughter. Her kind heart. The way she loved the Butterflies and they loved her. The way she'd looked at him after their kiss beneath the mistletoe after a snowy sleigh ride.

He flexed his jaw, shrugged, then said, "Nothing happened in Kentucky."

"Yeah, right." Lukas laughed. "You forget who you're talking to, but whatever. Come on and meet my daughter."

Lukas knocked on the door, then they entered the hospital room. Kelly, looking lovely as ever, lay in the bed, a blanket tucked up around her waist, and a wrapped-up bundle in her arms.

Lukas crossed the room, kissed his wife, then grinned down at the baby she held. "Isn't she the most beautiful thing you've ever seen?"

Bodie stared at his friend in amazement. Was this really the same tough, take-no-prisoners man he'd rather have had at his side during battle than any other? Lukas had loved the adrenaline rush every bit as much as Bodie had. Yet in this quiet, domestic moment, his friend looked completely happy.

Good for him.

Now that Bodie was returning to work, he'd be happy, too.

Well, if not happy, he'd be content to be back to doing what he loved, to be able to feel whole again.

What he wouldn't do is look at his friend and wonder if he could have ever been happy with that type of life—with a wife, a child, a home he could return to at the end of every day. If things had been different then maybe it could have been him with Sarah welcoming a child.

But things weren't different. This was the life he had.

Every muscle in his body tightened, making taking his next breath difficult.

"Get over here and see your goddaughter," Kelly ordered when Bodie lingered near the door. "And thank you for doing this so Lukas can be here with us."

Shoving his wayward thoughts aside, Bodie smiled at the woman who he'd grown to genuinely like during the time he'd lived with them, and who obviously made his friend a happy man. "No problem. I appreciate you forcing his hand into letting me get back to work sooner rather than later."

"You're ready?" she asked, concern visible in her eyes.

He understood why she asked. She'd seen the darkness in him, had heard him cry out with the nightmares.

For those same reasons, he understood why his

friend had wanted him to take those few extra weeks that the V.A. doctors had thought he needed.

They'd been right. Although he had been physically ready for any job handed to him, his mind hadn't been in the right place.

He hadn't been in the right place.

Being around Sarah, soaking in her goodness, had soothed his tortured soul, made him want to be better than what he was. For that, and so much more, he'd be eternally grateful.

Knowing he told the truth, he nodded. "I'm ready."

"Everything's ready for tomorrow?"

Snuggling beneath the quilt her mother had made her father, Sarah took a sip of hot tea and nodded. "I wouldn't be here if it wasn't."

Her father laughed. "There is that."

Although she'd started the day early, doing one last walkthrough to make sure everything was perfect for the open house, Sarah had spent most of the day with her father. They'd gone to Maybelle's for a late Christmas Eve lunch, then they'd met up with the Butterflies and others from church to go caroling, then they'd attended a Christmas Eve service.

She'd had a busy day. A good day. And yet...

"I was at Lou's yesterday," her father continued. "Everyone I talked to is excited about the Open House tomorrow."

"Me, too." Mostly. Because no matter how much she tried she couldn't quite get past the wish that Bodie would be there.

He wouldn't be.

"Your Aunt Jean would be very proud of what you've done with Hamilton House, Sarah."

Sarah's gaze lifted to her father's and she fought tears. "You think so?"

He nodded. "The only thing she loved more than that old house was you. That you are there, breathing life into those walls again, would have meant the world to her. I know she's cheering you on from heaven, and that Roy and your mom are right there with her."

Putting her hot tea down on a side table, she got up, crossed to his recliner and gave him a hug. "Thank you for always knowing what to say to make me feel better."

"Not always," he admitted. "I didn't know what to say when that idiot Richard left."

Settling back onto the sofa and pulling her mother's quilt back up around her, Sarah shrugged. "Richard did me a favor by leaving. If he'd stayed, I might have settled."

Her father grimaced. "You should never settle, Sarah. What about that last one, Bodie?"

"Bodie was my handyman, not my boyfriend."

"I'm a preacher, Sarah, not a blind man."

"Meaning?"

"Meaning I saw how you looked at him," he said.

"Not sure what you think you saw, but I never thought there would be anything permanent between Bodie and I."

"Then you were the only one."

"The Butterflies don't count. They're perpetual matchmakers. I'm surprised they haven't driven you crazy over the years with trying to remarry you."

Sadness flashed in his eyes. "Your mother was my

soul mate. I never met anyone else who came close. It wouldn't have been fair to marry when my heart would always belong to her."

"You, Aunt Jean, Maybelle," Sarah sighed. "I'm surrounded by people who loved and lost."

He shook his head. "I loved, Sarah. There is no lost. Some never experience what I shared with your mother. I've no regrets." He studied her a moment. "But I get the feeling your comment had more to do with a certain handyman than it did me, Maybelle, or your aunt."

"I don't love him," she denied, then took a sip of her tea. "I mean, had I not known he was leaving from the beginning, I might've fallen in love with him. But I did know—so I refused to get attached."

Much.

Her father looked empathetic. "If that's what you need to believe, I won't correct you."

"It is what I believe," she defended, annoyed that he'd implied otherwise. She did not love Bodie.

She missed him, longed for him to be at Hamilton House, because he'd been great company. She missed their conversations, his smile, the fluttery feeling she got when he laughed, his intelligence, and thoughtfulness. She missed Harry, too.

But that didn't mean she loved Bodie. She didn't.

I'm falling for you. His words echoed through her mind. If only, he really had fallen. If only he hadn't left. If only...

She glanced at her father, saw that he was smiling.

"You ever consider going after him?"

"What? That's the most ludicrous thing I've ever heard you say." She couldn't believe her father even asked such a silly thing. Of course she hadn't considered going after Bodie. Her life was in Pine Hill. Who knew where in the world he was?

His friend Lukas would know. She had his number from when Bodie gave it as a reference.

For that matter, she had Bodie's cell number.

But she wouldn't use it. He'd left. Even if she called, it would change nothing.

"Did you tell him what you told me, that if he'd stayed in Pine Hill that you could have fallen for him?"

"What would be the point in telling him that? He was always leaving."

"I want to see you happy, Sarah. If he makes you happy, then you need to be with him."

Had her father not been paying attention? Bodie had never meant to stay. He'd come to say thank you, had stayed to help her, and then he was gone.

"I am happy," she assured her father. She was. She had her father and the Butterflies, her friends and church, and Hamilton House. "I don't need Bodie to be happy or for anything else."

She didn't. Hamilton House would open tomorrow, on Christmas Day, and she'd begin a new adventure.

Just as Bodie had begun a new adventure.

But friends did wish each other Merry Christmas and later that night as she lay in her childhood bed, she sent a text.

She really did hope Bodie had a Merry Christmas.

"I shouldn't be here. Not on Christmas Eve," Bodie complained to his best friend as they chilled in Lukas's living room. Kelly had gone to the nursery to feed Lucy and put her down to bed just a few minutes after Bodie had arrived.

He'd come straight from the airport and was exhausted.

"You really think Kelly would let you go to a hotel room after your flight came in this evening?"

"You didn't have to tell her when I'd be back."

"Because she didn't know when I was scheduled to return?" Lukas challenged, then gestured to the dog lying across Bodie's lap. "Besides, somebody missed you. Never seen him just sit and stare at the door the way he has the past two weeks."

Harry had practically tackled him when he'd walked into Lukas's place. No one had ever missed him the way the dog apparently had.

Bodie stroked his hand along Harry's spine. Harry lifted his head, gave Bodie's cheek one appreciative lick, then settled back down.

"Thanks for watching him while I was away." Closing his eyes, Bodie leaned his head back against the recliner.

He had missed Harry. Missed a lot of things.

But the mission had been good.

An extraction of a well-connected Middle Eastern family who'd gotten trapped behind enemy lines as political winds had shifted. Bodie and his team had gone in, gotten the family out, and moved them to a safe location.

They'd run into resistance, which had tested Body's readiness, but he'd had no difficulties doing what needed to be done.

Afterwards, flushed with success, he had felt alive, whole.

And yet, he'd also felt as if something were missing. Someone.

"You planning to stick around until the new year?"

Opening his eyes, he met his friend's gaze and shook his head. "Figured I'd head out in the morning for Texas." That way Lukas and Kelly could spend Christmas morning together without his intrusion.

"You're welcome to stay until January when you go to D.C."

"For my glorified babysitting job?"

Lukas laughed. "Sorry. Most of our jobs aren't like the one you just pulled off."

Bodie's phone vibrated and, shifting Harry around until he could reach his pocket, he pulled the phone out.

Merry Christmas.

The same fluttery feeling he got anytime he thought of Sarah filled him. He hadn't expected to hear from her, to have any contact with her ever again. That she'd reached out to tell him "Merry Christmas" fit, though. Sarah wanted everyone to have a good Christmas. It was just who she was.

"Everything okay?" Lukas asked when Bodie remained quiet, staring at his phone.

He glanced up at his friend and nodded. "Fine."

"You're a terrible liar," Lukas pointed out. "That from Kentucky?"

Bodie glanced at his friend. "Since when did being my boss give you rights to my private life?"

"Since when did you have a private life?"

Since he'd gone to thank an elderly lady for his quilt and met a young, beautiful woman who lived to serve others. A woman who smiled and lit up a room. A woman who smiled and lit up him.

Wondering what had happened to the exhaustion he'd felt moments before, Bodie stared at the message, started to type back a message, then hesitated.

He shouldn't text her, shouldn't encourage her to remember him.

The sooner they both forgot what they'd shared, the better.

Only, he didn't want Sarah to forget him. Not ever.

CHAPTER SEVENTEEN

"NOT THAT I EXPECTED OTHERWISE, but it looks like today is going to be a big success."

Sarah clasped her hands together and smiled at Maybelle. "It does, doesn't it? Let's just hope people actually come by."

She'd been so nervous all morning. She'd stayed the night at her father's but left early to get everything just so prior to time for guests to arrive.

Maybelle had shown an hour early to help with last minute items needing attention, saying the other Butterflies would be there soon to do their part in helping with the Open House.

"Whether locals come to your Open House or not, Hamilton House will be a success." Maybelle wiped her finger over a piece of furniture, inspecting to make sure there was no dust. "You going to leave that out?"

Sarah followed Maybelle's line of vision and nodded. She'd considered packing the quilt away, keeping her secret safe a while longer. Instead, she'd left it right where it was. Right where it had been since the day Bodie had left.

"Everyone in our quilting group is going to recognize it as the one you donated to Quilts of Valor after Jean died."

"Doesn't matter."

"That's why he came here, to find you," Maybelle mused, then walked over to the quilt, picked up one corner from where it draped over a rocking chair. "Why do you think he left it?"

Sarah knew why.

"He didn't need, or want, it anymore. He told me once that when he received it, it made him remember why he did what he did. In the end, I think it reminded him of things he'd rather forget, including me."

Maybelle's gaze cut to her. Sarah waited, expecting the woman to offer some tidbit of wisdom or some dry remark meant to make Sarah feel better. She did neither.

"I'm sorry he left."

Sarah was sorry about a lot of things. Like how foolish she'd been the night before when she'd texted him. He hadn't texted back. Not even a simple "Thanks" or "Merry Christmas back." Would it have hurt him to have shown that courtesy?

Or maybe he wanted to make sure she got the message loud and clear that he'd left, and that he didn't want reminders of her.

"It doesn't matter." Sarah waved off Maybelle's concern. She wouldn't cry over things she had no control over. Today was Christmas. The best day of the year. She wouldn't let thoughts of Bodie dampen her joy. Today was a good day. A great day.

"I may have forgotten to mention," Maybelle said

slyly, "but I invited a friend to come up to interview you."

"Interview me?"

"Really, he's more the son of a friend," she clarified. "But same difference."

Sarah grimaced. "You're not matchmaking, are you? Because I don't need that today."

Or any other day. She planned to spend the foreseeable future focusing on Hamilton House and her work with the church. It was a good life.

"Matchmaking wouldn't do a bit of good right now with you hung up on Bodie. So, no, I'm not matchmaking. Just doing my part to get the word out about Hamilton House."

"Where does he work?"

Maybelle named a travel magazine Sarah had contacted months ago. She'd been disappointed but unsurprised that she hadn't heard back from them. That they'd respond had been a long shot.

"You're kidding," she gasped, staring at Maybelle in disbelief.

"I don't kid," Maybelle reminded drily and with an expression so regal she must have royalty somewhere in her bloodline.

"There is that. Wow, Maybelle. Thank you. Thank you." She hugged the woman, then took a deep breath as she heard the front door open.

"We're here!" Rosie called as several people entered the house.

The Butterflies must have ridden over together.

Sarah went into the foyer, then stopped short. Ruby, Charlie, Claudia, Claudia's husband, Rosie, and Sarah's father were just inside the door. As was a trunk with a big red bow stuck on it, two lamps with green ribbon tied around them, some brocaded pillows, and several more items that looked wonderfully familiar.

"Surprise!" Ruby said.

"Merry Christmas, Sarah!" Rosie and Claudia said at the same time.

"We would have wrapped everything but didn't want you to have paper and packages everywhere for your Open House," Maybelle said from beside her.

"You want us to carry all of this upstairs?" Charlie asked.

"I..." Sarah looked at the items again. "These were Aunt Jean's." She stared at her friends, wide-eyed. "In Aunt Jean's ledger, you're 'B'!"

"B is for butterfly," Rosie reminded her.

"You bought these things from Aunt Jean."

"Stubborn woman had too much pride to accept our help, started selling off her things to an antique shop in Louisville. Rosie commented how much she'd like to buy one of the wardrobes upstairs. Jean offered to give it to her, but finally agreed to sell it." Maybelle's blue eyes sparkled. "Next thing you know, we were all in the antique buying business."

They'd bought some of the antiques from the upstairs rooms.

"That is so wonderful. I know she had to feel relieved that they were going to people she loved." Meanwhile, Sarah was relieved to know the Butterflies had at least some of her aunt's treasures. Treasures she'd thought she'd never see again. And now, they were trying to give them to her. She shook her head. "I can't take these."

Maybelle's brows veed. "You're rejecting our Christmas gifts to you?"

She hadn't meant to offend Maybelle, but she couldn't accept such extravagant gifts. "They're too much."

"Nonsense, girl." Ruby came over and gave her a hug. "Each of us brought you a gift today, something of Jean's that we want you to have. Call it a Christmas present or a housewarming gift or whatever, but these are for you. It's what we always intended."

"I..." Sarah's eyes watered as she looked at the wonderful women who'd had such an impact on her life. "I don't know what to say."

"You say thank you," Maybelle reminded with her usual sass. "Then, you tell Charlie and your father to get this stuff carried upstairs and out of the way before your guests arrive."

A tear trickled down her cheek. "I love you all."

"Telling us that is much better than Maybelle's suggestion," Rosie assured, then hugged Sarah. "We love you, too, honey."

There was a flurry of hugging, then carrying items up the stairs where they put them in one of the mostly empty suites.

"I have the bed, chest, and dresser that went in this room," Maybelle informed her. "Someday, I'll give them to you as a wedding gift."

Sarah crinkled her nose. "I'd rather you sell them to me once I'm ready to open these rooms up to guests."

Maybelle shook her head. "No. When I bought the set, I told Jean what I was saving it for. She loved that idea."

Rosie cleared her voice. "The wardrobe I have matches."

"Do I have to wait until I get married on that, too?"

Rosie's eyes lit with delight. "Of course. It's a matching set."

Ruby and Claudia both looked about to burst.

"Okay, what are you holding ransom until a wedding that's never going to happen?"

"I have the curtains, those heavy brocaded ones that match these." Ruby held up one of the pillows.

"And I have the tapestry that used to hang on the wall over there," Claudia confessed with glee.

She couldn't help but smile at them as she shook her head. "Truly, it would be better if I bought them back. Waiting for years on a wedding that might never happen to bring this room back together seems a shame."

"There's no rush. You can always use other pieces until that day comes."

"Assuming it ever does."

"You never know when the right one will come along and sweep you off your feet."

Something in the way Rosie said the words had Sarah's gaze dropping to her hand.

"Rosie!" she exclaimed as she took in the glittering diamond. "You said yes."

Rosie lifted her chin and fluffed her bright blue hair. "Couldn't break Lou's heart on Christmas, now could I?"

Once they were all back downstairs, Ruby went to give Charlie the grand tour, while the others asked what they could do to help. Sarah assigned each one a room, putting her father, Maybelle, Claudia, and her husband in the kitchen to make sure guests got cookies and drinks as needed.

She stationed Rosie in the living area. When they returned, she put Ruby and Charlie in charge of the downstairs suites.

"Y'all just make sure y'all behave," Sarah told them, getting a giggle from Ruby as she and Charlie exchanged looks.

Oh, to have that kind of love. The kind where you loved and were loved in return and never doubted each other's affections.

Bringing a tray of sandwiches with him as a housewarming gift, Lou was the first visitor to arrive and got a round of congrats from everyone. Carrie and her family were right behind him. Within minutes, the house had a steady stream of visitors.

None stayed long, they all just toured the home, sampled some of the goodies, promised to rave about the place to any friends or relatives, then they gave their best wishes and left as others arrived.

The magazine journalist showed, snapped hundreds of photos, asked about that many questions, and told Sarah he'd shoot her an email when the article went live on their website.

A dozen or so guests were still there when the two-hour open house ended. One by one, Sarah saw them off.

After they were all gone, Ruby gave her a big hug. "Sorry Charlie and I can't stay longer. Our grands are coming over tonight for board games."

Claudia glanced at her watch. "Oh, we've got to be heading out, too. The hubs here has a surprise gift for me that wasn't under the tree this morning. I get to open it when we get back."

"If he's smart, it's a trip to anywhere but here," Rosie mused.

Sarah caught Maybelle and Claudia's husband exchanging a look, saw the glimmer of amusement in Maybelle's eyes, and knew the woman knew exactly what Claudia's husband had planned.

Not only that, but she'd played a role in it coming about. God love her.

Maybelle and Sarah's father stayed a few minutes longer, then both claimed they had to leave as well.

From the front porch, Sarah watched them drive away.

The open house had been a big success. The local paper and the magazine were both doing features. Dozens had attended.

She should be ecstatic.

Instead, she was haunted by thoughts of that one person who should have been there but wasn't.

Had she been secretly hoping he'd come to the open house? That she'd be talking to one of the Butterflies, turn, and there he'd be, smiling at her and stealing her breath?

How foolish. What would change if he had? She was tied to Pine Hill. Tied by strings of history, family, friends, community. Strings she cherished and didn't want to break.

But that didn't stop the ache of Bodie not being there, his not having come to the open house he'd help make possible, his not being there to receive his share of all the compliments on the classy way he'd created a modern bathroom yet kept the historic feel of the home.

His just not being there, period.

Get a grip, Sarah.

Struggling with her emotions, she went back inside Hamilton House.

She wandered from room to room, looking around with pride, flipping lights off as she went. As she walked into each room, she let memories from the past fill her mind. Aunt Jean, the Butterflies, all the open house visitors, even Bodie.

Inside these walls were so many memories.

She paused in the foyer, her eyes going to the photos over the staircase. She studied each one. Roy's parents wedding photo, Aunt Jean and Uncle Roy's, and the silly snaggle-toothed photo of her that Aunt Jean had adored.

She came from a long line of lovers. Loyal lovers who loved once and only once.

She would only love once.

A chill hit her.

She went to the living room, picked up Bodie's quilt, sat in the rocking chair that had once been her grandmother's, and wrapped herself up in the patriotic cover.

Had she been right in what she'd told Maybelle why Bodie had left it?

Or had he thought she needed the quilt more than he did?

In that moment, she realized she did need the comfort it provided. It wrapped around her like a gifted hug from him. Was that how he'd once felt about the quilt?

Was that what he'd wanted to give back to her? Knowing she'd need it more than him?

Having constantly checked her phone during the night to see if he'd texted back, she hadn't slept well. As she rocked, her eyes became heavy and she drifted off.

In her dreams, Bodie had never left. They'd replaced the photo on the stairs with a photo of them, a black and white one taken inside the church. The upstairs suites had been returned to their beauty and grandeur, filled with the wedding gifts from the Butterflies.

Hamilton House's walls threatened to burst from all the new memories being made within them. Memories that were happy and full of love.

Somewhere in the recesses of her mind, she knew none of it was real.

She also acknowledged how desperately she wished it were. Because like it or not, Bodie had taken something of hers when he'd left.

Her heart.

Her lucid dreaming continued, and she welcomed the illusion of Bodie's smile and laughter as the Christmas gift it was. From far off in her dream, she heard Harry barking, and she wished he'd hurry and join them so she could pet him.

His barking was growing louder, more persistent, and not fitting with her dream.

Opening her eyes, she glanced around the living room, eyes settling on her twinkling Christmas tree as she tried to orient herself from her dream-filled nap.

She was awake now. The barking should have stopped.

It hadn't.

Adrenaline shot up from her belly to her throat. Was she not really awake? Was this still part of her dream?

The barking had gotten closer, louder, as if...as if Harry were on her front porch.

Pulling the quilt off, she tossed it onto the rocker. Then she hurried to the front door and flung it open, not really expecting to see anyone, expecting to awaken and be disappointed that the barking hadn't been real.

There, on her front porch, was Bodie squatted down, telling Harry to quit barking.

He glanced up, met her gaze with his beautiful blue eyes, and grinned. "Merry Christmas, Sarah."

"I...what are you doing here?"

Not exactly the welcome Bodie had hoped for, but at least she hadn't slammed the door in his face or ordered him off the property.

Bodie's body seemed frozen in place, but Harry had no such issues and leapt at Sarah, barking, nudging her with his nose and licking her like crazy.

At his launching at her, Sarah stumbled back a step before steadying herself, laughing at Harry's exuberant hello as she loved on the dog.

"I missed you, too," she told Harry, hugging him to her and giggling as he attempted to lick her face.

"Down," Bodie told him, but for once, Harry didn't listen, just kept excitedly greeting Sarah. "Harry," Bodie said in a deeper tone.

"It's okay. He's not bothering me," Sarah assured,

scratching Harry behind the ears and moving her head around to keep Harry's licking from the chin down.

Maybe he should have left Harry in the truck until he'd told Sarah what he'd come to say. Then again, she'd looked stunned to see him on her porch and it was only after Harry went nuts that she smiled and laughed.

When Harry had calmed enough that conversation was possible, Sarah spoke first.

"You didn't answer my question. Why are you here?"

"Today is your open house."

She didn't look up from where she petted Harry. "The open house was from twelve to two."

He'd left in what should have been plenty of time to get there, but had run into bad traffic.

"I'm sorry I missed it. Maybe you could give me a private showing?"

Her gaze lifted. "Why?"

"I'd like to see what you did with the suites after I left."

She straightened, motioned for him to go inside. He followed her through the hallway to first one suite, then the other.

"I like the furniture and how you decorated. It all looks simple but beautiful."

"I can't take the credit. It's the furniture Aunt Jean's in-laws bought more than half a century ago. There's still cookies and drinks in the kitchen if you want some."

He'd grabbed something during his last pit stop to let Harry out and to stretch both their legs, but he wasn't one to turn down Sarah's cookies.

He started to follow her to the kitchen but, with her face looking a little pale, she stopped him. "I... Wait in the living room, and I'll bring them there."

With that, she went to the kitchen and left him in the hallway. Bodie watched her go, then went back to the foyer to make his way to the living room. In the foyer, he paused to look at the photos on the stairwell.

Specifically, the photo of Sarah.

He took a deep breath and went to the living room. Barely inside the doorway, his gaze immediately went to where his quilt lay on the rocker. Walking over to it, he picked it up.

It was warm.

When he'd gotten there, Sarah had been beneath the quilt.

"I figured I should use it since I couldn't regift it to Quilts of Valor. They only accept new quilts."

Continuing to hold the quilt, he turned to her. "If they'd have taken it, would you have given it to another soldier, Sarah?"

Her gaze dropped to the quilt. Her eyes closed, then she shook her head. "No."

"Because?"

Opening her eyes, she took on a steely resolve, lifting her chin and asking, "Why are you here, Bodie?"

But Bodie wasn't stopping until he had answers, until he gave her answers. They had a lot to discuss and it all began with the quilt he held. "Why wouldn't you have given the quilt away again, Sarah?"

"Because I... It's your quilt, Bodie. I made it for you."

"You didn't know me when you made this."

"As crazy as it sounds, I still made it for you." She

set the tray of cookies and drinks on a side table, turned to stare at the quilt he held. "My mother made a quilt for a soldier once. It wasn't a Quilt of Valor, but a quilt of love she made for my father while he was overseas. She poured love into every stitch." She pointed to his quilt. "Every Quilt of Valor quilt Aunt Jean made was for Roy. I did the same thing when I made that quilt."

She gave a self-derisive laugh, then met his gaze. "I was grieving for Aunt Jean, poured my heart into making the quilt because I knew that's what she did with Roy. Only with my quilt, I dreamed of you, my very own soldier, with every stitch I sewed. I didn't know you and yet," her shoulders moved in a slight shrug, "I did."

She crossed the room, took the quilt from him, and tossed it back onto the rocker. "There's my Christmas confession. Now, tell me why you're here."

"To tell you Merry Christmas."

"You could have just called." Her chin lifted a notch. "Or texted."

Knowing he had zero experience with romance and would probably completely botch this, Bodie reached into his jacket pocket and wrapped his fingers around what he'd put in there hours before.

"I could have, but then, I couldn't have done this."

He pulled out the sprig of green he'd borrowed from Kelly and Lukas and held it out to a stunned Sarah.

Was Sarah still asleep and dreaming? She decided she had to be. No way was Bodie in Hamilton House holding out a piece of mistletoe.

"I—I don't understand."

"No, I don't suppose you do." He placed the mistletoe in her hand, closing her fingers around the greenery. "I got ahead of myself."

Sarah opened her palm, looked down at the mistletoe, then back up at Bodie.

"When I left here, I believed I needed my job with iSecure in order to feel whole again, to fill the missing pieces while I put myself back together. To find purpose by serving and protecting others."

Although he was saying things she already knew, Sarah listened closely, trying to decipher what had brought him back to Hamilton House, afraid to let her mind wander as to why he was here, why he'd given her mistletoe.

"Lukas had planned to start me on easy assignments and let me work my way back up to high stakes again, but Kelly went into labor a month early, less than a day before Lukas was supposed to be on a plane for a major operation overseas. He was left with the choices of going himself, canceling the mission, letting the rest of the team handle it alone, or sending me in his place on the team."

"He sent you."

Bodie nodded. "When I got his call saying he needed me, I checked out of the hotel and drove straight to the hospital to meet him. I got my assignment, left Harry with him, and flew out that day. I got back to the States last night."

Sarah was glad she hadn't known where he was, what he was doing. Just thinking that he'd left had worried her enough. Had she known he was on some high-stakes mission out of the country, she'd have been a nervous wreck.

"I've always done my job well, Sarah. This time was no exception." He paused, walked over to the Christmas tree, touched the snowflake he'd put there the day after the On-the-Square Festival. "The problem is, I thought I had to go back to that life to be myself again. That if I didn't, I'd be letting that IED steal my life the way it had stolen my friends."

She watched him tighten his fingers, then flex them.

"Maybe I needed to prove to myself, to everyone, that I could still do my job."

"That's what you did?"

He nodded. "Lukas has offered me my pick of assignments."

Sarah bit the inside of her lip. She was happy for him, but...

"Congratulations, I think."

"I told him I had reconsidered my position at iSecure."

"What?"

"I don't want to be sitting in some desert on a stake-out, Sarah. I want to be here, at Hamilton House."

What was he saying? Why were her insides trembling?

"You do?"

He nodded. "Think you have a room for me?"

Her head spun. "You want to stay at Hamilton House?"

"If you'll have me here."

"Of course. That's fine. I...how long do you plan to stay?"

Rather than answer, he walked to where she'd put the quilt back on the rocker. He picked it up as if it were something precious, then moved to where she stood. He smiled down at her with something in his eyes she'd never seen before, something that stole her breath and made her knees shake.

"How long do I plan to stay?" he repeated. Taking the quilt, he wrapped it around her shoulders and pulled her to him. "Forever."

Forever? That's what shined in his eyes. *Forever.*

"You going to use that mistletoe?"

Sarah held up the green twig over their heads as he pulled her into his arms.

Epilogue

"Something borrowed," Ruby said, fastening an emerald bracelet around Sarah's wrist. "My Charlie gave me this for our forty-fifth anniversary."

"Something old," Claudia said, adjusting Aunt Jean's wedding veil on Sarah's head.

"There she goes talking about you again," Rosie said half under her breath while eyeballing Maybelle.

"Shush your mouth, woman," Maybelle ordered. "Can't you see we're getting ready for a wedding here?" Maybelle turned back to Sarah and placed a velvet box into her hands. "Something new. These are from all of us, even from your something blue over there."

Sarah eyed her bridesmaids, not a one of them under sixty-five, and fought getting too emotional.

She could not cry. She'd ruin her makeup and they didn't have time to repair it. She had a very important date to meet her father in just a few minutes.

"I don't know what I'd do without you," she told them, opening the box.

"Let's face it, neither does the rest of the world," Rosie bragged. "Butterflies are essential."

"Certainly, essential in my life." Sarah laughed, then gasped as she saw what was in the box. Lifting her gaze, she met each woman's eyes, seeing the pride and love shining there. "Really?"

They all nodded.

"Well, don't just stand there. Put them on."

With shaky fingers, Sarah removed the earrings from their box, sliding each one onto her earlobe, then walking to the mirror to admire her gift.

"I love them."

The women beamed behind her.

"Of course, you do. What's not to love about a butterfly?"

Sarah gave each woman a hug, then glanced at the clock on the wall.

"Still time to change your mind."

"Bite your tongue, Rosie Matthews," Ruby ordered.

"Oh, no, she can't change her mind. Bodie is taking her out of the country for their honeymoon," Claudia said matter-of-factly, then touched Sarah's arm. "You're going to love traveling, Sarah. When we went to Europe in the spring, it was so lovely." Thanks to some Maybelle meddling, Claudia had been on three vacations that year. "I hope Bodie is taking you somewhere lovely for your honeymoon."

"He's still not told you where he's taking you?" Rosie asked, sounding disappointed.

Sarah shook her head. "He says it's a surprise."

Maybelle tsked. "He should have at least told us."

"And risk you showing up? He's smarter than that," Sarah teased, checking her reflection one last time. Where they went didn't matter, not as long as she was with Bodie.

Ruby nodded. "Smart enough that he moved to Pine Hill and took a job with Sherriff Roscoe."

That he had. Bodie was a full-time sheriff's deputy, Hamilton House's maintenance man, and Sarah's best Christmas gift ever.

Music began playing over the intercom system.

"Oh!"

"That's our cue."

"Line up, ladies."

The Butterflies gathered at the door, then slipped into the church hallway to make their way up the aisle to where Bodie, Lukas, and Harry waited.

When the Butterflies had taken their place at the front of the church, Sarah's father held out his arm.

"You ready for this?"

From the moment Bodie had asked her to marry him, she'd been ready.

"Ready to replace that awful photo on the stairwell?" she asked. "Absolutely."

Her father laughed. "Glad I know that's not your only motive."

"I might have one or two others."

Like the wonderful man waiting for her to walk down the aisle. She wanted to glance around the church, to see her friends, Bodie's mother, stepfather, stepsisters and their families, but she couldn't take her eyes off the man smiling at her with love in his eyes.

When her father handed her off to Bodie and then stepped up to perform the marriage ceremony, Sarah smiled at her soon-to-be husband.

"I can't believe you made me wait a year for this day."

"You know Christmas is the best day of the year," she reminded him. "How could we have gotten married on any other day?"

"There is that," he whispered back. "Merry Christmas, Sarah."

Sarah's heart filled with joy.

Christmas really was the best day of the year.

THE END

CINNAMON SWIRL BREAD

A Hallmark Original Recipe

In *Wrapped Up In Christmas*, one of the ladies at Sarah's church is famous for her cinnamon bread recipe. Others attempt to copy it without success. Here's that secret recipe, filled with cinnamon and covered with yummy icing. The trick to beautiful swirls is in folding the dough into thirds so you get an extra layer of the delicious cinnamon-sugar blend. This bread is perfect for a Christmas celebration, like Sarah and Bodie enjoy together, or for any time of year.

Yield: 2 loaves (16 servings)
Prep Time: 3 hours
Bake Time: 45 minutes
Total Time: 3 hours 45 minutes

INGREDIENTS

Dough:
- ¼ cup warm water
- ½ teaspoon granulated sugar
- 1 envelope active dry yeast
- 1 cup whole milk
- 3 tablespoons unsalted butter, room temperature
- 4 cups bread flour
- ¼ cup granulated sugar
- 1 teaspoon kosher salt
- 1 large egg, beaten

Cinnamon Sugar:
- ½ cup brown sugar
- ¼ cup granulated white sugar
- 1½ tablespoons ground cinnamon
- 4 tablespoons unsalted butter

Vanilla Cream Cheese Spread:
- 2 ounces cream cheese, room temperature
- 1 cup powdered sugar
- ¼ teaspoon vanilla extract
- 1 to 2 tablespoons whole milk

DIRECTIONS

1. To prepare dough: combine warm water, ½ teaspoon sugar, and yeast in a large bowl. Let stand at room temperature for 10 minutes or until foamy.

2. While yeast is activating, combine milk and

butter in small saucepan and heat briefly to melt butter. Remove from heat; cool.

3. Combine flour, ¼ cup sugar, and salt in mixing bowl fitted with a paddle attachment and beat until fully blended.

4. Add milk/butter mixture and egg to yeast mixture and gently stir to blend. Slowly add to flour mixture and beat until dough pulls away from sides of bowl.

5. Turn dough out on a lightly floured surface; knead dough for 1 minute. Transfer to a bowl that's either buttered or sprayed with cooking spray, cover loosely, and set in a warm, draft-free spot to rise for about 60 to 75 minutes, or until dough has doubled in size.

6. Gently punch dough down and turn out onto a lightly floured surface. Fold in the two outer sides of dough to meet in the middle, then fold in the upper and lower sides of dough to meet in the middle, forming the dough into a square shape. Cover loosely and let stand for 10 minutes.

7. To prepare cinnamon sugar: while dough is resting, combine brown sugar, white sugar and cinnamon in small bowl and mix to blend. Heat butter in microwave-safe measuring cup for 30 to 45 seconds, or until melted. Reserve.

8. Grease two 9x5-inch loaf pans with butter or cooking spray.

9. With a floured rolling pin, roll the dough into a 26x12-inch rectangle on a lightly floured

surface. Brush top of dough with melted butter; sprinkle 2/3 of cinnamon sugar blend evenly over dough. Slice dough in half, forming two 13x12-inch halves.

10. For each half: fold dough into thirds, forming a 4x12-inch rectangle. Pinch outer edges of dough gently to seal seams. Roll dough out into a 7x13-inch rectangle. Brush top of dough lightly with butter and sprinkle half of remaining cinnamon sugar blend evenly over the top. Starting at long end of dough, roll up jelly roll-style. Place, seam side down, in buttered loaf pan. Repeat with remaining dough. Cover loaf pans loosely with film wrap; let rise in a warm draft-free place for 1 hour, or until almost doubled in size.

11. Preheat oven to 400°F.

12. Bake for 45 minutes, or until golden brown. Cover each loaf pan loosely with aluminum foil during last 20 minutes to prevent over-browning. Remove loaf pans from oven; cool for 5 minute, gently remove bread from loaf pans.

13. To prepare vanilla cream cheese spread: combine cream cheese, powdered sugar, vanilla and 1 tablespoon milk in bowl and whisk until smooth. Add additional milk, as needed, to form a spread-like consistency.

14. Serve cinnamon bread warm with cream cheese spread.

STARS AND STRIPES
A Quilts of Valor Group Project
Pattern instructions:
Copyright 2019 Ann Parsons Holte,
www.AnnHolteQuilting.com

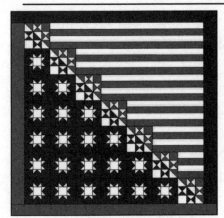

Finished Size: 71" x 71"
with 4" border

Designed by Kelly Harvey and Patty Gallmeyer, this quilt was chosen for the cover of **Quilts of Valor: A Fifty State Salute** (Schiffer, 2018). The book, written by Sue Reich, Renelda Peldunas-Harter, and Ann Parsons Holte, tells the story of the Quilts of Valor Foundation, gives a history of quilts that were made in response to war, documents the story of the makers and recipients of quilts pictured in the book, and features patterns for sixteen of those quilts. The Foundation is pleased to make this pattern available for quilters who want to participate in this important project to comfort those touched by war.

This pattern was adapted with quilt groups in mind. Often, volunteer quilters get together to make Quilts of Valor. As with any group project, things go more smoothly if the process is broken down into logical steps so that the parts can come together in the end. We hope that your group will enjoy making a quilt to thank a veteran for his or her service.

Fabric Requirements:

This quilt can be made from only three fabrics: red, white, and blue. However, assorted prints create an interesting, scrappy look. Note that these instructions are for 100% cotton, first quality, quilting weight fabric that is at least 40" wide. You will need approximately:

For Blocks: 2-1/4 yds White, 1-3/4 yds Blue, 1-3/8 yds Red
For Borders: 3/4 yd Blue, 3/4 yd Red
For Backing: 4-1/2 yds
For Binding: 3/4 yd

Cutting and Organizing the Fabric:

There are three elements to the main quilt top:
- red+white stripes
- blue+white 9" Morning Star blocks, and
- red+white+blue 9" Split Star blocks

Whether you are sewing alone or with a group, a good idea is to make **labels** before you cut the fabric.

Label	Fabric	Cutting Instructions
Borders		
Left/Bottom Borders	Red	(2) 4-1/2" x WOF*
Top/Right Borders	Blue	(2) 4-1/2" x WOF
Stripes		
Red Stripes	Red	(11) 2-3/4" x WOF
White Stripes	White	(11) 2-3/4" x WOF
Morning Star Blocks		
Star Center Squares	White	(21) 3-1/2" squares
Star Points	White	(168) 2" squares

Star Corner Squares	Blue	(84) 3-1/2" squares
Star Background	Blue	(84) 31/2" squares

Split Star Blocks

Corner Square	White	(7) 3-1/2" squares
HST/QST Squares*	White	(25) 5" squares
HST Center Squares	Blue	(11) 5" squares
Corner Squares	Red	(7) 3-1/2" squares
HST/QST Squares*	Red	(14) 5" squares

*Note:

- "WOF" means Width of Fabric.
- "HST" means Half-Square Triangle.
- "QST" means Quarter Square Triangle.

These squares will be cut larger than needed and then will be trimmed to the correct size after the units are sewn.

Label and Assemble Red+White Stripe Units

If you are working in a group, this page is for the people who will work on the Stripe Units.

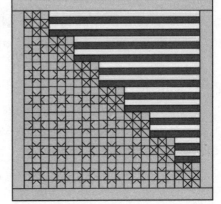

Make labels that say:

- 9-1/2" Segment
- 18-1/2" Segment
- 27-1/2" Segment
- 36-1/2" Segment
- 45-1/2" Segment
- 54-1/2" Segment

Cutting:

- You have already cut (11) 2-3/4" x WOF assorted red strips and (11) 2-3/4" x WOF assorted white strips
- Cut these strips into various lengths from 9" to 12" long

Make Strip Sets:

- Attach short, scrappy red segments together with diagonal seams to make approx. 400" long strip

- Repeat for scrappy white segments

- Trim seam allowances to 1/4"

- Press diagonal seams open

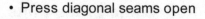

- Attach the long red and white strips on a long edge to make a two-strip set that is approx. 400" long

- Cut in half and sew the two halves together to make a four-strip set that is 9-1/2" wide x approx. 200" long

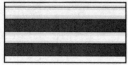

- Press the long seams toward the red fabric

- Cut the four-strip set into segments and attach the labels that you created

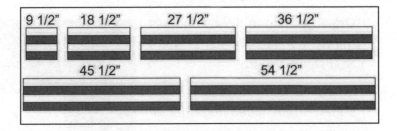

- Set the segments aside until time to assemble the quilt.

Blue + White Morning Star Blocks

This page is for the people who will work on the (21) Blue + White Morning Star Blocks.

If you make "block kits," each block will need:

- (1) 3-1/2" Star Center Square (White)
- (8) 2" Star Point Squares (White)
- (4) 3-1/2" Star Corner Squares (Blue)
- (4) 3-1/2" Star Background Squares (Blue)

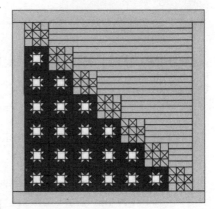

Make Star Point Units:

- Draw a diagonal line across the wrong side of each 2" white Star Point square

- Place 2" white Star Point square right sides together in a corner of a 3-1/2" blue Star Background square, as shown

- Sew just next to the drawn line in order to place the seam line just a bit closer to the corner (this allows for the "foldover" on the corner)

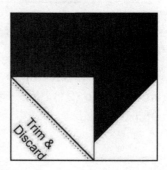

- Trim excess fabric and press seam allowance open

- Repeat at adjoining corner of 3-1/2" blue Star Background square

- Press and trim to 3-1/2", if necessary

Assemble (21) Blue+White Star Blocks:

- For each nine-patch block, you will need:
    - (4) Blue Star Corner squares
    - (1) White Star Center square

- (4) Star Point Units from previous step
- Attach square units as shown
- Set the blocks aside until time to assemble the quilt.

Split Star Blocks

This page is for making the (7) Split Star Blocks.

You have already cut and labeled:

- White (7) 3-1/2" Corner Square (set aside)
- White (25) 5" HST & QST Squares
- Blue (11) 5" HST Center Square
- Red (7) 3-1/2" Corner Squares (set aside)
- Red (14) 5" HST & QST Squares

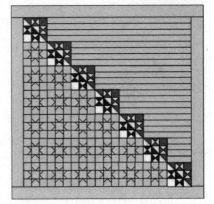

Please note:

- The squares for the Half-Square Triangles (HSTs) and the Quarter-Square Triangles (QSTs) were cut larger than needed and then will be trimmed to the correct size after the units are sewn
- Some HSTs will be trimmed to 3-1/2" square
- Some HSTs will be used to make QSTs and trimmed afterwards

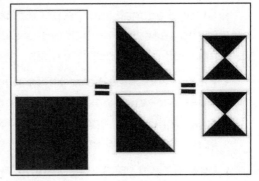

Make HST units from oversized 5" Squares

- Draw diagonal line on back of all (25) white 5" squares
- Place white squares right sides together with all red and blue 5" squares
- Sew 1/4" on each side of the drawn line
- Cut apart on the drawn line
- Press seam allowance toward darker fabric
- You will now have (22) Blue+White HSTs and (28) Red+White HSTs
  - **TRIM ONLY** (7) of the Blue+White HSTs to 3-1/2" and set aside for Centers
  - **TRIM ONLY** (14) of the Red+White HSTs to 3-1/2" and set aside for Corners

---

Make QST units from the remaining (15) Blue+White HSTs and (14) Red+White HSTs:

- Draw diagonal line perpendicular to the seamline on half of the blue and half of the red HST units
- Place two same-color HSTs right sides together, nesting the seam line, with light and dark fabrics opposite each other
- Sew 1/4" on each side of the drawn line

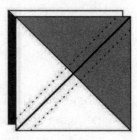

- Cut apart on the drawn line

- Press seam allowance open or "spin" the seam allowances so they all go in the same direction and then press

- Trim to 3-1/2" square, being sure to line up the center of the QST at 1-3/4" in both directions

Assemble (7) Split Star Blocks

After all units are trimmed to 3-1/2", for each block, you will need:

- (1) White Corner Square
- (1) Red Corner Square
- (1) Blue+White HST
- (2) Red+White HSTs
- (2) Blue+White QSTs
- (2) Red+White QSTs

Assemble Quilt

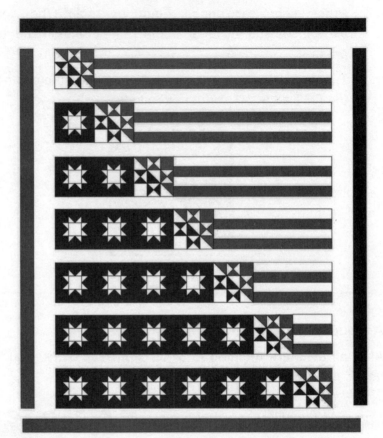

- Attach the rows of blocks as shown above.

- Add the strip sets to complete the rows.

- After the rows are attached to each other, the top should measure 63-1/2" square.

- For the borders:

- Cut (4) 4-1/2" x WOF strips each from Red and Blue fabric

- Attach strips end-to-end or by using diagonal seam method to make long strips

- Cut (1) Red and (1) Blue 63-1/2" for Left and Right Borders
- Cut (1) Red and (1) Blue 71-1/2" for Top and Bottom Borders
- Add the Left and Right Borders first. Then add the Top and Bottom Borders.

Thanks so much for reading *Wrapped Up in Christmas*. We hope you enjoyed it!

You might like these other books from Hallmark Publishing:

A Down Home Christmas
A Royal Christmas Wish
A Gingerbread Romance
An Unforgettable Christmas
Journey Back to Christmas
The Christmas Company
A Timeless Christmas
At the Heart of Christmas

For information about our new releases and exclusive offers, sign up for our free newsletter at hallmarkchannel.com/ hallmark-publishing-newsletter

You can also connect with us here:

Facebook.com/HallmarkPublishing

Twitter.com/HallmarkPublish

ABOUT THE AUTHOR

Author Janice Lynn loves to spin a tale that puts a smile on her reader's lips and a tear in their eye as they travel along her characters' journey to happy ever after. Her favorite read is one with a strong heroine who is able to laugh at herself and a hero who appreciates the heroine's strengths and imperfections.

Janice's books have won numerous awards including the National Readers' Choice Award and the American Title, but she is most proud of her seven children. From actor, engineer, nurse, student, to Army National Guard, they are her greatest accomplishments.

Janice lives in Tennessee with her family, her vivid imagination, lots of crafting and quilting supplies, and numerous unnamed dust bunnies.